# Charm Me Again

## by

## Tena Stetler

*Charm Me, Book 2*

This is a work of fiction. Names, characters, places, and incidents are either the product of the author's imagination or are used fictitiously, and any resemblance to actual persons living or dead, business establishments, events, or locales, is entirely coincidental.

**Charm Me Again**

Cover Art by *Kristian Norris*

The Wild Rose Press, Inc.
PO Box 708
Adams Basin, NY 14410-0708
Visit us at www.thewildrosepress.com

Publishing History
First Black Rose Edition, 2019
Print ISBN 978-1-5092-2972-7
Digital ISBN 978-1-5092-2973-4

*Charm Me, Book 2*
Published in the United States of America

Suddenly, the wind changed direction, a thin maroon line formed along the flat bottom of the dark clouds spreading across the sky where moments before there'd been only a few fluffy cotton ball clouds in a sea of blue. The maroon line widened then switched to vertical and spread open to reveal a shimmering interior.

Shadows emerged from the cloud then disappeared. As he was about to comment, huge raindrops plopped on the ground followed by pea size hail that grew to softball size.

Josie ran for cover and he followed. Protected under a ledge, she cupped her hands over her ears as the roaring of the storm combined with huge ice balls smashing against rocks echoed through the canyon. She elbowed him and cocked a brow in question, pointing to the vegetation that remained unharmed.

His eyes narrowed. Something isn't right. I can feel it. Magic is spinning this storm. But who—how and why? At a loss for answers, he shrugged and urged her further under the ledge to wait out the storm. Brushing the wet strands of hair out of her face, he smiled. She looked like a drowned rat but the fragrance around her reminded him of sweet spring flowers. He leaned into to her and brushed his lips over hers. Immediately, he straightened and backed away. Her eyes were still closed. Maybe I could've lingered…

Her eyes blinked open and she licked her lips. After a beat, she waggled a finger in front of him. "Not a good idea."

## Dedication

To my READERS, for whom I write the stories!
To all the supportive people in my life,
personal and professional, who help me realize
my dreams every single day.
Special thanks to my own hero, my husband,
who shines as bright as my characters
regardless of the situation.
My editor, Lill, who goes above and beyond.
You Rock! Thank you!

Chapter One
A Surprise Visitor

In the dusky light, a shadowy figure stalked up the sidewalk in a neighborhood of predominately large turn-of-the-century homes. One stood out from the rest. The building had obviously been remodeled. Taking a closer look, Daylan finally spied the hand-carved wooden sign with large sweeping letters: Welcome to Earthbound Yoga Studio. The sign complemented the house's architecture, and something was familiar with the style. Shrugging, he crept closer. This had to be it. All his research indicated this was where she'd surfaced.

The windows were dark as he climbed the three steps leading to the porch and eased down on the top stair. A streetlight in the middle of the block blinked on and off, casting shadows from the large trees surrounding the area. *How can I do this? What makes me think...* He'd spent most of the night sitting there trying to figure out how to execute his plan. *Yeah, it isn't much of a plan, either.* At least the Scotsman hadn't made an appearance...yet. He blew out a breath.

The sound of a vehicle caught his attention. The street was awash in headlight beams as the truck coasted to a stop in front of the building. He jumped up and sprinted to the north side of the house, blending into the bushes, his heart nearly pounding out of his chest as he waited.

A chime sounded as a tall muscular man opened the driver's side door. Light spilled onto the street as he stepped out followed by a large furry dog. The canine hesitated and sniffed the air, a low menacing growl rising from its throat.

Daylan froze as the dog crept in his direction, nose to the ground, hackles raised. The man sauntered to the passenger side of the truck and tugged open the door, offering a hand to the person inside.

"Piper, you get back here. Right now," a woman's voice commanded. She had one foot braced on the truck's running board and took the offered hand to step out of the vehicle. The dog stopped in its tracks and turned toward the voice.

He breathed a tiny sigh of relief. The dog continued to growl, turning its massive head back a couple of times as it hesitantly returned to the truck.

"What's the matter, Piper?" She bent down and rubbed the dog's ear as the man glanced uneasily up and down the street. "Come on, girl." Letting go of his hand, she motioned the dog to her side and took several steps before the man reached out and caught her elbow.

"Just wait a minute." The man stood a few yards from the SUV and drew in a long breath. "There's an unfamiliar scent lingering. Probably what has Piper on guard. I'll check the perimeter of the building after you get inside."

The woman's hair was longer than the last time he'd seen her. Her melodic voice floated in the air, and her no-nonsense gait made him sure it was Summer Rylie.

She turned her head, looking up and down the

street. "I don't see a thing." Pausing a minute more, she shook her head. "Don't sense anything either."

The man held her arm, leaned in, and gave her a long affectionate kiss. "I'll walk you inside. Don't want those unruly yoga mats to attack you in the dark." A deep resounding laugh wafted through the early morning air.

Yanking her arm from his grasp, Summer swiped at him. "You'll never let me live that down, will you?"

"Nope. It's way too entertaining." He wrapped his arm around her waist and whistled for the dog who'd wandered off the sidewalk into the grass with her nose to the ground.

"Piper would rather stay outside sniffing than go inside. I'll take her for a walk after sunrise."

She hesitated, closed her eyes, and reached out with her magic to scan the area. When she opened her eyes and took another quick look around, she shrugged. "Nothing unusual."

"I'll take Piper with me to check the area just to be sure." Her male companion followed her to the door.

"Probably a good idea. Josie will be here within the hour. She has an early morning class. I promised to have the studio open and ready since I'd be in early to do paperwork before we leave."

The keys jangled as she took them out of her backpack and unlocked the intricately carved wooden door. Count down beeps began as Piper trotted inside ahead of them. Another short beep indicated the alarm had been disarmed. The man gave one last look and the heavy wooden door groaned closed.

"Damn." He cursed and disappeared, reappearing on the other side of the street, re-masking his magic signature as well has his scent. *That went well. Not.*

A second later the door squeaked open and light flooded the front yard as man and dog walked around the house. When they finished, her companion shoved open the door. "Nothing out here. I'll pick you and Piper up around noon. Then we can head up the mountain to the cabin for the weekend."

"Sounds great. See you then." She stood in the doorway with the dog at her side and waved.

After she closed the door, the man drove off. It was a good thing he waited a few minutes before crossing the street. The SUV circled the block again, driving by slowly before it continued down the street. This time he remained hidden until the red taillights were no longer visible.

Crossing to Earthbound Yoga, he walked up to the door and shoved it open. The door groaned his arrival, and a dog bounded across the floor growling and snarling. He stopped dead in his tracks, threw a freeze spell at the dog, and yelled, "Summer, call your damned dog off."

Summer rounded the corner from the office into the open studio floor. Her eyes flew open wide and her mouth dropped open. Quickly regaining her composure, she fisted her hands on hips. "What the hell are you doing here? You didn't just spell my dog—did you?" She rushed to the dog, who was frozen in an aggressive stance. She narrowed her eyes, never taking her gaze off the man, and waved her arm, deactivating the spell, and the dog rushed forward. "Halt, Piper, sit."

The dog's butt hit the ground, but she continued to growl menacingly with her ears pinned against her head.

"Summer, I'm sorry about showing up here unannounced, but I had to talk to you. I wasn't sure—hell—I didn't know how to contact you after you disappeared."

She knelt beside the dog, scratching its ears, her head tilted to keep an eye on him. "There's a good reason for that. How did you find me?"

"That's not important. What is—is that I need your help."

"Figures." After getting to her feet, her hands resting on hips, she gave him an eat-shit-and-die look while surveying him from head to toe. "What kind of trouble are you in this time?" She strolled to the huge stone fireplace that took up nearly one whole wall and with a wave ignited the logs stacked in the hearth.

"Not really trouble, more like…need a change of scenery." He paused, jamming his hands in the front pockets of his jeans and swallowing hard. *She'd always assumed the worst.* He gave a mental shrug. *Guess I've given her reason for that reaction.*

Her eyebrows drew together, and eyes narrowed to tiny slits. "Yeah, right. Now out with it."

A bead of nervous sweat trickled down his temple. He wiped it away with the back of his hand. "See, there's this seventeenth-century Highland ghost who seems to have attached himself to me. No matter what I do, where I go, it won't leave—I mean he won't leave."

She whirled around to face him. "A ghost? So you're being haunted? I suppose you brought the ghost with you. Here," she said incredulously, adding emphasis to the last word.

He leaned back and shifted from one foot to the other. "Not exactly. I've not seen him since I left

Martha's Vineyard. But I feel him. I know that sounds crazy, but…"

"Downright creepy." She tilted her head to the side and peered at him, her curiosity obviously piqued. "Do you know who this ghost is or why he has attached himself to you?" She hesitated at the door to her office. "If you want to talk, you'll need to come in here, and make it quick. I've got a lot of paperwork to do before leaving at noon."

The front door banged open and a tall willowy girl rushed in. "Sorry, I'm late. That damn Kurt was lurking out in front of my apartment this morning. I had to climb out the back window and shimmy down the fire escape to avoid him. Missed the last step and fell on my ass." She stopped and brushed at her behind, fingering a tear in her pants.

Her long raven black hair hung to the middle of her back in a thick braid. Her enormous turquoise eyes widened as she continued her tale. "Couldn't get to my car, so I had to walk here. Thank God it's only a mile or so. I was afraid he was going to catch me." She shrugged out of her coat, tossed it on the rack beside the door and turned, almost crashing right into him. "Guess I'll… Whoa. Who are you? Where's Summer?" she sputtered, back-peddling several steps.

Mesmerized by her, he had trouble pulling his gaze from the girl…woman with bronze skin. She'd nearly collided into his chest. He took a step back. Long, thick, dark eyelashes framed her beautiful eyes and accentuated her sculpted facial features and high cheekbones. Dimples appeared in her cheeks as a shy smile curved the corners of her full pink lips. He shook his head.

"Josie, I'm in the office. You're probably staring open-mouthed at my brother, Daylan." Summer snickered as she stuck her head out of her office.

"Not the one that was—involved with the woman you didn't like?"

"I only have one brother, Josie," Summer said curtly. "Let's not rehash ancient history." She eyed Josie's disheveled appearance and the tear in her clothing. "Better get changed. Students will be arriving soon."

Josie's gaze wandered over his face for a moment, then switched quickly to Summer. "Boy howdy, the family resemblance is strong."

"Yeah, well, we're twins," he offered. A slow smile curved the corners of his mouth as he took a few steps toward her. "Pleased to meet you, Josie." He extended his hand to her. "Is that short for Josephine?"

She grinned and took the offered hand. "Nope. Named after a cartoon character. Ever heard of Josie and the Pussy Cats?"

"A long time ago." He grinned, brought her hand to his lips, and brushed his lips over her knuckles. "Well, that's unique, like you."

"Oh my," she breathed. Red patches bloomed on her cheeks.

"Don't let him fool you," Summer called from her office. "Daylan is a devil. You better run upstairs and change your clothes. Do you have spares here?"

"Yeah, I think so," Josie stammered, still staring at him.

"If not, there may be a couple of pairs of yoga pants I left in the apartment for emergencies."

"Thanks."

7

"What kind of emergencies do you have in a yoga studio?" he asked incredulously, then released Josie's hand and winked. "I'd better get back to my sister, but it was a pleasure to meet you." Turning on his heel, he strode toward the office door where Summer was waiting, tapping her foot lightly. He paused in the archway and gave Josie a long appraising look as she rushed up the stairs. His sister grabbed his arm and hauled him into the office.

"What's her story? Is she seeing anyone?" he asked.

"None of your business. She's off limits. Understood?"

"Yes, ma'am." He nearly brought his hand up for a sloppy salute, but at the last minute thought better of it. *I need her help.*

"What do you expect me to do about the ghost?" she hissed. "Very few people know what I am, and I want to keep it that way."

"Who's the big brawny dude that dropped you off?" He gave the dog a wide berth as she trotted into the office, curled her lip in a silent snarl, and positioned herself between him and Summer.

His sister slipped into her chair with a smug look indicating she was enjoying his discomfort. "I'll ask the questions. How long are you planning to stay?" Shuffling the papers on her desk, she glanced at him over the computer monitor and nodded to the chair in front of the desk. Reaching over, she turned on the computer and waited as it buzzed and whirred to life.

He slid into the chair, still keeping an eye on Piper. "As long as it takes to get rid of him. I've spent the last several months trying to convince him to leave."

"Months?" she huffed. "And you're just now enlisting my help?"

He leaned back in the chair, arms crossed. "You were a bit difficult to find. At first, he appeared once in a while at my forge. It was distracting, to say the least. Nearly jumped out of my boots the first time he appeared. He seemed to know a lot about the trade. Actually, he taught me a few things about sword and knife smithing." He paused for a beat.

"Then he began popping into my apartment in the evening. You know when—at the most inopportune moments. After you dispatched my last romantic interest, it was hard enough to get a date, but with him around it's damn near impossible. On top of that, he claims I'm the only one who can help him. Insists I'm his namesake."

She raised a brow. "Are you?

"Don't know." He shifted uncomfortably.

"So as long as you benefited from his appearances it was fine. But if there's no benefit, you want him gone? Rather crass of you, don't you think?" She rested her hands on the desk.

"Not really. I didn't ask for his help. I went to Mom and Dad first, but they have no idea who he is—or was. They're still searching the family archives to…"

"If you are the only one that can help him, what do you expect me to do?"

"I thought maybe you could talk to him."

Rolling her eyes, she made a sound of exasperation. "Why don't you simply ask him what his name is and what he wants?"

"Well, I kinda pissed him off." He shoved to his

feet and paced until Piper stepped in his path growling.

"Gee, now there's something new." Summer paused, pointing to the corner. "Piper, get on your blanket."

Piper grumbled but trotted over to the green plaid blanket on the floor and curled up, back to Summer, but kept her gaze on him. "How did you piss the ghost off?"

He waved his hand dismissively. "It's not important. I had this dream. There was this gorgeous woman, with long dark hair, pointed ears, laughing at a younger version of the ghost who was obviously distraught. Another woman was weeping on the floor, looking up at him. Pointed ears looked straight at me and pointed a finger. I woke up soaking wet with sweat and with a terrible feeling of foreboding."

"Have you seen the ghost since?"

"No."

"Problem solved." Summer turned back to her pile of paperwork. "I need to get all this taken care of before noon when I leave town for the weekend."

"You're not going to help me?"

"Not today. Devlin and I are going to the cabin for the weekend to relax, enjoy the peace and quiet of the mountains." She stared pointedly at him. "Serenity has never been in your aura. Chaos and destruction follow in your wake. To be honest, that is the last thing I need right now."

He trudged toward the door. "Okay, I'll find somewhere to stay until you return. I can't leave this situation as is. Somehow I know it has dire consequences for—someone—maybe our family?"

Chapter Two
Sink or Swim, But It'll Be in the Apartment

"Okay fine. I'll see what I can do when we get back. But you do realize I've not spoken to family or friends in Martha's Vineyard since leaving. That big hunk, as you called him, is my fiancé. I'll not have him dragged into this situation. Is that clear?" Summer pushed up from the desk and shoved a finger in his chest.

"Your fiancé?" he sputtered. "You serious?"

"Yes. I've made a life for myself here. Made friends. Devlin, and his family are wonderful. I disappeared for a reason. I torched that female vampire because of you. Because you wouldn't listen, and she nearly drained you dry. I'm the one who has to live with what I did. Luckily there weren't any repercussions."

"I know. I can't tell you how sorry I am. But I can't change things, or I would." He stared down at the floor and closed his eyes.

"Yeah. Now you come hunting me down." She pursed her lips. "It's not appreciated. I have a new life and new friends. We're planning our quickly approaching wedding, and Devlin's whole family will be here, which is stressful enough." Throwing up her hands, she blew out a breath. "Out of the blue, you show up. Whatever you're mixed up in is not my problem. Every time I help you, things go south because you aren't entirely honest with me."

"The problem is—if he's family—it could affect you, Mom, Dad, me…it's hard to tell how far-reaching."

The wind howled around the building, the outside door banged a couple of times, and then a blast of cold spring air swept through the room. Summer walked out of the office. "What's going on?"

Josie and several students were standing around the front door, which was swinging on its hinges. "I don't know. All of a sudden the door swung open and now it won't stay closed. I think the wind must have tweaked it." Josie pushed her back against the door in an attempt to keep it closed. "The deadbolt is stuck. Does Devlin have time to come by and fix it?" The door flew open again, this time flinging Josie across the floor. She landed with a thud and stared wide-eyed at the door, then at Summer. "What the hell?"

Daylan rushed to her. "Are you all right?"

Josie nodded as he helped her to her feet, and she brushed at her yoga pants and stared up at him.

All the color drained out of his sister's face as she looked accusingly at him. "I'll call Devlin. Until then, Daylan, see what you can do to fix the problem temporarily." She turned on her heel and marched into the office.

Josie motioned the students to follow her to the far side of the room near the roaring fire in the hearth before continuing the class.

He strode to the door, forced it closed, and turned the deadbolt, murmuring a few words to make sure the door stayed closed. The ghost's presence swept through him. "If you want my help? You'll stay away from my sister," he whispered menacingly. "You're only making things worse."

"Did you say something?" Summer hurried out of her office. "Devlin will be here in thirty minutes."

He shook his head wearily. "You don't need to bother him. I've got it under control."

Summer frowned then lowered her voice to a whisper. "He's here?"

"No, he's gone. Sorry about that. It won't happen again." *I hope.* "I'll let you get back to work. Sorry to have bothered you." Shoulders slumped, he slipped out the door into the light rain and closed it quietly behind him. There was a little motel down the road. He'd stay there until the situation got sorted out. No way was he returning to Martha's Vineyard. There was nothing there for him.

Realizing how bad he'd hurt Summer over the vampire situation was difficult. At the time she'd been forced to torch his girlfriend before the vampire sucked all the life blood out of him. Anger and fear had consumed him. Concerned only over his loss and recovery, he hadn't given a thought to the mental anguish taking a life had caused his sister.

Looking back it was obvious the coven's chilly attitude toward her was on him, as was the strain the situation put on their parents. Straightening his shoulders, he pulled up the collar of his jacket and hastened his pace. The rain increased, turning to sleet, and he didn't know enough about this place to use magic out in the open to keep himself dry.

Her voice wafted through his mind. *Daylan, come back to Earthbound. Devlin is here and we'll try to work something out.* He answered in kind, *I'll see you on Monday.*

A split second later, out of the corner of his eye, he saw a blur. He looked up in time to back-peddle to a halt before running into the hulk of a man that had been with Summer this morning.

"Hello. You must be Daylan," the man said pleasantly, side-stepping out of the way and extending his hand.

"I am. You're Devlin? How'd you find me so fast?"

"Yep, I'm Devlin." Devlin reached out to shake the offered hand. "Pleased to meet you. I believe your sister invited you to return to the yoga studio. You know her as well as I do, maybe better. When she gets something in her head, she isn't going to let it go. So it's better for everyone concerned if you come back with me. Get this situation settled so Summer and I can go on up to the cabin. You don't want to spoil my planned getaway. Do you?" Straightening to well over six feet, he took a deep breath and trained his gaze on Daylan. "Or piss her off again."

Undaunted by the man's stature, he looked up and met his gaze. "How long have you known my sister?" He narrowed his eyes.

"Long enough to know what she had to do to save your sorry ass. So I suggest you don't go there. Protective brother doesn't fit you. Our wedding is less than a month away and nothing or no one is going to spoil our day," Devlin said in a deceptively calm voice.

Daylan took a couple of steps back, leaning away from the bigger man. "Understood. I meant after what happened she could be vulnerable—and…"

Putting his hand up, Devlin shook his head, and a wry grin turned up the corners of his mouth. "Stop right there. Summer is about as vulnerable as a wounded coyote and just as vicious. So don't worry about her. Now back to the matter at hand. You coming?" He turned and motioned forward.

Hesitating only a couple of minutes, his shoulders slumped as he pushed the long wet strands of reddish-blond hair from his forehead and fell into step, slightly behind the other man's long strides. "How'd you meet my sister?"

"At Moon Ridge Gun Club."

"A gun club. What the hell was she doing there?"

"Enrolled in a women's weapons class," Devlin said conversationally.

"She doesn't need a—"

"Apparently, she thought she did."

"See, that's what I mean. Someone there took advantage of her. Talking her into taking a class, probably into buying a weapon, and costly membership fees." Daylan's voice dripped with ire.

Stopping mid-stride and whirling around on his heel, Devlin caught Daylan by the shoulders to keep him from running into him again. "Jumping to conclusions must be your modus operandi. Bet it's got you in more than one difficult situation."

He smiled sheepishly. "Maybe. But…"

"Summer stopped by the gun club of her own volition—wanted to be able to protect herself—using mortal means and do it legally. She qualified for a concealed carry permit. It wasn't until we'd been dating a while that I understood her motive."

Running his fingers through his wet hair, he

grimaced. "Still, the manager or owner saw her coming."

"I highly doubt that. Moon Ridge doesn't operate that way."

Daylan looked dubious. "Sure about that?"

"Positive—I own the gun club."

He swallowed hard and licked his lips. "Shit, guess I'll shut up now."

"Good idea."

When Devlin shoved open the door to Earthbound, the class was gone. Summer and Josie were deep in conversation. The women's heads swiveled as he walked through the door a few steps behind Devlin. His gaze met his sister's hard stare. *This doesn't bode well.* Straightening his shoulders, he followed Devlin.

"Look what I found wandering around out in the rain. Didn't have the sense to come in out of the wet." A devilish grin spread across Devlin's face as he strode to Summer and kissed her. "Why so serious?"

She held her brother's gaze for a beat, then turned her attention to Devlin. "Josie seems to have a suitor that doesn't take no for an answer." Summer's brow creased in concern. "I really feel bad leaving her on her own this weekend with him stalking her."

Devlin frowned and glanced from Summer to Josie, rocking back on his heels. "Can't you stay with friends?"

Josie stared at her hands for a beat, then looked up. "Not really. He's alienated most of my friends. They don't want him around, nor do they want to be involved in an altercation with him. And I don't blame them." She chewed on her bottom lip. "He's caused trouble before."

"Do you want to come up to the cabin with us?" Devlin offered.

"Oh no, I wouldn't dream of intruding on your weekend. Besides, I teach two classes on Saturday. I'll be fine, really. Don't worry." She waved a hand dismissively.

The studio was quiet except for thundering paws coming out of the office into the studio and skidding to a halt. For the second time that day, Piper stood growling at Daylan.

"Knock it off," Summer commanded. The dog turned to greet Devlin, still keeping a wary eye on him.

Summer glanced at Devlin, who laughed. "Guess she figures we have him under control."

"Well, she didn't this morning."

"But I wasn't here," Devlin said.

"True, she knows an alpha when she sees one." Summer giggled.

"It's clearly an inside joke," Daylan interjected. "If I may, perhaps I can help."

All eyes turned to stare at him. Piper lifted her lip in a silent snarl.

"I could meet Josie at her apartment before work, escort her to the studio on Saturday, stick around during the classes, and make sure she gets home safely," he offered.

"No—No—Absolutely not." Summer glared at her fiancé.

"Now wait a minute," Devlin interrupted. "It's not the worst idea I've ever heard." He held his hand up to Summer. "Just hear me out. Daylan needs a place to stay. There is the extra room behind the studio on the first floor. Josie could stay in the apartment above the studio, since you've moved out. Daylan could keep an eye on the situation while we're gone."

"But you don't know what Daylan brought with him," Summer protested. Then her hand flew to her mouth.

Tilting his head as a quizzical expression creased his brow, he said, "Brought with him?"

Grabbing Devlin's arm, she pulled him into the office, leaving Daylan and Josie standing in the studio staring at each other.

"What just happened?" he asked, eying Piper who'd parked her butt between him and Josie. *That dog doesn't like me.*

"Oh, apparently Summer wanted to bring Devlin up to speed on something she didn't want us privy to. Happens all the time. Don't take it personally." Josie shrugged. "So you're Summer's twin brother." She surveyed him head to toe and shook her head. "You two sure look alike, but you don't have her confident, no-nonsense demeanor."

"You don't even know me. How could you even begin to…"

"It's a gift." She shrugged again. "I can read people really well."

"Then how did you get into this situation with Kurt? Didn't vibes tell you to stay away?" He smirked.

"Staying away didn't have anything to do with it," she said tersely. "He was a student in an advanced yoga class that Summer was teaching, and I was assisting. He came on to her. Devlin stopped by to pick up Summer and intervened, shut Kurt down and showed him the door." She paused. "Kurt is only a few inches shorter than Devlin, but he can be very intimidating."

"Tell me about it. Devlin must work out 24/7."

Josie smiled. "He looks like it, huh? Anyway, the next day Kurt came to the early beginner class. I was instructing it alone. He came on to me and became aggressive when I rejected his advances. In class, no less. Can you believe it?"

"Not really. Did you call the cops?"

"I threatened to call the police. But he left, so I didn't give it much thought. Until a few days after that, when I'd see him down the block from the studio. He'd show up where my friends and I hang out. He didn't make contact so…" She shrugged. "A few days ago he created a scene at a nightclub we were at and one of my girlfriends' boyfriend punched him. Knocked his ass out cold. We poured a mug of beer on him to bring him around. He got up and took off. But in the morning all my friends' tires were slashed, mine included.

"So he knew or found out where you all lived?"

Josie nodded. "I guess so. Couldn't prove it was him, but… Called the police. They told me to stay clear of him. Not enough evidence to…well, you get the picture. He disappeared for a while. Figured he'd turned his attention to someone else until Mandy, she's the other instructor here, saw him lurking down the street from the studio and told Summer. She hauled me in the office and wasn't any too happy I didn't tell her what was going on. Geez…she's my boss. I didn't want to get fired."

"I'll bet she wasn't. With good reason. You should have told her. Devlin might have handled…"

"I don't want anyone fighting my battles for me. I can handle myself." She glanced up at him. "Protectiveness run in the family?"

He ignored her snarky comment. "Yeah, like climbing down the fire escape to avoid him and landing on your ass. What are you, maybe one hundred ten pounds soaking wet? The guy must be a lot bigger than you."

She put her hand on her hips. "One hundred and twenty-five, but I'm nearly five feet ten inches tall," she said proudly.

Raising an eyebrow, he frowned. "Oh, wow. He could have slung you over his shoulder and we'd never see you again. He's trouble, Josie."

"I know it. That's what Summer and I were discussing when you and Devlin crashed our talk."

The cute little pout on Josie's lips was his undoing. "You need protection and I'm available to help out. What do you say?"

"Not so fast, Casanova." Summer's irritated voice echoed through the studio. Devlin grabbed her around the waist, pulled her to him, kissed her cheek, and whispered something in her ear.

She batted at him and jerked out of his hold. "I know, I know, but…I don't have to like it."

Devlin sauntered up to him. "Here's the deal. There's a spare room with a bed, dresser, chair, and desk behind the studio." He pointed to an intricately carved door with a glass doorknob, across the room. "The apartment above the studio," he jerked his chin toward the wooden staircase, "is unoccupied since Summer and Piper moved in with me."

Summer interrupted. "We propose that Josie take the apartment for the weekend. We'll discuss longer arrangements when we return." She poked a finger in his chest. "You can stay in the spare room, saving you from finding a motel. In return you provide security for Josie—no hanky-panky or so help me, I'll kill you and no one will ever find the body."

He clicked his heels and gave a sloppy salute. "Yes, ma'am." He sent a covert glance to Josie, who blatantly ignored him.

"If you think for one minute I won't..." She grabbed a hold of his ear and yanked.

"Down, girl." Devlin released her fingers and pulled Summer against him and away from his ear. "He gets the point."

"As far as the other ghost of an issue, we'll leave that to Daylan until we return."

Devlin snapped his fingers. "I knew it'd come to me. Daylan—is that Scottish, or maybe English, meaning enchanted blacksmith?"

He felt the heat rise in his cheeks. "Sort of. Historical blacksmith with supernatural powers, if you must know." It had been years since someone made that reference to his name. He glanced at Summer, then Josie. "But I assure you I'm nothing but a hardworking blade and blacksmith. Nothing more. Or I was. My forge is back east in Martha's Vineyard."

"Well, I'll be damned. We gotta talk when Summer and I get back." Devlin grinned, slapping him on the back. "That is, provided you survive." He chuckled and winked at Summer. "Shall we?"

"I'd like to accompany Josie to get a few things from her apartment and get her settled in here before we leave. Daylan can stay here and get settled."

"Your wish is my command." Devlin slid his hand on the small of Summer's back, guiding her to the door. He looked back. "Coming, Josie?"

Sprinting to catch up with the couple, she turned, beaming at him out of his sister's line of vision, and called out, "Right behind you."

He accompanied them to the door and stepped outside. The rain had turned to a light drizzle and mist crawled along the ground. Out of the corner of his eye, he caught sight of a hooded figure loitering at the end of the block. He tensed, ready to give chase. When he opened his mouth to say something, Devlin was already looking in that direction and gave a slight shake of his head.

He returned to the studio, where the door let out a loud, long groan as he closed it. *Going to work on that door first thing.* He glanced at the yoga mats stacked neatly in the bin beside the carved door to the spare room. Without warning, the crystal doorknob turned, and the door creaked open. Daylan rubbed the back of his neck, blew out a breath, and strode toward the doorway. *This can't be good.*

Chapter Three
A Ride Home & the Real Josie Is Discovered

Josie scrambled into the back seat of Devlin's truck and pushed her damp hair away from her face. "Thanks so much for doing this. Kurt is beginning to scare me."

Piper trotted around to Devlin's side and waited for him to open the back door. He chuckled and held the door open while she jumped inside, settling next to Josie.

"Beginning?" Summer raised an eyebrow. "You should have told us before." She climbed into the front seat and twisted around to glance at her. "You put yourself at risk as well as the students."

"I know that now. Won't happen again."

"You bet it won't." Summer faced front again.

Out of the corner of her eye, she caught the cease-and-desist look Devlin shot to Summer, then bit the side of her cheek to keep from smiling. Summer could be tough as nails, but she had a soft heart for those she cared about. Which brought her thoughts back to Daylan and why Summer was so hard on him. Twins were supposed to be close.

"Did you see Kurt at the end of the block when we left Earthbound?" Devlin wanted to know as he glanced in the rearview mirror at her.

Josie shook her head.

"Need to be more aware of your surroundings. I

know Daylan saw him." Devlin switched on the ignition, and the engine roared to life. He grasped the steering wheel and turned out of the studio's parking lot onto Cascade Avenue. "How far is your apartment?"

"About a mile and a half. Turn right just before the bank building on the left-hand side." She peered at Summer. "I'm sorry. Figured he'd get the brush-off and go on his way. Like he did when Devlin showed him the door. He didn't. Guess I'm not as intimidating." She snickered under her breath and looked out the back window. "At least it doesn't look like he followed us." She reached out and stroked Piper's soft fur.

"You do know this isn't a laughing matter." He arched a brow and peered in the rearview mirror at her.

"Yes, sir. I was laughing at the absurdity of the thought. Not at the situation. Sorry."

"I figured as much. But still, I'm counting on Daylan to keep Kurt busy if he tries to follow us." Devlin pointed to a red brick building on the left. "Turn right here?"

"Yes. It's the purple house on the right with pink shutters and magical creatures painted on the outside."

Devlin raised a brow and glanced back at her for a second. "Interesting motif."

"We were bored last summer, and the landlord wanted the main house and carriage house painted. It was weathered and some of the wood was rotting, especially the fascia boards. There are only six tenants in the building, counting the carriage house apartment out back. So we offered to paint it for him in exchange for deduction in our rents. He paid for the wood, paint, brushes, nails, and screws."

"You mean he approved that paint scheme?"

She giggled. "Not exactly. It was a creative endeavor that made the front page of the local newspaper after we were done. A bonus was the guy downstairs is an electrician and he brought the electrical system up to code. Jimmy, our landlord, paid for the supplies. Jack donated his time. Got a couple of months' credit for his work."

"I'll bet it did. But I kinda like it." Summer took her phone out of her backpack and snapped a couple of pictures.

"It's nice that you have a fair and understanding landlord. You hear so many tenant horror stories."

"Yeah. He's great, but Jimmy's getting up there in years. We worry what will happen when he can no longer manage it himself or sells the place. The other tenants and I have talked about buying it from him, but..." She shrugged.

"Hmm... Could be a good investment, close to downtown." Summer paused for a couple of beats. "Are you into magic, fantasy, that sort of thing?"

"Kinda. I love a good paranormal romance. One takes me away from my humdrum life for a few hours. The heroes are swoon-worthy. And the women have to be strong, or I won't read it." She sighed. "Too bad there aren't men like that in real life."

Summer stole a covert glance at Devlin, who smirked and slowed to a stop in front of the house. "Okay, Josie, make it quick. Don't want an altercation with your friend."

"He's not my friend." She huffed out as she slid off the seat and jumped to the ground. "I'll be right back."

Summer opened the door, grabbed for her arm, and nearly toppled out of the truck. "Hold on there. I'll go in with you."

Leaning back in the seat, Devlin waved the girls on. "Piper and I'll wait in the truck. Give you a heads-up if I see anything suspicious." He wiggled his cell phone back and forth in his hand. "Are we sure this guy works alone? Seems to me it would have taken him a long time to acquire all your friend's addresses, then go to each place and slash the tires."

"Most of my friends live in the vicinity. So it wouldn't have taken long," she offered before sprinting toward the front door, Summer on her heels. Piper barked her protest at being left in the truck.

She blew out a breath as she reached the door and paused a moment to touch the new leaves budding on the trees near the entrance. They were wet from the recent rains and glistened in the sunlight that peeked through the clouds. She turned her eyes skyward for a moment.

Following her gaze, Summer glanced up. "Looks like the storm is over for the moment, but clouds are boiling up over the mountains fairly quickly."

Inside the old house renovated to apartments, she sprinted up two flights of stairs, stopped at the top, and pointed to a door at the end of the hall. "That one's mine. I need to stop here and tell Lizzy what going on. She'll worry about me otherwise."

"Okay but don't tell her where you are staying or how long you'll be gone," Summer said gently.

She put a hand on her hip. "I'm not stupid. But Liz would never tell Kurt anything."

"You don't know what circumstances Kurt could put Liz under. If she really doesn't know anything, it's best for everyone. I believe Kurt is dangerous. Not just a bother, as you've been treating him."

She picked at the hem of her worn wizarding sweatshirt from a popular movie. "Didn't think of that." Knocking on Lizzy's door, she grinned when the middle-aged woman with brown hair pulled back in a braid that hung nearly to her waist answered the door. Lizzy was dressed in a bright orange broomstick skirt that swept the floor and a butter yellow peasant blouse with tiny pastel fairies embroidered around the neckline, tied at the top with a multicolored cord.

"Hey, Josie, what brings you here in the middle of a workday?" Liz narrowed her eyes. "Anything wrong? You're not in some kind of trouble, are you?" Her gaze bounced between Josie and Summer. "Come in, come in. Don't want the whole world knowing your business." She eyed the door across the hall as it opened a crack, then closed quickly.

The woman held the door open wide. Josie stepped inside, followed by Summer, and closed the door. "Spill."

She hesitated then finally said, "No trouble—not really."

Summer gave her a stern look and opened her mouth. Before her boss could get a word out, she interrupted.

"Well, sorta. Kurt is hanging around here again. You know, the guy we chased off a couple of times a month ago. I had to use the fire escape this morning to avoid him." She frowned. "Tore a hole in my brand new pink yoga pants. So I'm going to grab a few things from my apartment and stay with friends for a few days. I didn't want you to worry."

"Thanks. I appreciate that. Where can we reach

you if necessary?"

She hesitated for a beat, peering at Summer. "Uh...if you need me, call and leave a message at Earthbound." Josie hugged her friend.

Lizzy scowled at Summer. "And who might you be?"

Summer grinned. "I'm Josie's boss. Well, a friend, too. I own Earthbound Yoga Studio. Kurt's causing problems for Josie—I don't like it."

Liz's face broke into a wide smile. "Me either. That guy is bad news! You'll take care, Josie."

"Yes, of course. Keep an eye on my apartment, please?"

"Will do. Don't be gone too long. We'll miss your sunny smile and contagious giggle around here."

Opening the door, she gave Liz a quick wave and hurried down the hall. She paused at the door with a faerie painted in the center, then opened the door to reveal a neat apartment nestled in the corner of the building. Large windows occupied one wall. A contoured ceiling line, with a border of small light pink flowers and a whisper of mint green ivy accents on a sandy background finished the décor. Landscape paintings hung around the rooms, a few on the floor leaned against the bedroom wall. It was an open-concept-design living area.

Summer cocked her head and touched a finger to the "JMac" scrawled in the bottom corner of one painting. In an awestruck voice, Summer asked, "Josie, did you paint these?"

Heat rose in her cheeks. "Yeah. Painting helps me relax." She bent down and yanked out a tie-dyed duffel from under her bed.

"These are beautiful. Think we could hang a few in Earthbound?" Summer perused a few of the paintings that lined the bedroom wall and found a beautiful painting of Piper on black canvas. She sucked in a breath.

"Oh, heavens no. They aren't that good." She grabbed necessary items from the bathroom, went to her dresser and took underwear from the drawer, shoved it inside the bag, then stopped at her closet. "I'll get a few things and come back if I need more."

"Better get enough for a week." At the look of despair on her face, Summer added, "Just to be safe. By the way, I'm taking this picture of Piper. How much do you want for it?"

She smiled wistfully. "It's one of my favorites and my first attempt at painting on black canvas. But you can have it. Piper is such a sweet companion. I love her."

"Oh, I know a few people who would disagree adamantly with you." Summer quickly pulled bills out of the wallet in her backpack and stuffed them into Josie's duffel. "This one is going to the cabin. Turning, she pointed to a woodland scene and a snow-covered mountain landscape. I want those for Earthbound. Name your price and I'll take them with me today. Devlin can frame them with aspen wood at the cabin. They'd be a wonderful addition to the studio."

"No, no. They aren't worth anything."

"Oh, they're wonderful. You're an extremely talented artist." She picked up the paintings. "I'm going to take these to the truck." Summer peeked out the window at Devlin's vehicle below. "It's starting to drizzle again. Do you have a sheet we could cover them with?"

"Sure." From the floor over in the corner, she picked up a turquoise sheet with dried paint spatter and tossed it to Summer. "You can't tell any of our students they're mine. Okay?"

"Of course, but they'll figure it out." Summer wrapped the sheet between the paintings. "You should be proud."

Her cheeks heated at the compliment. She'd never thought about anyone liking her work. It was a stress release for her. Putting the stuffed duffel on the floor, she pulled several outfits on hangers from the closet. "I think this will do."

Summer dug through her backpack, took out her cell phone, touched the screen, and put the phone to her ear. "Devlin, we are going to need help up here. Any problems down there?" She paused. "Great, we're on the third floor, the last door on your right. See ya in a minute." She tapped the screen again and stuffed the phone in her backpack. No sooner had she set the backpack on the floor than three sharp, staccato beeps sounded from the pack. Yanking up the bag, she found the phone and stared at the screen. "What the hell?"

"Isn't that the ring tone for your alarm company?" She asked worriedly. "Did Kurt get into the studio?"

"Doubt it." Summer touched the screen. "Hello. No, I'm not at the location, but my brother is. Let me check with him and call you back." Disconnecting the call, she made a growling sound in her throat as she paused for a moment, touching her finger to her lip. 'I wonder." She touched the screen again and held the phone to her ear. "Daylan? It's you." Summer's shoulders slumped and she eased into a chair. "Scared me half to death for a moment. I've nothing to hide, but I wish you'd respect my privacy. This is not the way to…"

A sharp knock had Josie rushing to the door, where she hesitated. "Devlin?"

"Are you expecting someone else?" he answered in an amused voice.

She opened the door and pointed to Summer.

Hoisting the paintings, Summer finished the phone conversation and glanced at Devlin. She tapped the screen a few more times and dropped the phone in her pocket, giving Devlin a significant look. "We'll work on a price for these when we get back."

Devlin raised an eyebrow but took Josie's duffel and the bundle of paintings from Summer. "Is this all?"

She glanced from Summer to Devlin. *None of her business.* She shrugged.

"For now. I want to come back and take a better look at Josie's paintings. You might find some that will look good in the gun club." Flipping through several canvases, she pointed at one in particular. "And see that one of Pikes Peak in autumn?" Summer jerked her chin toward the painting leaning against the wall.

Devlin glanced around the room. "Been hiding your real talent, huh?" He chuckled. "They are quite eye-catching." Picking up the Pikes Peak painting, he added it to the bundle, then wrapped the sheet around all of them and headed out the door. Summer followed him, while Josie slung the duffel over her shoulder and locked the door behind them.

Lurking on the first landing was a red-haired teenage boy with freckles. "Where you going? You're not moving out, are you?"

"Nope. As if it's any of your business." She ruffled his hair. "Doing a little camping. Be back soon."

He rolled his eyes and frowned, brushing his hair into place. "See ya later." He shoved his hands in his pockets and meandered down the hallway toward the stairs.

"Who was that?" Devlin inquired, stopping on the landing.

With a nonchalant wave of her hand, she watched as the boy clomped down the stairs. "Joe. He lives on the second floor with his mom."

"What's he doing on the third floor?" Devlin asked, carefully picking his way down the flight of steps.

She shrugged. "Don't know. He's always around."

Summer pursed her lips and looked over at Devlin. Outside he hustled to the truck and gently laid the paintings in the pickup bed and closed the cover.

Seeing the exchange between Summer and Devlin, she huffed out a breath. "Trust me. He's just a neighborhood kid." She waved her hand dismissively. "According to Lizzy, his family was one of the first tenants in the complex years ago. Hence he wanders the hallways as if he owns the building."

"Pays to be cautious. Then you don't end up climbing out a window and hot footing it to work." Summer snickered.

Devlin coughed to hide a chuckle. "Ladies, let's get going."

*Never going to live that down.* Josie stowed her duffel on the floor, clambered into the truck, and settled beside Piper. "Hey, Summer, what's the story on Daylan? Weren't you two close growing up?"

"We were. But…it's a long story."

"I've plenty of time."

"What about you? Never talked much about your family." Summer twisted in her seat to face the girl.

*Slick change of subject.* She smiled. "It's a long story. Short version, I'm the black sheep in my family. A free spirit. Parents didn't like that. Finished college with a liberal arts degree rather than a law degree. Studied Yoga with the old ones after college, then traveled around. When they threatened to cut off funding to bring me back into the fold, I told them that was fine. Been on my own ever since."

"I see." Summer nodded.

"As far as I can see, money only creates different problems. Mom and Dad were always looking for something better, a new house, a new car, a brilliant child, a new spouse. Well, you get the picture. My sister fulfilled their dreams and I went my own way. My brother was a lot older and buckled under parental pressure. He's a corporate attorney in Georgia or somewhere in the south. Married, has a couple of children."

"That's too bad. Family is important." Devlin glanced in the rearview mirror at her.

"Family can also be difficult. You're lucky to have such a supportive family. Some of us just don't fit the mold," Summer said wistfully.

"Is that what happened between you and your brother?" Josie knew she was poking the bear, but…

"The dynamics in our family are difficult. We simply grew apart as adults and went our own ways."

"Okay. Don't tell me," she said quietly. *I'll figure it out. Painting isn't my only talent.* "He seems like a lonely wanderer."

Summer cocked an eyebrow and scowled. "Daylan's got a way with women. So watch yourself. He's mucked up opportunities. Fell in with the wrong crowd. Now he's paying the price." She turned to face front.

Devlin slowed the truck. Gravel crunched under the vehicle's tires as he took the alley and turned into the parking lot behind Earthbound. Summer hopped out of the vehicle. Waiting for Devlin to release Piper, she called the dog to her side and strode toward Earthbound.

"Hey, wait a minute." Josie jumped out of the truck. "We weren't finished."

"As far as Summer is concerned, you are," Devlin said with a grin, glancing around in the darkening afternoon mist. "You want to know what makes Daylan tick? Observation is the key."

Chapter Four
Only the Beginning, But How Do You Keep a
Ghost Quiet?

Daylan tiredly pushed through the door. On the bed
sat the Scottish Highlander fading in and out with a
smirk on his ghostly lips. "What the hell you do want?
Spit it out in words I can understand. Your Scottish
brogue is hard enough to understand, without the thee,
ye, kens, and other mumbo jumbo."

The ghost tilted his head to the side as if to
question, then appeared to think better of it. "Seems
your sister's mate kens what ye have failed to see."

Wrenching the chair out from under the makeshift
desk, Daylan flipped it around and straddled it,
narrowing his eyes at the ghost. Exasperation crept into
his voice. "And what would that be?"

"Magic powers of the blacksmith," the ghost said
mysteriously.

"I'm a warlock, plain and simple. Nothing magical
about my forge or talent for blades—which, by the way,
comes from practice and hard work." He jumped up
from the chair and paced the room, stopping
occasionally to frown at the ghost.

"Ye could not be more wrong, laddie."

"So say you." He plopped into a worn recliner,
covered with a brightly colored patchwork quilt that
matched the thick comforter on the king bed on the far

side of the room. "You got a name. Right?"

"Of course I have a name. But the curse prevents me from telling ye. What I can say is: ye are the seventh son of the seventh son, by the same name, and able to break the curse, provided..." The ghost began to fade.

"Hey...don't you dare disappear. I'm not through talking to you."

"I have said too much already. Don't wanna draw attention to ourselves, because he may wait and listen in the Fae realm, always vigilant as his revenge continues."

"Who's he? A faerie? You're scared of a faerie? You gotta be kiddin' me."

Shaking his head sadly, the ghost faded, leaving only a wisp of mist floating in the air.

Shoving up from the chair, he stormed around the room cursing vehemently. After a few minutes, anger spent, he braced his hands on the window frame and rested his forehead on the cool glass. "This gets better and better," he vented to the empty room. "How the hell am I supposed to help someone who talks in riddles?"

He kicked the massive sleigh bed frame and yelped.

"Hello...hello... Anyone here?"

Standing on one foot, he quietly put his other foot down on the floor and limped to the bedroom door and opened it. A young couple stood beside the massive wooden door. "I'm sorry, we're closed." He stared down the hall to the "open" sign in the window. "I forgot to flip the sign."

"Oh...do you happen to have a schedule of classes? What form of yoga do you teach? Vinyasa, a physical yoga like Hatha, Ashtanga, Iyengar, Bikram, any Restorative?" The young woman tilted her head up to meet his gaze.

He stood rooted to the spot and glanced around the room before meeting her gaze again. "Whoa...you're talking to the wrong person. This is my sister's studio. I'm visiting and haven't a clue about yoga." He paused, remembering the stacks of paper on the bookshelf in Summer's office. Holding his index finger up, he said, "Wait here a moment." He limped toward the office.

She followed him, chatting a mile a minute. "Sure. We're new in town, and a clerk at the motel down the street recommended this place. Kinda hard to find. Missed the sign a couple of times." The young woman shifted from foot to foot outside the office door.

In the office, he made a beeline to the bookcases where stacks of information sheets on types of yoga, instructors' experience, and a schedule of classes were neatly arranged. "Aha..." He picked up several papers and hobbled out of the office. Waving the sheets in his hand, he said, "Found 'em."

The man stretched out his hand and grasped Daylan's. "Todd, and this is my wife Winnie."

"Nice to meet you." Releasing Todd's hand, Daylan gave the instruction sheets and schedule of classes to him. "These should answer any questions you have. If not, give Summer or Josie a call. The number is at the top of the schedule."

Winnie took the papers from Todd and reviewed them. "Thank you. We'll be back in the morning."

"I'll tell Summer to expect you."

The couple waved, and Todd yanked open the door and let it close behind them.

Daylan locked the door, flipped the sign to Closed and padded over to the fireplace. The flames had died down, so he hefted a couple of logs onto the fire, waved his hand, and flames raced around the logs. Crackling, hissing, and popping sounds came from the hearth as the fire roared to life. Standing in front of the fireplace, he rubbed his hands together, his stomach gurgling.

Earlier in the day, he'd noticed a convenience store down the block. The rain had subsided, and he needed to check for Kurt anyway. He stepped out the door, circled the studio, and limped down the sidewalk to the store. Once inside, he picked up a six-pack of soda and several sticks of beef jerky. When he returned, magic allowed him to reenter the studio, since he'd locked the door on his way out.

He took a bite of the jerky. Twisting the cap open on the cola drink, he wandered around the studio sipping his drink, the pain in his foot nearly gone. Pausing at the ornately carved newel post and banister, he glanced up the stairs. *If I'm supposed to keep Josie safe, I'd better familiarize myself with the layout.* Sliding his hand on the banister, he plodded up the wooden stairs to the apartment and wiggled the handle. It was locked. Hesitating only a couple of beats, he waved his hand over the door handle and it clicked open. His hand on the knob, he started to push it open.

Lifting a foot, he stopped at the threshold. *Am I trespassing inside my sister's place? She allowed me to stay in the room downstairs but didn't say I couldn't wander around. She's not living here now anyway.* He stepped inside and surveyed the rooms. A sixty-inch television hung on the wall with surround sound speakers strategically located around the room. *Nice.* In the cozy living room sat a mismatched couch, loveseat, and recliner. Peeking into the bedroom, he noted a matching log bedroom set. Quickly backing out, he padded to the kitchen.

The kitchen was state of the art, new appliances, cabinets, center island with a natural stone countertop. Maybe granite? He ran his fingers over the smooth, cool surface, then noticed the surveillance camera. *Uh-oh. If I'm not supposed to be up here—busted. I better come up with an explanation pronto.* A recessed panel in the kitchen caught his eye. He touched the edge and the panel slid open to reveal a silent alarm, counting down. *Shit.*

The cordless phone on the kitchen counter rang. Nearly jumping out his skin and his heart thundering in his chest, he stared at the device, then glanced at the caller id. His sister's name came up. *Busted big time.* Picking up the phone he said, "Sorry. I came upstairs to make sure everything was secure. Guess I should have asked first—but you weren't here."

An exasperated voice answered. "Daylan. It's you." She blew out a breath on the other end of the line. "Scared me half to death for a moment. I've nothing to hide, but I wish you'd respect my privacy. This is not the way to…"

He raked his fingers through his hair. "I know, I'm sorry, didn't think. Won't happen again."

"See that it doesn't. We'll talk when I return." She paused. "No Kurt?"

Breathing a sigh of relief, he leaned heavily against the counter. "Nope. I took a walk around the premises. No sign of him." He wasn't about to tell her he'd left the area to grab a snack and used magic to get back into the studio. *At least I locked the door.*

"Okay. See you soon." She disconnected the call.

Wow, his sister was serious about security. There were alarms on the windows, glass-break modules, an alarm panel and computer monitoring system set up. He walked to the door, turned the lock, and closed the door.

Downstairs, he nosed around a bit more and discovered the same tight security. The system in her studio must be monitored in her office. He returned to the fireplace and sat on the end of the raised stone hearth finishing the soda and a piece of jerky. Pulling his phone out of his jeans pocket, he disabled the WIFI and GPS. Hesitating for a couple of beats, he finally touched the screen and held it to his ear.

After three rings, a man's voice answered. "Hello."

"Dad…glad I caught you."

"Daylan, where are you? Did you find Summer?"

"Yeah, I found her. She wasn't any too glad to see me." He picked at the cement between the rocks.

"Where is she?"

"Safe, happy, and settled. Pissed as hell that I hunted her down. So for the moment, I'm not going to disclose her location. I'll let her tell you when she's ready." He let out a long breath, expecting backlash from his dad.

"All right," his father said hesitantly.

Relief flooded through him. "The reason I'm calling is the ghost is back. Got a little more information for you." Daylan repeated the exact conversation he had with the ghost. "Any idea who the faerie—Fae is and what revenge he is referring to?"

"None. But it gives us more to go on than we had

before. Sounds like a battle of power over someone or something ended badly. Please tell Summer to call us, if only to check in. Your mother will be disappointed that you won't disclose your sister's location."

"I know, but if I want her help, I gotta stay on her good side. You understand."

"Understood. Don't like it."

"Call me if you find anything."

"Will do. Keep on him. We need more. Your sister is more the family historian, so if you can enlist her help…"

"I know, but she's left that part of her life behind."

The wooden door banged open. Piper came thundering through, followed by Summer and Josie.

"Dad, I gotta go. Talk to you soon." He disconnected the call and pushed to his feet, ambling over to take Josie's duffel from her, and carried it upstairs. His phone buzzed in his pocket. He let it go to voice mail.

Pounding back down the stairs, he stopped on the bottom stair as Piper planted herself on the floor in front of him, lips curled but no sound.

Stifling a giggle with the back of her hand, Summer called, "Piper, leave it. Let Daylan pass." The dog stepped sideways a couple of feet and sat down again.

"Oh, so funny." He walked carefully past Piper, slowly reached into his pocket, and drew out a small piece of beef jerky and dropped it on the floor. "I hope beef jerky is okay?"

"It would've been nice if you'd asked first, but it's one of her favorites. Smart move."

Piper remained where she was, glancing from the

jerky on the floor to Daylan, and turning a pleading gaze to Summer. "Get it, Piper." She pointed to the treat. Piper gobbled it up and stared at Daylan, who was now standing beside Devlin. She huffed and trotted to her water bowl by the door.

"Looks like you are free to move about the studio." Devlin chuckled, carefully placing the paintings on the floor then turned his gaze on Summer. "I assume you'll decide what to take with us and what to leave here?"

"Nope. They all go to the cabin so you can frame them. We'll hang the pictures when we get back."

He groaned. "This is supposed to be a relaxing weekend."

She caressed his back, leaned over and nuzzled his neck, and breathing a kiss below his ear she whispered, "You'll be well compensated."

He wrapped his arm around her waist and pulled her against him. "I'll hold you to it."

"Yewww. Guys, get a room." Josie grinned and pointed to the door. "Don't you two have somewhere to be? We have things handled here." She grinned up at Daylan and shivered.

"Are you cold?" He glanced around the room for a sweater or jacket.

"No." Her cheeks blushed crimson.

"That's what I'm afraid of," Summer said on a laugh, letting Devlin guide her to the door. She whistled for Piper and motioned her to follow.

Crossing the floor, Daylan caught Summer's arm. "Oh, I almost forgot. A couple, Todd and Winnie, stopped by. I told them the studio was closed today but gave them literature on Earthbound I found in your office, the class schedule, info on instructors, and yoga types practiced here. They'll be back tomorrow. So I guess Josie will handle it?"

Summer smiled at her brother. "Wow, I'm impressed. Thank you for doing that. You know how to reach us. See you on Monday."

"And the world better be coming to an end if you call us," Devlin added, his lips twitching as Summer jabbed him in the ribs. "Oh, Josie, we'll stop back by your apartment and bring your vehicle over here before we leave town. If you'll toss me your keys?"

She sprinted to the office, came out rummaging through her backpack, and pitched a single key to Devlin. "It's my spare. Just park my SUV in the lot and be on your way. We'll be fine. Have a great weekend." She closed and locked the door behind them. Turning to Daylan, she asked, "What do you want to do for dinner?"

"Hadn't thought much about it. I'd rather stay in. Anything to eat around here?"

Josie paused for a beat, glancing upstairs. "Probably not. My staying here was kinda spur of the moment, and Summer hasn't been in the apartment for months." She snapped her fingers. "Hey, we could call out for pizza."

"Sounds good. Tomorrow between classes we can grab a few groceries."

She nodded her head as she scrolled through her phone. "Great idea. Do you cook?"

"Of course. Do you?"

"I have my specialties. To be honest, I eat out a lot. What do you want on your pizza?"

"Meat."

She touched the screen and put the phone to her

ear. "Delivery. Yes, that number and address are correct." She paused. "One half mega meat, extra cheese, and sauce all around, then only beef on the other half—yes, that's correct. Thirty minutes will be fine." She ended the call.

"Wow, they had your number and the studio's address?"

"Yeah, we order lunches quite often. They have lots of other delicious things besides pizza, too. Italian is my favorite food group."

"Good to know." He stood hands in his pockets waiting for her to make the next move.

Josie bounced across the room and hesitated at the stairs. "Want to come up to the apartment, watch TV until the pizza comes? More comfortable than standing here staring at each other. I don't bite—too often." She giggled.

*That woman has more energy than a kid on a sugar high.* Then the words she said hit home. *Did she know about his ex-girlfriend? Did she know Summer was a witch? Oh, I should have asked Summer before she left.* He touched his phone in his pocket. *Not earth-shattering, it could wait until Monday.*

"Hey, only kidding. Why are you looking at me like I could be from outer space?"

"Sorry. Thought of a couple of things I should've asked Summer before she left." He shifted from one foot to the other. "Maybe…"

"Hey, I can probably help you. What did you want to know?" She cocked her head to the side and smiled at him.

"Just family matters. Forget it. Did she leave any movies up there?" He glanced at the stairs.

"You bet. Devlin has his own supply of every movie ever made, according to Summer. And a spectacular home theater in the cabin. There's microwave popcorn in the office. It's not as good as homemade, but it'll do tonight. Don't you think?" She sprinted up the stairs, leaving him staring up after her.

Watching her cute butt bounce up the stairs was a turn-on. One he couldn't afford. "Sure, works for me." He climbed the stairs slowly, hoping to cool down his reactive body parts. This weekend could be a challenge. It had been a while since he'd been with a woman, and Josie had stirred his blood from the first time he saw her. *Not good.*

Chapter Five

Dark, Brooding, and Probably Dangerous—Just Her Type—But What Was He Hiding?

Josie unlocked the door to the apartment, pushed it open, and deactivated the alarm. *Has someone been in here? It smells—almost like—Daylan?* She flicked the light switch and the room was bathed in subtle light. At a soft touch on her back, she jumped and squeaked.

"Sorry, didn't mean to startle you. Is there a problem?"

"No—no, just detected a strange scent." She waved her hand in a dismissive gesture. "I have a sensitive nose."

"I was up here earlier, but the door was locked. Maybe that's what you smell."

"Yeah, could be." *But the scent is all over the apartment. He was in here. How'd he get in? I have the key. Maybe Summer gave him a key.* She gave a slight shake of her head. *Not likely.* She turned to face Daylan. "So what's your story?"

For a moment she stood hands on hips, her gaze locked on his emerald green eyes, then on his high sculptured cheekbones and full sensuous lips. She turned abruptly, crossing to the kitchen, opened the microwave, tossed in the package of popcorn, and turned on the timer.

"No story. A family situation called for a

46

discussion with Summer. So I looked her up and here I am."

"Well—I'd believe that if Summer hadn't given you such a cool reception. Your sister told me she was estranged from her family, sooo—" She dragged the last word out. "Oh, never mind, it's none of my business. The movies are in the cabinet under the TV, bottom drawer."

The apartment filled with the delicious aroma of buttered popcorn. Josie took the steaming package out of the microwave and poured it into a bowl. She inhaled deeply. "Wow, I love the smell of fresh popcorn. What do you want to drink? We've got pop downstairs in the fridge. Glad we're planning on shopping, 'cause tomorrow the cupboards are bare. Like ol' mother Hubbard's. Refrigerator too." She giggled.

"I'll run downstairs, retrieve the soft drinks, and check on pizza delivery."

"It's only been ten or fifteen minutes. It'll be at least thirty. That's why I made popcorn. I'm starved."

"Okay, be right back. You're talking about the fridge in Summer's office. Right? Any chance there's beer in there?"

"Nope, not unless Devlin left a couple out of a six-pack. It'd be taking your life in your own hands to drink one without asking." She snickered. "You don't want to get on his wrong side. Seems you've enough trouble with your sister."

"You got that right. We'll pick up beer tomorrow." He paused. "Summer will allow—never mind."

"She won't care as long as the beer is up here in the fridge. Devlin leaves a bottle or two on occasion. Usually after doing handyman stuff around here.

Summer isn't about to say anything to him. The sun rises and sets in that man, according to her. Lucky gal."

She opened the freezer to check for ice cubes, then remembered Summer left the ice maker on up here because the fridge in her office didn't have one. *Convenient.* Filling two glasses with ice, she listened as Daylan made his way to the first level. His footsteps faded as she got out paper plates. Walking to the coffee table, she set the glasses and paper plates on the table, then scooted to the door.

A shiver shot up her spine as she looked into the darkness of the studio. Only a sliver of light shone beneath the office door. A shadow crossed the light and opened the door. She blanched even though she knew it should be Daylan.

"Hey, Josie, anything wrong?" Holding a six-pack of soda, Daylan's long legs carried him across the studio floor in record time.

She sagged against the door frame, knees wobbly. *Guess the Kurt situation has taken more of a toll than I thought.* "Nope. Noticed the alarm was still off in the studio. I'll set it from up here. That's all."

Daylan swept into the apartment, set two cans on the table beside the glasses, and put the rest in the fridge. "So tell me about this Kurt. There has to be more to the story than you told Summer. Otherwise, you wouldn't be trembling." He wrapped an arm around her in a friendly gesture, holding her until the trembling stopped.

For a moment, her traitorous body curved against him. Was it security or need? She didn't want to find out. Summer was quite clear he was off limits. Patting his arm, she slipped out of his hold and padded to the alarm panel. "I need to set the alarm. Summer is a stickler for security. Something bad must have happened to her." At the sound of tires and squeaky brakes out front, Josie turned toward the window.

"She's always been that way," he said nonchalantly. "Now about Kurt?"

"Give it a rest." Josie peered out the window. "Pizza's here. I'll pick the movie. You get the pizza."

"Okay, but don't set the alarm until I get the pizza." He glanced at the open alarm panel. "Summer will have a conniption if the alarm goes off."

"How would you know?" She closed the panel staring at him.

"Because I—know my sister," he finished lamely.

Snickering, she flashed a mischievous smile. "I'll set it after you bring the pizza up. Make sure you lock the door and set the deadbolt." She tossed him the keys, grabbed a handful of popcorn and took a bite, then flipped through the DVDs and Blu-rays, selected an action/adventure, and reached for the remote.

The TV blinked on as the sound system came to life. By the time Daylan strode through the door, she had returned to the security panel, flipped through the screens from the cameras downstairs, and set the alarm.

"Don't you check the building before setting the alarm?"

"Already did." She settled onto the couch, one foot under her, and started the movie.

Pizza box in hand, he flipped it open. She put a slice on the paper plate. He plopped a piece on his plate and flopped into the lounger, biting into the pizza with gusto. "Wow, this is excellent."

"Told you." She tossed the movie cover to him.

"This one okay?"

Raising his hand in the air, he caught it and turned it over in his hand. "Looks good. I haven't seen it but planned on it. A lot of hype when it first came out; tall, blue aliens in an inhospitable environment to humans wasn't on my radar at that time."

"What was on your mind?" she asked coyly.

"Making a living, keeping my forge running, and keeping my mind off my personal life."

She clung to that last phrase. "Bad breakup, huh?" She tossed a piece of popcorn up in the air and caught it in her mouth.

"Kind of. I don't want to discuss it." He took a bite of pizza and washed it down with a swig of cola. "Did you actually date Kurt?"

"Heavens, no! He was a student, as I said." Taking her pizza from the plate, she bit into it. Cheese strung from the piece to her mouth.

"So you don't know any background on him?" He narrowed his eyes at her as she slid the DVD into the player and clicked play.

She bit off cheese and wrapped the extra around the piece of pizza, then wiped her fingers on a napkin next to the box. "No. I've been over this with Summer and Devlin. If we see him again, we'll call the police to file harassment and stalking charges. End of discussion." She popped her last bite of pizza into her mouth and reached for another. "Yum!" Around the bite, she asked, "What do you forge?" Taking a sip of cola, she looked expectantly at him.

"I do a bit of farrier work, custom blades, swords, that kinda thing." He paused the movie. "Do you want to talk or watch the movie?"

"Both. Can't we do both?"

"Not really. I've never seen the movie, so I'd like to watch it uninterrupted. I don't mean to be rude, but I'm not much of a multi-tasker."

"I suppose." She sulkily curled both feet up under her on the couch.

"Thank you. We can talk afterward," he offered, leaning back, stretching his long legs out.

"If there's time. I have an early yoga class tomorrow. If I don't get enough sleep, I'm cranky and it takes me a while to get limbered up. So I am usually in bed around nine."

"Sure. Don't forget Winnie and Todd will be here in the morning. Guess they want to sign up for classes." He clicked the remote and the movie resumed.

She watched the movie, checked her email on the phone, poured another glass of cola, and took a drink. "Ohhh, I love this part. It's so romantic with the tree and them coming together."

He gave her a sidelong glance, then returned his attention to the movie. "It's a great movie."

As the movie credits scrolled on the screen, she stood and stretched, picked up the pizza box and a glass, and took them to the kitchen. She stuffed the box into the garbage, turned on the water in the sink, squirted dish soap, then held up a wet sudsy hand to cover her wide yawn.

"So why did you become a yoga instructor?" He picked up the soda cans and a glass and followed her. Standing behind her, he leaned against her at the sink as he dropped his glass into the sink of soapy water. It bobbed in the water for a second, then sank. He backed away.

"I was looking for peace and harmony in my life." She paused and grinned up at him. "And because, at the time, it pissed off my parents."

"Why?"

"I wasn't cut from the same cloth as they were. My much older brother followed in their footsteps. They figured the rest of the children should too. My sister tried but fell in love with a doctor. They had kids right away, so she's a stay-at-home mom. Still, even that kinda fit with their plans for her."

"You didn't conform to their wishes?"

She shook her head. "When I was younger they referred to me as their "free spirit." Thought it was cute. But as I grew older, it wasn't cute anymore and didn't conform to their plans. We butted heads a lot. I wasn't having any part of their pre-law studies in college or attending law school. A nine-to-five job or practicing law wasn't what I wanted out of life."

"Ohhh, that doesn't sound much like fun. Not a suit-and-tie guy myself."

"I would guess not—owning a forge and all." She snickered. "Anyway, I graduated with a liberal arts degree and traveled the world until they cut off my funding. Studying yoga with the old ones gave me a sense of belonging. Eventually, I wound up here. The previous owner had lots of personal problems, was always late and wanted me to start the class. So I kinda took over for her until Summer came along."

"It didn't bother you that my sister came along and took over?"

"Not at all. I didn't have the funds to keep this place afloat. The previous owner's downward spiral continued until Summer bought the place and took over the classes. She made lots of upgrades and asked me to stay. Mandy, the other instructor, fills in for us when we need her. It's a great arrangement."

"Sounds like an ideal situation for a free spirit." He nodded in agreement watching her stifle another yawn. "Looks like you're beat. I'll let myself out and take the trash with me." He reached down and yanked the trash bag from its container. "See you in the morning."

"Nite." She followed him to the door and locked it behind him. After taking a nice warm shower, she fell into bed and slept fitfully. Dreams of magical creatures, stalking menaces, and a woman on fire sent her into an adrenalin overload. Waking up damp with sweat, and her hands clammy, she crawled out of bed and pushed open the kitchen window. *Nope, not a full moon.*

Only a sliver of the moon shone in the inky darkness, casting silvery shadows over the silent landscape. Gulping in the crisp air, her head began to clear. *Wow, what a wild night.* The blue numbers on the digital wall clock indicated it was almost four a.m. *Not going back to bed after that.* She wiggled into her orange yoga pants and matching yellow-and-orange striped shirt.

Returning to the kitchen, she turned on the coffee maker for hot water and searched the nearly empty cupboards for an orange spice tea bag. On the top shelf of the cupboard was a tin marked TEA. Standing on tiptoes, she found her fingertips barely touched the rim of the tin. The container tumbled forward and bounced on the edge of the counter. Before she could catch the falling tin, it clattered to the floor. She cursed loudly, swooped down, and grabbed the canister. When she finally pried the top open, the tin nearly slipped out of her hand again.

*Way too early in the morning to require this kind of dexterity.* Inhaling deeply, she smiled. *Ahhh...orange spice tea, my favorite.* She paused for a moment, listening. Was that a door opening? Had she woken Daylan up? *Shit.* His concerned voice wafted up the stairs.

"You okay?"

"Yeah." The hot water streamed into her cup. Holding the mug, she swished her tea bag around as she slipped her feet into her shoes and padded downstairs. Rifling through the fridge in Summer's office, she found a nearly empty tub of blueberry shmear buried behind a bag of bagels. She took a bagel and popped it into the toaster oven sitting on the makeshift counter, flipped the knob to three minutes, and waited impatiently. After slathering the bagel with shmear, she scarfed down breakfast while wandering around the studio.

The hearth was set with logs and crumpled newspaper, but no matches or a lighter in sight. She wrapped her hands around the nearly empty but still warm mug, then turned up the thermostat. It took a long while for the furnace to heat the large, tall-ceilinged studio.

Which was why there was always a roaring fire in the hearth when she arrived for work. She could never find where Summer kept the incendiary devices.

Come to think of it, she'd never seen her boss light the fire. Standing at the window, watching the first yellow rays of sunlight spread across the eastern horizon, she was sipping what was left of her tea when the old house groaned, the stairs squeaked, and what sounded like a door creaked. She spun around, her heart beating a tattoo in her chest as the mug slipped out of her hand and shattered on the floor.

Chapter Six
A Rude Awakening Before His Morning Coffee—
What a Way to Start the Day

Juniper Dupree still haunted his dreams as she had since her fiery death. He knew Summer had no choice. If only he'd paid more attention to the warning signs or listened to his family, none of this would have happened. Yet here they were, two years since Summer had used witchfire to kill his fiancée before she could drain him dry.

Did Juniper ever love him? Was he just a dalliance for her? He'd allowed her to feed from him during their lovemaking, reveling in the sexual euphoria he experienced. *Looking back, not his wisest idea.* Still, his heart ached when he thought of her. He'd been head over heels in love with the beautiful woman—vampire.

Yet on that fateful night, she wouldn't stop. He'd shoved at her, but she was overpowering. Pinching the bridge of his nose, he closed his eyes. Yet the scene played out in front of him as if it were yesterday. Juniper raised her blood-smeared mouth from his neck, making a purring sound, her fangs dripping with his blood. The sound still haunted him. She turned his head and sank her fangs into the other side of his neck, sucking hard and long.

After the sexual euphoria subsided, he'd wavered in and out of consciousness, but she kept feeding.

Suddenly, she'd sat straight up with a loud growl and her eyes wild. A fiery arrow drove straight through her heart, followed by another and yet another. Juniper had let out a blood-curdling scream and clutched at the arrows with her hand. Summer appeared beside them, kicked the flaming vampire to the floor, and watched her burn to ash before covering his naked body with a blanket. "What the fuck were you thinking?" Those were the last words she'd said to him for several weeks.

With a flick of his wrist, a bottle of aged Jamison's whiskey appeared out of thin air and poured into a glass hovering over the night table beside his bed. With a snap of his fingers, the bottle vanished with a pop. He sat up, snatched the glass, and gulped the amber liquid. He hissed as it burned his throat.

"Rough night, laddie?" The ghost materialized at the end of the bed.

He opened his mouth to scream, but no sound came out, only a fine puff of mist.

The ghost held a finger to his lips and shook his head. "Don't want the lassie above you to hear you scream like a little girl."

*That damn ghost will be the death of me.* He stared at the ceiling, for the first time realizing Josie was in the apartment above his room. "What the hell are you doing here?" He growled menacingly yet kept his voice low.

"Simmer down, lad. You be thrashing about. You all right?"

"No thanks to you," he ground out, noticing the ghost's speech pattern had changed. He was much easier to understand. *Well, at least that's something.*

"Lad, I had naught to do with your dream turmoil. Women are the bane of our existence. Which brings me to my dilemma. Time is running out. I need your help."

"How do you expect me to help you when I can't even help myself?"

"A foul mood you be in." The ghost disappeared into a cloud of mist.

He had just swung his legs out of the bed, feet on the floor, when a loud crash reverberated overhead. He jumped to his feet and barreled toward the door. He yanked open the door to hear Josie cursing up a blue streak. "You okay?" he called out.

"Yes." Her irritated voice spewed from the second floor. "Dropped the tea canister. Sorry about the noise."

"You better be," he muttered under his breath, glancing at his wristwatch. Rubbing his eyes, he paused and looked at the watch again. *Might as well be the middle of the night.* The duffel and suitcases he'd brought in last night still sat next to the small dresser. Rifling through the bag, he pulled out a clean pair of jeans and a long-sleeved T-shirt.

He stashed the rest of his clothes in the dresser or hung them up in the closet. He opened the door a crack and peeked out. Josie was standing in front of the big picture window, sipping her tea. His stomach growled. Opening the door wider, he stepped into the studio.

Suddenly, she whirled around and dropped her mug. It shattered on the floor. She stared at him.

He returned her glare for a beat, then surveyed the surroundings. "A bit jumpy today?"

"I guess so."

"What time is your class this morning?"

"Eight." She picked up the pieces of the mug and wiped the floor with a paper towel.

"How about we grab a fast-food breakfast and

bring it back here? You've plenty of time before class. I'm starved."

"I had a bagel and part of a cup of tea." She looked forlornly at the pieces of pottery as she deposited them in the trash. "My favorite mug." She glanced up at him. "I can fix you a bagel. There are several kinds in Summer's freezer."

"Doesn't sound like much of a breakfast. Come on. Let's go. I'm buying." Tugging at her arm, he scooted across the floor, looked from the alarm to the door, and back to Josie.

"Okay. But I usually don't eat much when I have an early class." She entered the alarm code, and it switched from blinking blue to solid green. "Go on outside. I'll reset the alarm to away."

He stepped out the door and glanced across the parking lot. *Nothing unusual. Good.* A soft glow from the streetlights pooled on the side of the road, then blinked off as the sun crested the horizon. He waited for Josie to exit, then insisted they walk around the property before leaving. A lone mid-sized SUV sat in the parking lot. "Is that your vehicle?"

"Yeah, Devlin brought it back before they left for the cabin. Had to have transportation, since I assume you don't have any."

"No—I didn't plan ahead. Figured I'd rent one, if necessary, until sis and I work things out."

She shrugged, fobbed the doors open, and slid into the driver's seat. "There's a twenty-four-hour pancake place a couple of miles from here. They also serve lattes. I'd like one, and you could get a hot meal. Fast food isn't good for you. We'd still get back in time for class."

"Sounds like a plan." His stomach rumbled again, and she gave him a sideways glance.

Inside the restaurant, bacon sizzled, and aromas of freshly baked cinnamon rolls, hash browns, and eggs filled the establishment. Josie slipped into one side of a brown leather booth with log accents and he eased into the other side. Brushing aside the cream-colored lace curtains, he looked up and down the street.

A worry line dug itself down her forehead as she watched him. "Expecting someone?"

He leaned back against the booth and stretched his legs out. "Nope. Just familiarizing myself with the surroundings. If the food here is as good as it smells, I'm going to be a regular customer." He took the menu from its holder on the table and glanced at it. "Everything looks good."

A tall slender woman with brown shoulder-length hair stopped at their table and smiled. "What can I get for you?" She tapped her pen on a pad and looked expectantly at them.

"I'd like a mocha latte, please, with two slices of wheat toast."

He looked at the waitress's name tag. "Jill, I'll have the ham-and-cheese omelet, with hash browns, bacon, and hotcakes." He paused for a beat. "Add a small glass of tomato juice, and coffee, please."

"I'll have it out for you shortly." She hurried off.

"Only the one mixed class this morning?"

"Yep. This afternoon we have an advanced class. Saturday we only offer the two classes, and we're closed on Sunday."

Quick as a wink Jill was back with juice, coffee, and the latte. She set the drinks down and flitted away.

"We better do grocery shopping between classes." He took a drink of the tomato juice.

"Food in the apartment would be good," she agreed, blowing on the steaming latte. Foam clung to her upper lip as she took a sip. She licked it away with the tip of her tongue.

That was enough to engage his unruly male parts. *Don't women know better than to do that kind of thing in front of a man?* He squirmed in his seat trying to relieve the uncomfortable tightening in his crotch. His attraction to her was growing, and he couldn't seem to control it. He'd found women attractive before, but nothing like he felt when she was around.

She looked across the table and raised an eyebrow but said nothing.

He poured a packet of sugar into his coffee, added milk, and stirred a little more vigorously than necessary. The liquid sloshed over one side onto the table. He quickly wiped it up with a napkin.

Saved by the waitress. She returned with his steaming omelet plate, balancing it on one hand while she wiped the table with a clean, damp cloth, then set the plate in front of him. With a quirky smile, she said, "Can I get you anything else?"

"I believe we are good for now." He glanced over at Josie to confirm. She nodded.

He forked up a bite of omelet, the cheese stringing across the plate. He popped it into his mouth, chewed slowly, then swallowed. "We have the whole weekend in front of us. Do you have plans for Saturday night or Sunday?"

"Not really. Been keeping a low profile since the Kurt incident."

He nodded, forking up another bite of omelet. "Understood. How about going to a movie tonight?" Pausing, he glanced at her. The last thing he wanted to do was make her uncomfortable. "Then if you have time, would you mind showing me around town on Sunday?"

"Are you asking me out on a date?" Pretending to be shocked, her eyes widened, and she covered her mouth with her hand. "Your sister told me you're a devil and can't be trusted. So let's keep it platonic." She feigned a cough to cover a snicker which wasn't lost on him.

"Date? Nooo. Only looking for ways to pass the time since we're stuck with each other until Summer and…" He paused. What he really wanted was to keep her away from the ghost. Summer would kill him if she encountered the ghost this weekend or any other type of supernatural behavior.

"Devlin. Her fiancé's name is Devlin." She tilted her head up to meet his eyes. "I was only kidding. Sure we could go see that new superhero flick tonight, in 3D at the IMAX." She glanced at the clock on the wall. "We'd better get back. Didn't you say that couple would be at the studio early this morning?"

"Yes." He shoved up from the table.

She rifled through her bag, pulled out a wallet, and flipped open the clasp.

He put a hand over hers and the wallet. "Breakfast is on me. Remember?"

"Sure. I was checking to make sure I had money to go to the movie tonight." She slid out of the booth and winked at him.

*She's flirting with me. Talk about mixed messages.*

"The movie is on me, you buy the popcorn." He chuckled, turned, and waved to the waitress. "Bill, please."

"Gawd, popcorn and a drink are almost as much as the movie ticket." She hip-checked him and, forgetting about Kurt for the moment, flounced out the door.

"Hey, wait a minute." He slapped a twenty-dollar bill down on the table and rushed after her. Catching her outside the door by the arm, he said gruffly, "I'd rather you let me exit the buildings first. If something happens to you this weekend, my sister will kill me."

Since Kurt, she'd been a bit jumpy and worried, but she couldn't have Daylan thinking she was a wimp. "Hey, I can take care of myself." She whirled around and deftly slipped out of his grasp. Hands on hips she glared at him. "You are not my babysitter."

"Nope, but I sure as hell am your bodyguard this weekend," he shot back. "As far as taking care of yourself, it was you who shimmied down the fire escape and landed on your ass yesterday morning trying to avoid your stalker. A stalker you didn't take seriously until he forced an altercation with your friends." At the look of hurt turning to fury on her cute face, he immediately wished he could take back those words.

She sprinted to her vehicle, jumped inside, and the engine roared to life. She squealed tires leaving him standing on the edge of the parking lot.

He considered his options. What he really wanted to do was simply disappear and reappear in the passenger seat of her vehicle. But that wasn't an option. Walking to the studio would take too long, and what if Kurt was waiting for her. Using magic was risky, should someone see him disappear or reappear out of thin air. But he'd rather risk that than his sister's wrath. Especially if something happened to Josie, proving him an incompetent ne'er-do-well again in Summer's eyes. *No way.*

Jogging across the parking lot, he ducked behind a blind corner of the building. Using a bit of magic, he disappeared and reappeared in his room, the only safe place he was sure no one would see him. He listened for voices and sounds indicating she had arrived safely. The studio was eerily silent. Willing his mind's eye open, he searched the perimeter. No Josie.

He opened the bedroom door and had started across the floor when her vehicle squealed into the parking lot, spewing rocks and gravel in her wake. Retreating to the back of Earthbound, he peeked out the window, watching her stomp to the front door. He walked through the doorway and waited. Being caught in the studio without explanation as to how he got inside without a key or setting the alarm off wasn't a smart idea.

She unlocked the door, stepped inside, and slammed the door behind her. Two beeps told him she'd deactivated the alarm. A few minutes later, the sound of an engine caught his attention as another car pulled into the parking lot. He held his breath but relaxed when the couple he'd met yesterday exited the vehicle talking and laughing. Several minutes passed before he exited out the back door and the alarm chimed. He paused for a beat, then waved a hand to lock and shut the door quietly.

"Damn it," he muttered and sprinted to the front door, calculating enough time had passed that she'd assume he walked back to the studio. To his relief, the door to Earthbound was ajar. He pushed it open and pasted a smile on his face. Her little tirade and unsafe behavior would be addressed later.

"Good morning, Winnie and Todd," he said graciously, passing by the office door. "Nice to see you again."

They smiled and waved to him, unlike the stony look Josie gave him, which melted away as she switched her attention to the couple standing in front of her.

Motioning for them to sit in the chairs across the desk from her, she walked toward the office door, then turned. "I'll just be a moment. Daylan—"

Reluctantly, he paused just past the door. *Shit, she'd heard the chime.*

"Did you try to come in through the back door?" She glanced at the alarm. "I thought I heard the backdoor warning sound." Pinning him with her gaze for a beat, she then glanced toward the back door.

"Yeah, I jiggled the handle, but it was locked. Would that set off the warning?"

"Not usually." She narrowed her eyes at him.

"I'll check it. You go ahead and take care of the customers." He nodded toward the office door.

She stood for a moment as if deciding whether or not to check it herself, then turned on her heel and returned to the office.

Breathing a sigh of relief, he sauntered across the studio's polished hardwood floor, glanced back at the office to make sure she wasn't watching him, then pushed open the door to his room and gasped.

Chapter Seven
A Haunted Yoga Studio Does Not Make a Calm Environment

Josie straightened her shoulders, took a deep calming breath, and ambled toward the office, where a couple stood just inside the door with yoga mats in hand. *How did that guy get under my skin so fast? Calm and balanced, centered. Remember?* She released her breath slowly and stepped into the office. "Good morning. Sorry for the interruption. I thought I heard the backdoor chime."

"I heard it too, as we came in the front door," Winnie said. Her husband nodded. "We can wait if you need to go check on it."

She smiled. "No, it's taken care of. The owner's brother is staying here for a few days. He'll check it out. Now, what kind of classes are you looking for?"

"Mostly intermediate. I have a bad back and use yoga to stretch the muscles and help me stay limber," Todd said.

She nodded and glanced at Winnie inquiringly.

"Oh, I'm kinda high strung. Yoga settles me and helps me find balance. You know what I mean?" Winnie glanced at her husband and smiled. "I guess you'd consider me..." She waffled her hand back and forth. "An intermediate or advanced beginner also."

After a few more minutes of conversation, she gave

them a quick tour of the studio and returned to the office. She pulled out the paperwork and slid it across the desk. "If you could fill out the application and waiver, you'll be all set. We happen to have a class I believe you'll enjoy starting in about half an hour."

"That's what we thought when we reviewed the schedule." Winnie smiled, reaching down to pick up her bag.

"Great." She waited for them to complete the paperwork, then stood. "Feel free to make yourselves comfortable on the couch in the main room or spread out your mats and stretch out." She walked the couple to the office door and showed them to the area where the class would be held. Winnie and her husband spread their mats out and began stretching. When she returned to the office, she closed the door and pulled out her purple yoga mat.

Sitting cross-legged, her hands on her knees, thumb and third finger touching, she took in a long breath and closed her eyes. The hair on the back of her neck stood on end as a feeling of being watched broke her concentration. Jumping to her feet she looked around. Nothing—there was nothing there. *I'm losing it.* She slumped, her back against the wall.

The whole Kurt thing had her on edge, that was all, and her imagination was working overtime. Easing down onto the floor, she kept her back to the wall and faced the doorway as she tried to relax and find balance moving through a few yoga poses. After several minutes, she huffed out a breath, rolled up her mat, and paced the floor. *How am I going to lead a class when I can't find...*

A long mournful creak interrupted her thoughts as

students murmuring greetings trickled in the front door. They began unrolling their mats on selected places on the floor, then quietly visiting in small groups. Before class, she walked the entire building, upstairs, the studio, everywhere except Daylan's room.

If there was a problem there, he'd have to handle it. Nothing appeared out of place. With a sigh of relief and a determined stride, she returned to the studio and stepped to the front of the class. "Let's begin with Mountain pose, then into Vransana and Adho Mukha Svanasana."

By the end of the one-hour class, calmness had settled over her and she felt more like herself. New energy by the name of Daylan in the studio had to be to blame for her jitters before class—and of course the situation with Kurt. What she couldn't figure out was why Daylan had such an effect on her. Normally she could take or leave a man, but him—she couldn't get him out of her head or her nether regions. Damn her traitorous body.

The students gathered their things and ambled to the front door. Tug and pull as they might, the door refused to open. That eerie feeling of being watched washed over her. The hair on her arms stood up, and she rubbed at them until the feeling went away.

"You cold, Josie?" Winnie asked, glancing at the fireplace where kindling and logs were neatly stacked on a bed of crumpled newspaper.

"I have matches." Todd volunteered, holding up a pack of incendiary devices.

"Sure, that would be great." Josie turned toward the room Daylan was staying in.

"Hey, don't you have a back door? Maybe we

should use that exit." One of the other students suggested.

"Can't. It's locked with an alarm bar during class hours. So no one can sneak in when we are in class. I'll be right back." She quickened her pace to Daylan's door. Raising her hand to knock, she paused and listened. Was there someone in there with him? Or was he talking to himself? She sucked in a breath and knocked on the door.

Chapter Eight
What the Hell? He Was Warned, But This Was Unexpected

Daylan stepped inside his room and closed the door. What the hell? Mist floated in the corner of the room toward the ceiling. His ghost. "What have you done?" He strained to keep his voice low. The clothes he'd hung in the closet were strewn across the bed. His suitcase was lying on the floor wide open, and the six drawers from the dresser were upside down on the floor. The lamp next to the bed was tipped over.

He strode to the suitcase, leaned over, and sorted through the contents, straightened, then glanced around the room. The journal he'd left locked inside the suitcase was missing.

The ghost held his hands up in a gesture of surrender. "'Twasn't me. I've been keeping me eye on the young woman downstairs. She's a…"

He slapped his hand down on the table near the door. "You stay away from Josie. I don't need you spooking her and my sister throwing me out on my ear. You've caused me enough trouble. If you want my help, we have to keep my sister happy or I can't help you. She's the key."

The ghost spread his arms wide. "I tried to tell ye something like this could happen. A rogue Fae—"

Shaking a finger at the ghost, he said, "What do

70

you mean you told me? I have no idea what you are talking about. But you'd better get this place cleaned up pronto."

"Not afore ye make sure nothing is missing. Did ye have magical items secreted away in here?"

"No...I left most of that stuff back at the forge. Didn't know what my trip out here might entail. Appears only my journal is missing, and there's nothing magical about it. Only lists my clients and the blades that I've made. If I know my sister, this building is protected with magic. Are you telling me a faerie..."

"Fae," the ghost corrected. "Can't be very strong magic if the Fae penetrated it." He paused for a second, touching his chin with a finger. "Could have woven a faerie spell around it."

"I don't know...Summer is pretty thorough." He rubbed at the back of his neck. "Fae...came in here looking for something and made this mess?"

"Fae magic is ancient. A modern witch may not weave spells for such things. "The ghost nodded. "Do you possess the enchanted hammer, blade, anvil, or chain?"

"I have no idea what you are talking about. The hammer I use was passed down from generation to generation..." He paused, making a mental note to bring up Fae magic to Summer when she returned home.

The ghost's head blurred as he nodded his head vehemently.

"Are you telling me the hammer is enchanted?"

"Aye. The blade, anvil, and chain too, once upon a time. They were a great source of magic and power long ago."

71

"I don't have a chain."

"Aye, ye do, if you have the anvil. 'Tis wrapped around the bottom of the anvil for safe keeping. Once the spell is broken, the chain will do yer bidding."

He wiped a trickle of sweat off his brow with the sleeve of his shirt. "All those things were left in my forge back home."

"With naught for protection? Did your journal list the location of your forge?"

"The forge is alarmed," Daylan protested. "My business information is listed inside the front cover of my journal. Why?"

A heartbroken expression crossed the ghost's face. "Shameful...tools were passed down without the tale." He shook his head sadly. "We cannot release the curse without..." His head jerked up. "The Fae has the location of your forge from the journal."

He held his finger to his lips and shook his head. Quiet footfalls sounded outside his door, became louder, then stopped, and someone knocked. The ghost disappeared.

He sensed Josie and waved his arm. Without a sound, everything in the room found its proper place. *I'll do a more thorough inventory later.* Nonchalantly, he opened the door, leaning his shoulder against the framework. "To what do I owe the pleasure of your company?"

"Is there someone in here with you?" Josie peeked around his body into the room. "I heard voices."

"Not that it is any of your business, but no one is here but me," he said flatly.

She looked around and listened intently. "Must have been coming from outside. But I could have sworn— Anyway, the front door is stuck. Can you get it open? My students want to leave."

"Really. I thought— Never mind." He followed her to the door, where the yoga class was gathered around. When he touched the doorknob, a vision from the recurring dream he'd had before coming here flashed through his mind. Then it was gone, and the door swung open.

"You've the magic touch," one of the students declared as they filed out the door.

Josie's eyebrows drew together for a beat. Then she smiled and waved as the students left. "See you all next week."

He wiggled his fingers and grinned. "You must have loosened it for me. Ready to go shopping? We have a little time before the next class. Right?"

"We do, but..." She examined the door frame, then swung the door back and forth. It made the usual groaning and squeaking sounds but didn't hang up once. "Strange. First the door won't stay closed. Next thing you know, the door won't open." She shook her head. "Never had these problems before."

"Maybe the recent rains have swollen the door, so it won't close or sticks while it dries out, and then it's fine." He offered, feeling just a bit chagrined. *I'm sure as hell not going to tell her the truth—not yet. And definitely not without Summer's permission.* The vision of the beautiful woman and the dark-haired man haunting his dreams crossed his mind. He tucked them away for later consideration.

He motioned out the open door. "I'll step out. You set the alarm, lock the door, and we'll be on our way." Out of the corner of his eye, he saw movement and whirled around in time to see a hooded figure disappearing around the corner of the building. He sprinted out after the person, but by the time he reached the corner, no one was in sight.

Josie stood transfixed on the doorstep to Earthbound. "What are you doing?"

"Thought I saw something, but it must have been my imagination. There was nothing around by the time I reached the corner."

She touched his arm. "Daylan, I'm sorry about overacting this morning at the restaurant. I guess this whole thing with Kurt is getting under my skin. Normally, I'm not a fearful or skittish person, and having someone responsible for my protection other than myself grates. If you know what I mean."

He nodded. "I get that. The fact remains Kurt could be a dangerous person. He seems to have an unhealthy infatuation with you and could easily overpower you. Summer has trusted me with your well-being. I can't let her down. So your safety is my number one priority. Please don't try to get away again. He could be lurking around anywhere."

"I understand. It won't happen again."

"Thank you." Gently taking her by the elbow, he guided her toward her SUV. "Where's the nearest store?"

"We have several choices, but I like the store a few miles away on Palmer Park. Better prices and selection. Besides, I have several coupons for the items we need." She reached in her backpack, drew out the vehicle keys, and held up an envelope which she waved in the air. "Never pay full price if you can help it."

"Got it." He smiled and shook his head. A far cry

from the women who vied for his attention in Martha's Vineyard.

Approaching her vehicle, she stopped dead in her tracks. Her SUV sat lopsided. The two tires closest to her were flat and a hissing sound was coming from the other side of the vehicle. "Aww, shit. Those are brand-new tires."

"Did they come with a warranty?" Rounding the rear of the SUV, he bent down to assess the hissing tire. The air was leaking from a 4-inch slash next to the rim. "I don't think…"

"You're right, warranties don't cover vandalism." She stepped out from behind him and cursed. "I'm going to kill him." Reaching into her purse, she yanked out her phone and touched in numbers, then put it to her ear. "You sorry son-of-a…"

Daylan swiped the phone out of her hand and ended the call while dodging her grabbing hands as she attempted to get it back. "Your reaction is exactly what he's looking for. If you think Kurt did this." He walked around to the other side of the SUV and confirmed those tires had been slashed too. "Apparently, we interrupted your vandal. You still have one good tire." His lips twitched.

"Kurt did this, and I can prove it." Sprinting back to the studio she called over her shoulder, "We have surveillance cameras trained on the parking lot." She unlocked the door, shoved it open, and tapped in the alarm code. Inside, she rushed to the office. He followed close on her heels. She touched the keyboard and backed up the camera feed fifteen minutes.

A hooded figure rounded the corner from the west side of the parking lot. The individual wore gloves and carried a long blade that glinted against the sunlight. Pausing, he kept his head down but appeared to look up and down the street as he crept toward the vehicle. The person then bent over and slashed the first two tires, carefully keeping his back to the camera. Then he ducked behind the vehicle for a few seconds, suddenly bounding from behind the SUV and racing to the corner of the building. A few moments later Daylan and Josie appeared on camera.

"Run that footage back to the person's appearance." He stared at the figure. "The slasher is familiar with the layout here."

Tapping the buttons on the keyboard, she stopped the view and gestured to the screen. "See, I told you it was Kurt." She spat out the name, clenching and unclenching her hands as she paced in front of the monitor.

Hesitating for only a beat, he leaned in for a better look, resting his hands on the back of the empty office chair. "You still can't prove it. Never saw his face."

"Don't you think I can see that myself? But I know his build, his body language. It was him. I'm calling the cops."

"And tell them what? You don't have enough for a positive ID."

"Like hell I don't." She pointed to the screen. "See how he shuffles his feet, walks with his shoulders slumped? It's him."

"Okay. Let me play devil's advocate for a moment. If you were doing something you shouldn't be, would you be standing up straight, strutting around like you owned the place? Or skulking around? Half the young male population shuffle when they walk. It's in vogue."

"But...but..." She paused, some of the bluster leaving her attitude. "I know it's him. If only he'd looked up."

"Josie, he knows where the cameras are. That much is apparent." He shoved his hands into the front pockets of his jeans. "I think you're dealing with more than a jealous ex. Kurt's done this type of stuff before."

"Why do you say that?"

"He had gloves on, leaving no fingerprints, and no way to identify him. The knife wasn't a pocketknife, either. If I had to guess, it was a twelve-inch hunting knife. Little overkill for slicing tires."

She looked out the window at her disabled vehicle. "Guess I better call roadside assistance."

"Tell you what, go ahead and call the police. You're going to need the report for the insurance company. Those tires don't come cheap. I'll make a couple of calls. There's a tire store a few blocks down. Hopefully, they can replace the tires this afternoon. We'll plan on going to the store after classes are over." He tossed her phone to her.

Simultaneously her phone played a muted version of the 1812 Overture. As she caught the phone triumphantly she checked the screen for caller ID. "Oh, I got to take this. it's Lizzy."

"Who's Lizzy?" he asked as she put the phone to her ear.

"My neighbor. Lizzy is kinda the unofficial resident manager for our little band of misfits." She shifted from foot to foot. "Hey, Lizzy, what's up?" Josie listened, her forehead creased in concern. "Oh, well, sure, I'd love to take over the carriage house. Do you happen to know the rent difference?" She paused again. "I could handle that. Tell Jimmy I'll take it and have him call me. Better yet, have him draw up the rental agreement. I'll swing by and pick up the paperwork Monday when Summer gets back. If there's a problem, call me. Thanks for the heads up. See ya soon." She disconnected the call, squealed, and gave a fist pump.

"Good news?" Daylan rubbed his ear, which was still ringing from her piercing outburst.

"The best. The guy living in the carriage house is moving out. He bought a house. So I'm next in line. If I want it. And I do!" She plopped into an office chair. "Okay, we'll go with your plan. I'll need more than a few minutes to prepare before class. Calm and centered is going to be tough to achieve after today's events."

He stepped outside the studio and yanked his phone out of his pocket, touched the screen, then held the phone to his ear. At the first ring, a male voice answered.

"Daylan? I wasn't quite finished with our conversation."

"I know, Dad, but I have to be careful our conversation is not overheard. I'm not the only person here."

"Who else is there with you?"

"Never mind. Is everything all right at the shop?" he asked, concern reflected in his voice.

"I suppose. Haven't been there for a while but haven't heard from the alarm company."

He paused for a moment, glancing up and down the street. *How much should I say out in the open like this? Is the Fae still around?* "Would you mind checking for me? Make sure nothing is missing or out of place?"

"Now how would you expect me to know that?" his father asked incredulously.

"Something in that shop could be connected to the ghost and old magic. I want to make sure…"

"Oh, I get it. I don't have an eidetic memory like you and your sister, but I'll do my best. Call you back in a few."

"Great." He ended the call and walked to the SUV to check the tire size on the one remaining tire. He searched his phone for the tire store down the street, only to discover it closed at noon. *Shit*. He circled the vehicle twice, then raised an arm and a fog settled around the area, thickening near the SUV. After he whispered a spell and glanced at the vehicle, new tires appeared, and he ambled toward the studio surveying the area. After several minutes he waved his arm and called to the wind. A stiff breeze blew in, moving the fog slowly out of the area.

Commanding elemental magic of wind, water, earth, and fire came in handy, he mused, though his sister was much better at it. It wasn't breaking any magic rules he'd pay for later. After all, he was lending assistance to a mortal in need. A car door slammed, and cheerful voices came closer.

A couple hugged their coats around them as they sprinted up the sidewalk to Earthbound. At the door, a young man turned his face to the sky. "Wow, did you see how those clouds dropped and then the wind came up? We're in for a storm tonight, for sure."

"Yeah, an unstable trough of cold air mixing with the upper warmer one," the young woman said firmly.

"So you say. Everyone knows weather forecasters are only right about thirty percent of the time," the young man scoffed. "No disrespect, but your decision to study meteorology is flawed, if you ask me."

"I didn't ask." She huffed at him and yanked open the wooden door. It groaned at the intrusion.

"I gotta fix that damn door." He grinned at the couple's conversation, feeling a bit guilty weather forecasters would take the blame for his magic. The cell phone played a lively tune in his pocket. Pulling it out, he glanced at the screen and put the phone to his ear. "Dad, talk to me."

Chapter Nine
Classes Over, Dinner Looms on the Horizon, But Trouble Stirs

As the last class of the day said their goodbyes and dispersed without any further interruptions, Josie rushed to the locked file cabinet in the office and retrieved her backpack. Staring into the drawer for a second, she snagged the gun out of the drawer and slipped it into her pack. Usually, she didn't carry because it was too heavy, but with recent events, she'd bear the weight.

Passing by the office window, she saw the tires on her SUV had been replaced. Daylan stood beside the vehicle grinning at her and dangling keys from his index finger with a smug look on his face. Unable to help herself, she snickered. The man was such a puzzle. One moment he irritated the hell out of her. The next minute he had a way of making her melt inside.

Summer would not be pleased. She found a bit of subversive pleasure in that too. Waving at the window, she dashed from the room and skidded to a halt in front of the alarm control, where Daylan now waited. *How did he do that?*

"Ready?" A leisurely smile curved his lips as a mischievous sparkle glinted in his eyes. He raised an eyebrow as if to punctuate his question, dangling the keys over her head.

She gave him a sideways glance, jumped, grabbing the keys, and grinned. "Now I am. How about getting a bite before heading to the store? I'm starved."

"I like the way you think. Dine-in or fast food?"

"Fast food isn't good for you. There's a great steakhouse on Powers. It's still early, so there may not be a waiting list yet."

"Lead the way." He backed up a couple of steps and put his hand on the door handle, waiting for her to set the alarm.

It was clear sailing across town. After only twenty minutes, she wheeled into the steak house parking lot and cut the engine. "They have the best homemade rolls here. You can watch them while they make the bread."

"I haven't had a homemade roll in—quite a while." He rubbed his hands together in anticipation. "What else is good here?"

"I'm going to have the barbecued baby back ribs. They are to die for. But the steaks are fantastic too."

Daylan pulled the door open and held it while she entered. She turned around and flashed him a cheeky grin. "And they say chivalry is dead."

"Nope, it's alive and well, but hard to find. My dad always opens doors for Mom, and for my sister when she lived at home. He made sure I did too, or he swatted me upside the head. As a youngster, I'd dodge the blow, snicker, and run off. Always paid for it later." He shook his head. "Dad claimed there was no excuse for bad manners. As I got older and more defiant—well— let's just say manners were the least of my worries. Do you hear from your brother, sister, or parents often?"

"No. My parents and I aren't exactly on speaking terms. If my sister, Pam, or my brother, Rod, call me, it's usually to lay a guilt trip on me for not coming home or calling my parents on special occasions. Even though my appearance at those shindigs always turns out badly. Better I don't go."

A hostess came up to them with a basket of rolls and silverware wrapped in cloth napkins. "Follow me." She smiled. "Have you been here before?"

"Yes, several times," Josie said.

Daylan shook his head. "First time."

"Welcome and welcome back." She showed them to a booth and waited until they were seated. "Your server will be with you shortly." She handed them menus and scooted off to another table.

Josie glanced at the menu, then closed it, setting it on the wooden table. Two small pails sat on the table, one empty and one full of peanuts in the shell. "I absolutely love these." She cracked the peanut between her thumb and forefinger, then popped it into her mouth.

"Ready to order?" A woman asked in a friendly voice.

Josie grinned. "Yes. I'd like the half-slab of ribs, extra sauce, salad with ranch dressing, and baked potato with butter only." She picked up a roll, cut it in half, and buttered it, then took a little nibble.

Still munching on the peanuts, he handed the menus to the server and swallowed. "I'd like a porterhouse steak, medium, with baked sweet potato, brown sugar and cinnamon, please."

"You get one other side, sir."

"How about green beans?"

She smiled and scribbled on her pad. "Yes, sir. Anything to drink?"

"I'll take coffee with cream, please." He paused for a beat, then added, "Two glasses of water."

"Raspberry iced tea, thanks," Josie chimed in.

The faint sounds of the 1812 Overture started from her backpack. She grabbed the pack and yanked out the phone. "It's Lizzy again." Touching the screen, she put the phone to her ear. "Hey, Lizzy. What 's up?"

"Oh, Josie, I hate to be the bearer of bad news, but Jimmy won't give you a lease on the carriage house. Says he's going to sell the property, move closer to his kids and grandkids in Montana."

Her face fell as her heart sank to the soles of her feet. "Oh, no. I kinda had my heart set on moving into the cottage."

"You still can. He won't give you a lease because he doesn't know what the new owners will want to do with the place. If I were you, I'd move in and request a lease from the people who buy it. Possession is nine-tenths, as they say."

"Does he have a buyer in mind?"

"No, he hasn't even listed it yet. Said he hated to do it, but the upkeep is too much for him anymore."

"That's too bad. What's he want for the place?"

Lizzy cackled. "I've no idea. You got money to buy it?"

"Well, maybe we could all go together and buy it?"

Lizzy roared with laughter until she had to take a breath. "You know most of the people living here barely make their rent on time. Let alone come up with a down payment to pool together. You're dreaming, Josie!"

"But— Okay. Thanks for letting me know." Disappointment dripped in her voice. "Bye." She tapped the screen, disconnecting the call.

"What's wrong?" Daylan asked as she shoved her phone into the backpack.

She relayed the conversation to him, frowning. "I guess I'll take Lizzy's advice. I'll let Jim know I can move in as soon the tenant vacates the carriage house. Clean it myself."

"He doesn't have any buyers? Might be a good investment property."

"Yeah, but none of us have the means of securing a loan. A down payment—impossible." She sat back in the booth, shoulders slumped. "I really love that place. He doesn't have any buyers, hasn't even listed the place yet."

He paused for a beat, his brows furrowed. "Would you give me Jim's number? I'd like to talk to him about the property."

"Why? I can't afford to buy it, especially if I had to depend on the renters to pay on time to make the payment. Liz says they're always late."

The waitress arrived with salads and drinks. "Your main entrees will be out in a few. Anything else I can get?"

Glancing at her, she shook her head, while he peered at the waitress. "No, we're good for now. Thanks."

She picked her phone out of the pack, along with a pad and pen, then jotted down a phone number. She handed it to him and touched the screen of her phone. After a short pause, she said, "Jim, it's Josie. I'd like to move into the carriage house as soon as the tenant moves out. I'll clean it myself. Maybe you could give me a credit on the first month's rent? Also, a guy named Daylan Riley will be calling you about the property. I gave him your number. I hope you don't mind. Call me when you get this message." She disconnected the call, stabbed her fork in the salad, and took a bite.

Spooning up a crouton with dressing on it, he popped it in his mouth and chewed as his forehead creased. On a whim, he said, "How about we get out of town tomorrow? The studio is closed on Sunday. Right?"

"Yeah," she said tucking her phone back into her pack. "Maybe—"

"Ever heard of Hanging Lake near Glenwood Springs? I was looking for hiking places in the area—and before you say it, I know it's about a four-hour drive. But a great day trip. I'd love to see a lake on the side of a mountain."

"Oh, it's beautiful. The hike is not an easy one, but really worth it. Sounds like a great way to spend the day. But I-70 can make it more than a four-hour drive to get home. Especially on a Sunday afternoon. All the campers are trying to get back into town from their weekend trips." She sighed. "Maybe not such a good idea. Besides, you want to be at Hanging Lake by sunrise if you expect to get a parking spot."

"What about if we head up there tonight? Putting Kurt off your trail for a couple of days might not be a bad thing."

"We wouldn't get there until nearly midnight, have to find a place to stay, and..."

"Not a spontaneous type person?" he teased. "I'll drive. You can snooze. You've been up since the crack of dawn."

The waitress returned with a tray hoisted on her shoulder and a stand held in her hand. She flipped the stand and set the tray of steaming food on it. "Ribs, extra sauce, and potato, butter only." She set the plate in front of Josie. "Porterhouse steak, medium, sweet potato with cinnamon and brown sugar, and green beans." She whisked the plate from the tray to in front of him and checked her pad. "Anything else?"

"Nope, looks like you got everything. Thanks."

"Like to keep the customers happy." Tapping her pen on the pad, she shoved the pad and pen into her pocket. "I'll check on you later." The waitress rushed off to another table, one with a baby, a toddler, and a distraught mom and dad. The toddler tossed the napkin with silverware onto the floor as the infant started howling.

Josie winced. It never failed when going out to eat. She was a screaming-kid magnet. *What a talent.*

"So how about it?" He cut up his steak, waiting for an answer, and popped a piece in his mouth and chewed. "Mmm, this is excellent." Taking a drink of water, he looked up at her.

"What?" She glanced at him, then back to her plate, sprinkled a little salt on the potato, and forked up a bite into her mouth.

"Leaving tonight for Glenwood Springs."

"I've only half a tank of gas." She paused, her cheeks pinked. Taking an interest in her food, carefully she tore apart her baby back ribs and took a bite. The sauce was delicious and the meat tender. Looking at her sticky fingers and feeling barbecue sauce on her face, she picked up a napkin and wiped at her face and fingers. *I should have thought of this before I ordered.*

"I'll pay for the gas and lodging, since it was my idea, and I don't have a vehicle yet."

"Oh, I couldn't let you," she started to object.

"Why not? My sister told me to keep you safe. We've had two run-ins with numbnuts. I don't want a third on my watch. Besides, it's been several years since I've taken a vacation. My forge keeps me pretty busy and is a good source of income. Since Summer abandoned me for the weekend, I figured you could show me around until she gets back."

"Guess that's what you get for showing up without warning or invitation." She smirked. "Still I don't relish Kurt lurking around either."

"Let's leave from here."

Quiet for a couple of seconds, she touched her finger to her lips. "I always carry a change of clothes and hiking shoes in a bag in the back of my SUV."

"Great. Let's go." He scooped up the last bite of beans.

"What about you?" She glanced at his sneakers.

"I'll wing it." He paused for a beat. "There are stores along on the way. I'll pick up a few things."

"What if Summer comes back early?"

"Call her. Leave a message."

"You've got an answer for everything, don't you?" A sliver of excitement zinged through her body, and awareness of something else entirely different settled in her lower regions. *Summer warned me off him. Alone on the road, staying in a motel with someone I just met…not a wise idea. But…*

"I try." He shot her a mischievous grin. Signaling the waitress for a check, he finished off the last swig of coffee. "Ready?"

Chapter Ten
Hanging Lake Adventure, Mother Nature or Magic
Controls the Storm

Up before dawn, Daylan dressed in the jeans and hiking boots he'd purchased yesterday along with a thick hoodie. He slipped out the door, eased into one of two porch chairs set in front of his motel room in Glenwood Springs. As the sun peeked over the horizon, the dusky sky exploded with spectacular oranges, yellows, and reds reflected off the walls of Glenwood Canyon.

He couldn't believe his luck when the small motel he'd seen off I-70 had one vacancy, especially with the quaint little porches and tiny flower boxes in front of each room. Maybe his luck was changing.

Soft footsteps in the room and then the cascade of water in the shower told him Josie was awake. He leaned back in the chair, legs stretched out in front of him crossed at the ankles, and waited. After fifteen minutes she stepped out onto the porch dressed in faded blue jeans, worn maroon hiking boots, and a tie-dye rainbow-colored hoodie.

"Well, there'll be no losing you today," he teased.

She swatted at him, then dropped her day pack at his feet. "Hungry? There's a quaint little restaurant with great breakfasts just up the road."

He dodged the blow, catching her hand in his.

"Great, we'll grab breakfast. Stop and get lunch at a sandwich shop on the way, and arrive at the trailhead before the morning is even started for most."

"You want breakfast and lunch both?" She laughed. "I have a better idea. The restaurant will pack a lunch for us."

"Of course. We want a picnic after we get to the lake. Right? According to the flyers at the motel desk, it's quite an interesting climb."

"That it is. Only a little over a mile, but the trail is steep and very rocky. That's why I insisted you have hiking boots. Last fall, I came up here with friends, and there was a couple with only tennis shoes trying to hike the trail. Not having much fun. Surprised they didn't break their necks." She shook her head. "But the lake is worth the hike. Bet you've never seen anything like it. Hope you're up to it."

"Looking forward to it. I've done quite a bit of hiking in the Catskills. Don't have to worry," he shot back. Getting to his feet, he swung the day pack on his shoulder and followed her out to the SUV, tossing the pack in the back seat next to the bottled water. "Got everything in here we need?" Climbing into the passenger seat, he glanced at the pack.

"Almost. I purchased a few energy bars, chocolate candies, and snacks while you were shopping last night. They're all in the pack. I like to mix my own trail mix."

He raised a brow. "Candy?"

"Of course. I never hike without a mixture of chocolate, peanuts, and raisins. Love the stuff."

It was only a five-minute drive to the café, and the parking lot already had cars in it. "We better eat quickly, or there won't be any parking at the trailhead."

He pulled opened the carved wooden door and waited for her to enter. They slid into a brown leather booth by the door.

When the waitress offered menus Josie glanced at him and said, "If you don't mind, I'll order." He nodded. "We'll have two scrambled eggs each, whole wheat toast, hash browns, and orange juice. We're kinda in a hurry, hiking Hanging Lake this morning." Her lips curved into a bright smile.

"Add coffee too."

"Sure thing." The waitress shot him a quick smile, eyeing him, then shifted her gaze to Josie. "Got ya, Jos. Who's your friend?" She jerked a thumb toward Daylan.

"He's my boss's brother, visiting from back east. I'm showing him around. "

"Have a good time. I'll put a rush on the order. Be right back."

"Hey, Deb, would you mind putting together a couple of your famous meat sandwiches, with cheddar and mayo? Hold the rabbit food." She glanced at him again.

"Maybe mustard too?" he suggested.

"Figured you'd want lunch to go. No problem." Debbie grinned. "Was wondering when we'd see you. Been a while."

"Yeah, you know, working for a living cuts into my leisure time." She said to Deb's back as she barreled through the kitchen doors.

"You know the waitress?" Daylan asked.

"Yeah, during the summer I enjoy the drive, the hike, and the serenity of the lake at early morning. It's mid-morning before the lake fills up with people in the spring. Today's a perfect day for a hike. Not a cloud in the sky, and a slight breeze. I've come up here the night before only to walk out at dawn into the howling wind and pouring rain. Not a fun hike. Only did it once." She shivered. "Never again. Those rocks are slick as snot when wet."

Deb hurried over with their orders, set the plates of food on the table, and rushed back with a paper bag stuffed full. "Two hoagies, mustard and mayo, deviled eggs, chips, and two cans of partially frozen cola." She nudged Josie. "You're all set. Couple pieces of freshly baked cherry pie, too." She turned and headed for the next table.

"Thanks so much!" Josie beamed, then peered at him. "They make the best cherry pie in the world here. We'll have to forego the ice cream."

With little conversation, he tucked into his breakfast as Josie did. They were finished in record time. He left money on the table, picked up lunch, and winked at Deb as they flew out the door.

The parking lot was over half full when they pulled in. Josie blew out a breath as she put the vehicle in park and set the brake. "We made it. Would you look at the line behind us? Serenity is going to be few and far between today. Usually, I'm up here on the weekdays. Forgot how busy it can be. Off we go." She grabbed her backpack and a bottle of water and sprinted toward the trailhead. "Oh, use the facilities before we start up. None at the lake."

"Hey, wait for me." He stuffed lunch into the day pack, along with extra waters, swung it onto his back, and jogged after her. He made the suggested pit stop and met her at the base of the trail. "Ready?"

"Just so you know, we'll gain a thousand feet in elevation during the mile climb. Drink lots of water. I can't haul your ass off this mountain if you're incapacitated due to dehydration or altitude sickness." She snickered.

"I'll be fine." He fished the bottle of water from his belt pack and took a swig. "See, I'm prepared. Also bought a first-aid kit last night."

"Great, now we have two. I always have one in the SUV."

"Good to know. Not a lot of help on the trail or at the lake," he chided.

She smirked. "It's in the day pack you're carrying."

A little over two hours into the hike, he huffed and puffed as he struggled to keep up with lithe Josie, who had no trouble talking as she climbed.

Pausing on a footbridge, she waited for him. "This trail follows Dead Horse Creek. There are footbridges that span the creek along the way. Like this one." She picked up her booted foot and put it back down. "Ready?"

He nodded because he didn't have the breath to say anything.

As they climbed, the trail became steeper and rockier. He grabbed hold of the handrails, assuming they were provided for oxygen-deprived people like him. *How do people breathe up here?* Until now, he'd prided himself on being in excellent shape.

She turned and peeked over her shoulder. "You all right back there? We're almost to the top."

*About damn time.* Huffing out another breath, he leaned against a large boulder. The trail opened up and the lake came into view. He sucked in a breath at the geologic wonder before his eyes. Suspended on the edge of Glenwood Canyon's cliff, waterfalls spilled into a clear turquoise lake. Lush green plants trailed from the outcropping of rock on the walls surrounding the water. It was like nothing he'd ever seen before. "This is absolutely unbelievable."

She grinned. "Told you." Grabbing his hand, she tugged him to the boardwalk area surrounding part of the lake and plopped down. "Rest. We'll eat our sandwiches and then I'll show you around."

"Sounds good." He eased down on a rock and shrugged off his pack, opened it, and handed her a sandwich. He wolfed down his sandwich and chips and drank another bottle of water.

Opening a container of pie, he inhaled deeply. "Hmm, this smells fantastic." He handed the container to her, pulled out the other one, and fished around for the plastic forks.

She took the piece of pie and a fork from him. "It tastes as good as it smells."

They finished off the pie in record time. Hunger satisfied, he glanced around at the signs. "What's Sprouting Rock?"

"I'll show you. Come on." She stood and brushed at her pants.

He packed up the lunch stuff and slung the pack over one shoulder.

She led him a short distance and pointed. Water barreled through a narrow hole in the limestone cliff, creating an inviting spray. "That's icy water from snow-melt."

"Looks refreshing."

"Don't know. You don't want to venture into the spray because contaminants from your body will impact the fragile ecosystem. That's why there is no swimming, not even sticking your toe in the water," she warned.

Suddenly, as the wind changed direction, a thin maroon line formed along the flat bottom of the dark clouds spreading across the sky where moments before there'd been only a few fluffy cotton-ball clouds in a sea of blue. The maroon line widened, switched to vertical, and spread open to reveal a shimmering interior. Shadows emerged from the cloud, then disappeared. As he was about to comment, huge raindrops plopped onto the ground, followed by pea-sized hail that grew to softball size.

Josie ran for cover, and he followed. Protected under a ledge, she cupped her hands over her ears as the roaring of the storm, combined with huge ice balls smashing against rocks, echoed through the canyon. She elbowed him and cocked a brow in question, pointing to the vegetation that remained unharmed.

His eyes narrowed. *Something isn't right. I can feel it. Magic is spinning this storm. But who—how and why?* At a loss for answers, he shrugged and urged her farther under the ledge to wait out the storm. Brushing the wet strands of hair out of her face, he smiled. She looked like a drowned rat, but the fragrance around her reminded him of sweet spring flowers. He leaned in to her and brushed his lips over hers. Immediately, he straightened and backed away. Her eyes were still closed. *Maybe I could've lingered...*

Her eyes blinked open and she licked her lips. After a beat, she waggled a finger in front of him. "Not a good idea."

Chastised, he nodded.

Meanwhile, people were running for cover, screaming. The hard-frozen ice balls changed to slush pellets, then switched to large storybook snowflakes. The howling wind died down and the sun returned to a cloudless sky in a matter of fifteen minutes.

"Wow. I've never seen— Wow." She leaned over and scooped up a mixture of soft snow and hard ice balls just before it all disappeared. "Colorado is known for its changeable weather, but…" She shook her head.

"Crazy weather you have here." He glanced around, bemused.

"No…no…this isn't normal." She turned on her heel in a circle. "How…"

He reached for her, catching the arm of her jacket. "Someone pissed off mother nature. Come on, let's get going." He couldn't explain it, but there'd been a serious rift in the magic continuum, and it wasn't good.

"Well, on the bright side, the rocks won't be wet from whatever weather phenomenon caused the storm. It'll make hiking down much easier than slipping and sliding on icy snow, hail, sleet, rain—and battling wind during whatever."

"Yeah. Guess so." He was amazed at the nonchalant attitude she demonstrated while assisting several shocked families down the trail. She was quite a find and had no idea where or what he'd come from. Family money had been more of a curse than a blessing. He understood why Summer left and kept her secrets tight in this new life she'd created for herself.

*Did her fiancé know?* He was ripped out of his musing when his foot slipped and became wedged between two rocks, propelling him forward. "Shit. Oooff." Catching hold of a tree branch was the only thing that saved him from a face plant on the rocks. He righted himself and carefully dislodged his foot, hoping to lessen the damage. His ankle throbbed as he tried to put weight on it, still clinging to the tree limb.

Josie skittered to a stop and turned back toward him. "Daylan, pay attention. You'll break your neck. Then I'll have to explain what happened to Summer. Not going to happen on my watch." She grabbed his arm with both hands and steadied him, then backed off the trail and eased him onto a flat-top boulder.

He tried a half-smile looking into her piercing turquoise eyes. "Hey, I'm the one who's responsible for keeping you safe."

"Not if you fall to your death." She blew out a breath. "You all right?"

He groaned. "Yeah, I think so. Twisted my ankle— a little." He rubbed the side of his ankle just inside the boot collar. *Not the time or place to use healing magic.*

"Let me see." She unlaced his boot, pulled the top of his sock down, and let out a low whistle. "It's starting to swell. Swivel around for a second."

She opened the top of the day pack, rifled through it, and pulled out her first-aid kit. Opening the kit, she took out an ace bandage, shut the lid, and stuffed the kit back in the day pack, then took his boot and sock off.

"Hey, guys, need any help?" A young muscular man carrying a large backpack paused beside the rock.

"No, I think we'll be all right. He twisted his ankle."

"Oh that sucks. I have hiking poles." He reached over his shoulder and pulled a pole from the pack on his back. He tugged it out to full size and handed it to her. "It may help him make it down the trail." He started to pull out the other pole.

Josie hesitated, looking from the young man to him. She put a hand on the young man to prevent him from pulling the other pole out. "Yes, it would, but we'll need to get it back to you," she said, turning it over in her hand. "These aren't cheap."

"I'm planning to eat a snack in the car once I get to the bottom, so I can wait for you, or I can help get him down," he offered.

"I think we'll be okay. There's barely room for two on the trail. But thank you. We appreciate it." She unrolled the bandage and began wrapping the ankle.

"Okay, see you later." He waved, scrambled over the rocks, and returned to the path.

After wrapping the ankle, she eased the sock over the injury and helped put his boot back on, lacing it for support. "Now, can you stand on it?"

He got to his feet and put weight on it. "It throbs a bit, but I can make it down the trail." He wasn't about to let her know it ached like a banshee.

"Okay. Here's the hiking pole. Don't shift your weight on it, but use it for steadying yourself. Put your other hand on my shoulder if you need more support. I'll go down in front of you. We only have a quarter of a mile to go. Take it slow."

When they reached the parking lot, she glanced around for the young man who'd helped them. A loud whistle cut through the air—he stood under the open back of his SUV, waving.

After getting Daylan settled in her vehicle, she returned the pole to the young man with thanks.

Chapter Eleven
Family Secrets, Hidden Talents, and a Different World

Josie stopped the SUV under a security light in Earthbound's parking lot and cut the engine. The deserted landscape was awash with silvery shadows under the pale moonlight. A shiver skittered up her spine. "I don't see anything, do you?" She pulled her phone out of her backpack to check the alarm app on her phone. No one had been inside since they left. She opened the door, stepped out, snagged the groceries they'd picked up on the way down, and hurried around to the passenger side.

"Nope, not a soul." Daylan climbed out of the vehicle, testing his injured ankle as he stretched his long legs, then took a few steps. "If Kurt knows what's good for him, he'll keep it that way." Picking up the quart baggie of melted ice used to keep the swelling down on his ankle, he slung the liquid out onto the ground.

"Strong words for an injured bodyguard." She snickered, bending down to examine the ankle. "It didn't like the ride and there's swelling above the bandage. Lean on me. We'll get into the studio and ice it again."

"I'm all right." He limped toward the building.

"Okay, fine. You're a tough guy. But don't put any

more pressure on the ankle than necessary. You could do more damage, and then it'll take longer to heal." She caught up with him and slung his arm around her shoulder. "Shift part of your weight on me." When she unlocked the door and pushed it open, the alarm beeped. He leaned on the door frame while she deactivated the alarm. "At least no one tried to get in while we were gone."

Inside the studio, he paused at the couch. "I'm going to go on into my room after I check your apartment." He limped to the stairs.

"You'll do no such thing. I'll check the surveillance system. Since the alarm hasn't been tripped, I doubt there's anyone up there. Unless of course they magically appeared." She laughed, scurrying into the office.

"That's what I'm afraid of," he muttered under his breath.

She whirled around. "What? You're kidding—right?"

"Sure." He hobbled after her.

"Nope, no one up there. See." She swiveled the monitor toward him.

"Leave the door open when you put up groceries. Please."

"Of course."

He limped to his room as she ran upstairs, deactivated the apartment alarm, and opened the door. The temperature in the room dropped several degrees, and what she saw in front of her didn't appear as it had on the monitor. Someone had ransacked the room. Chairs were overturned, cupboard doors flung open, and cushions from the couch strewn on the floor as if someone had searched for something. The bags of groceries she'd been carrying dropped to the floor and she muffled a scream as she backed out of the doorway.

"Is everything all right up there?" Daylan called from his doorway.

She sucked in a breath. "Ummm. Yeah—No. I'll be right down." Thundering down the stairs, she took a hard right at the bottom and crashed into Daylan, flinging him against the wall.

"The alarm was active, yet everything is tossed around. It's a mess. Summer is going to kill me." She paused glancing into his ashen face. "Oh, sorry about that. You okay?"

"Yes. She won't kill you. Are you sure no one is in there?" Slowly, he made his way upstairs, pushed open the door, and surveyed the scene. He motioned for her to remain at the entryway while he hobbled through the rest of the apartment. After his search was complete, he returned to the door. "No one here—now."

Meanwhile, she picked up the groceries and set them inside the door. Then she reached for her backpack where she'd dropped it outside the door and yanked out her phone. "Shit."

"What's wrong?"

"Summer called several times." Josie touched the screen and listened to the messages. "Crap. Crap. Crap!" She touched the screen again and put the phone to her ear. It rang only once.

"Josie, what the hell is going on? Devlin and I are just leaving."

"Don't. Everything is fine. Daylan and I took a road trip last night, spent the night in Glenwood Springs and hiked Hanging Lake trail early this morning. I didn't check my phone last night 'cause it was so late. We were up early to beat the crowd, and cell service is spotty at best. I left a message on your phone and—"

"You're babbling, Josie. What's wrong?" Summer demanded.

"Daylan sprained his ankle, and it was a tough climb back down the trail. We just got back."

"Are you sure that's all that's wrong?" Summer asked, an edge of suspicion in her voice.

"Yes." She sucked in a breath hoping Summer believed her explanation. "I'm tired and headed to bed. See you in the morning?"

"Guess so. If you're sure. Is my brother close?"

"Yeah." Josie handed the phone to Daylan. "She wants to talk to you."

He took the phone. "Hey, Sis. Enjoying your weekend?" He paused, closed his eyes, and grimaced. "Yeah, I know, I should have called you. It was a spur of the moment thing. Thought it would be a good idea to get Josie out of the city for a while." Another pause. "I know. Won't happen again. See you tomorrow." He touched the screen and ended the call. "Whew—is she pissed."

"She'll cool off by tomorrow. Until we have to tell her what happened."

He rubbed his temples. "Let me handle that. She didn't get your message?"

"No. She could have been in a dead zone up there when I sent it and it's floating out in cyberspace somewhere. The message will probably show up on their way down the pass. Then our story will be confirmed, and she'll settle down." She picked up the sacks of groceries and carried them into the kitchen.

"One can only hope."

"The land surrounding their cabin has spotty cell service. Devlin put in an enhancer or something to make the cell signal stronger. Summer says it works well in the cabin but not so much in the acres around the house." She wrinkled her nose as she finished putting the groceries away and turned to face him. "Smells funny in here, and look." She puffed out a breath. "Why can I see my breath—inside the apartment, but a few steps outside the door and it's warm again?"

"Heating problem. I'll take a look at it. Better get this mess cleaned up so you can get some shuteye. You teach the early class in the morning?"

"Yeah. My bet, Summer will be here before dawn." Returning to the living room, she shivered, rubbed her arms to generate a little heat, and used her foot to upright a chair. She bent over, picked up the dish towel and peered into an open cupboard, then closed it.

After an hour, the place was back to normal. Hands on her hips, she chewed on her bottom lip. "Strange, not a thing is missing. How on earth did someone get in here without setting the alarm off, freeze the surveillance feed, and—I don't get it. Won't be sleeping up here tonight, that's for damn sure."

"Okay, I'll sleep up here. You take my room."

"Works for me." Josie turned on her heel and sprinted down the stairs.

"Let me get a few things out of there, and it's all yours." Limping down the stairs, he held his breath and opened the door to his room. He released the breath, relieved the room was as he left it.

"I hate for you to climb all those stairs again and in

the morning too." She picked at the bottom hem of her shirt.

"I'm sure the ankle will be much better in the morning." He grabbed shave cream, razor, toothbrush, and toothpaste, snagged a pair of sweatpants from the back of a chair, then winked at her. "See you in the morning."

"We could share the bed—I mean with our clothes on—staying on our own side," she stammered, heat rising in her cheeks.

He grinned. "Not going to happen. My sister would have my head before either of us could explain. But thanks. Sweet dreams."

"Yeah, right."

\*\*\*\*

Inside the apartment, he closed the door, flicked his wrist while opening his hand, and banished the residual Fae magic used to search the area. Then he wove a protection spell. It might not stop 'em, but at least he'd get a warning before another visit. The room reeked of magic but that stopped at the doorway. Sitting on the edge of the bed, he took his shoe and sock off and rubbed his ankle.

A subtle green light emanated between his hands and ankle for several minutes. Afterward, he wiggled his ankle back and forth, then stood. Testing it, he walked across the room into the kitchen and almost squealed like a little girl, clamping his hand over his mouth. The ghost stood in the dim moonlight flooding through the windows.

"What in the hell are you doing here?"

"Is that any way to greet the gent that saved your arse a few minutes ago?"

"What're you babbling about?"

"He was back, searched your room, again, and then here." The ghost spread his arms wide, turning in a circle. "Heard the lass coming down the stairs with you and I straightened your room. Figured you wouldn't want to explain another room in shambles."

"Thanks. I guess. Since all this is your fault in the first place." He took his shirt off and unbuttoned his jeans. "Now if you don't mind, I'm going to take a hot shower and go to bed. I'm beat." He strode across the room, his ankle feeling good as new, and pushed the bathroom door open.

"He's not going to stop until he finds what he's looking for."

"Who? The faerie…" He snickered.

"Fae," the ghost corrected.

"Okay. That explains the entrance without detection. He searched with magic. Didn't he?"

"Yes. If you think your piddly protection spell will keep him out, think again. Laddie."

"I've done a little research on my own. It'll hold until Summer gets here. Good night."

The ghost shrugged, shook his head, blurring around the edges, and was gone. "I hope so." His words echoed eerily inside the room.

"Always gotta have the last word." He returned to the nightstand, set his phone down, and sauntered into the bathroom. With a flick of the shower knob, warm water cascaded over his tired muscles and steam filled the room. *What in the hell am I going to do? What a mess.* Finishing his shower, he stepped out, toweled off, and fell into bed.

His cell phone vibrated across the nightstand and

crashed to the floor. Jumping out of bed, he whacked his knee on the nightstand and cursed in his search for the offending noise maker. The screen lit up as it hit the floor, he bent at the waist to pick up the phone, touched the screen, and put it to his ear. "Dad?"

"Who the hell else would be calling you in the middle of the night?"

"Hard to tell, after the last couple of days I've had. What's up?"

"The alarm went off in your forge an hour ago. I went to reset it, figuring the horrible storm we had here set it off, but no. Son, you need to come back here. Someone or something all but destroyed your forge."

"What?"

"Well, okay, 'destroyed' is too strong a word. Glass cases that display your work were smashed. Your tools were used to smash windows, slashes on the walls floor to ceiling, and…" He paused for several beats. "Nothing was taken, that I can tell, but the words scrawled—burnt is a better word—across the one undamaged forge wall didn't make any sense."

"What words?"

"You haven't been sleeping with someone's wife or girlfriend, have you? Someone powerful in the magic realm?"

Daylan released a heavy sigh. "Hell no…I'm not involved with anyone—at—all." He emphasized each word. "Mortal or magic."

In an ominous tone, his dad repeated the writing on the wall. " 'This is only the beginning if you don't give up what's mine.' Those are the words."

He repeated his father's words, shaking his head. "What the hell?"

"Anyway the police need you here to do an inventory. I called them. I didn't know what else to do to explain the damage. Customers have been calling wanting to know when you'll be back. I've taken several orders from people I met in town. Figured you'd be back—eventually."

He clenched his fists. "I don't know when I'll be back. Email the orders to me. I'll handle them myself. Thanks." Pausing again, he asked, "Mom discover anything about my ghost or family history?"

"No, she hit a dead end. Most of that kind of information she'd given Summer over the years before...and we don't know how to contact your sister." He cleared his throat. "Now if you'd enlighten us—"

"Nope. I'll talk with her and make arrangements to be home midweek. I've got something here to take care of first. Put the police off for a few days."

"Okkkay." He drew the word out. "I hope you know what you're doing."

"If there are any more incidents, please let me know immediately. Don't call the police again." After a long pause, he added, "We're dealing with ancient Fae or Faerie magic, so act accordingly. Be careful."

"Shit. If it isn't vampires, it's faeries. What're you mixed up in now?" His dad's voice had an edge to it.

"Apparently...it has something to do with an old family curse and my name. So that puts it back on you and Mom. Not my fault. Who was I named after?" he shot back, rolling his eyes.

"Your great, great, great—oh, I don't know how many generations—grandfather on your mother's side. He was a very talented warlock and blacksmith. You and your sister inherited his talents, making you a target in some ways."

"Does Mom have any pictures?"

His dad paused, then blew out a breath. "Doubt it, but I'll ask her."

"Great. I've got to get back to sleep. Talk to you later when I figure a few things out. Sorry for the rant. Nite."

"When can I tell the investigator you'll be here?"

"I'm not sure, but soon." He disconnected the call and tossed the phone onto the nightstand. *This is the last thing I need.* Crawling into bed, he pulled the covers over his head, wishing this was all a bad dream. Sleep eluded him, so finally, he sat up and reached for his phone. The door downstairs banged open and the alarm beeped.

Chapter Twelve
Investment Property? Family History with a Twist

Josie tossed and turned most of the night. When she heard the lock on the door click downstairs and the disarming beep of the alarm, she shot out of bed. Opening the bedroom door a crack, she heard the voices of Summer and Devlin echo through the empty studio. Paws pounding across the hardwood floor into the office were a welcome relief.

"You're here early," she called from the doorway of Daylan's room. "I'll be right there."

Summer walked out of the office, her brow arched. "No hurry. Wanted to catch up on paperwork, and Devlin needed to be at the gun club early. One of his employees failed to show up yesterday, and he's scheduled to open this morning."

Josie closed the door and hurried to dress in black yoga pants with a pink-and-blue print decorating the sides and a printed top that matched. Opening the door just as Summer raised her fist to knock, she squealed. "You scared the crap out of me!"

Lips pressed in a straight line, Summer stood arms crossed over her chest. "Don't mean to pry, but why are you in my brother's room?"

"Good morning, Sis," Daylan said in a sleepy voice from the top of the stairs. "Pretty quiet around here over the weekend, unless you count the slashed tires and skulking around of a male in a black hoodie, which is the reason we left town after class on Saturday night."

Summer moved to stand at the bottom of the stairs and craned her neck to see Daylan. "Why are you in the apartment? What happened last night? The alarm system blinked on and off for a split second, but when I checked the history, no record of an alarm event. I had a feeling something wasn't right when I talked with you, but Devlin insisted I was overreacting. Was I?"

"No. Let me get dressed, and I'll be right down." With a whoosh and a click, Daylan closed the apartment door.

Frowning, Summer backed up enough to let Josie pass by her.

She shifted from one foot to the other, facing her boss. "Daylan and I switched rooms because—well, I'm not sure what happened here, but—I'll let him explain."

"This should be good." Devlin came out of the office and plopped down on the couch.

"Don't you have to go to work?" Summer said.

"Nope, got a couple of hours before I have to open the gun club, no special classes today. Or so the calendar says. I want to hear what Daylan has to say."

"On another subject entirely, I could use some help moving from my apartment to the carriage house."

Summer grinned. "Wow. You've been waiting for a long time to get that space. Guy moved out, huh?"

"Yeah, he bought a house. But it's bittersweet. Jim won't commit to a lease because he's putting the property on the market. At least he is letting me move in." Josie's voice betrayed her disappointment. "Daylan commented that it could be a good investment for the right person. I floated the idea of the tenants buying the property—but no one has that kind of cash. Most live from paycheck to paycheck." She glanced at Devlin.

"Anyway, Lizzy says it's too much upkeep for him and he wants to move to Montana, where his kids and grandkids are. Can't blame him."

Summer nodded, shifting her gaze to Devlin. "It's got a lot of land in addition to the buildings. Great location. Don't think you'd ever have a problem keeping it occupied. It needs a little landscape work, but…"

Daylan bounded down the stairs. "Yeah, Devlin—Summer. Depending on the asking price, that property could be a great investment, and we have an onsite manager." His tennis shoes screeched a protest as he skidded to a stop behind Josie and patted her on the shoulder. "I've left a message for Jim to call me to discuss it. Figured if we got to him before he hired a real estate agent, we'd all come out ahead."

"Who's we?" Devlin asked. A slight grin curved the corners of his mouth.

"Didn't mean to be presumptuous, but it'll take me longer to get the financing lined up, being from out of town. Thought maybe we could go in together, since you're local." He turned toward Summer. "She knows I'm good for the money."

Hands on hips, Summer held her hand up, palm out. "Whoa. Can we table this discussion until I find out what happened last night?"

A melodic tone came from across the studio. She glanced at the office, then to Daylan as he turned toward Josie. "Jos, could you catch the phone?"

"Sure." She sprinted into the office.

\*\*\*\*

Daylan recounted what happened in the apartment and his room, then the conversation he had with the ghost. "If Josie doesn't know what you are...we are...she's going to have to be told. Especially if what I suspect is actually happening. There was this strange storm at Hanging Lake—rain, huge hail, snow, then poof, everything disappeared. I understand the weather in Colorado is unstable, but...this reeked of magic. When Dad called in the wee hours of the morning, he indicated there'd been a bad storm before the break-in at my forge."

Summer's jaw muscle worked overtime. "You brought this to our door. You can leave and take it with you." She strode over to the snack station in the studio and rinsed the glass pot out, filled it, added coffee, and opened the cupboard. "I've carved out a comfortable life here without the intrusion of magic until you showed up." She took out a can of mixed nuts, poured the contents into a bowl, then snatched a package of chocolate chip cookies and arranged them on a plate.

"I understand. But it's family business that brought me here. Mom and Dad reached a dead end. In fact, Dad called the police after my forge was broken into last night. It's clearly magic and related to the occurrences here. And the ghost. Still he..." He paced, then paused in front of Summer, took a deep breath, and blew it out. "Mom claims she turned all the family records over to you before you left. She couldn't find them, so figured you took them with you. Did you?"

"I didn't intend to. They were in the bottom of my oak hope chest grandfather built. I cherished that chest, and it's one of the few things I brought with me."

Devlin cleared his throat and stepped closer to Summer. "Before you send him packing, why don't you tell him what you discovered in your research this weekend? Sending him away may not be the answer now that you're involved."

Summer whirled to face Daylan, pointing a finger in his face. "You had no idea the tools of your craft were enchanted? Even after the assistance you received from the ghost?"

"Never occurred to me. They were basically what I'd term tricks of the trade. While I do weave magic into my creations on occasion, at the request of witches and warlocks in our community, those are learned enchantments from the family Book of Shadows passed down from generation to generation. Why would I suspect anything else? The bulk of my repeat business is non-magical customers. There are only a few magical clients. Speaking of the forge, I have to return home for a couple of days and take care of the situation with the forge. I'm going to need a safe place to store—hmm—the items in question. Any ideas?"

"What—are you crazy?" Summer exploded, pointing to the door. "I want you—"

Devlin touched Summer's arm as Josie bounced out of the office. "Let's try Jim again, Daylan," he said. "Always looking for a good investment."

A puzzled look crossed Daylan's face. "Okaaaay."

Josie skidded to a stop, her gaze bouncing from one person to another, finally landing on Summer. "The call was from a couple of college girls from down the street. They'll be coming in early to talk to us and fill out paperwork, maybe join or observe this morning's class. Do you want to take care of them, or do you want me to?"

Summer tapped her index finger to her lip, as if deep in thought. "You can take care of it."

When Daylan reached into his pocket, his cell phone chimed. He yanked it out and checked the screen. "Wow, you're clairvoyant. It's Jim."

"Great timing," Josie said. "Well, aren't you going to answer it?" She tapped her toe on the carpet.

He put the phone to his ear. "Hi, Jim. I'm a friend of Josie's, and she indicated that you are considering selling her building. We are interested in talking to you about buying it. Have you hired a real estate agent?" He paused for a beat, then smiled wide, pumping a fist in the air. "I'm going to put you on speaker phone so my sister and her fiancé can hear our conversation. Is that okay?"

"I guess so... As I was saying, I haven't gotten around to hiring a real estate agent yet."

"Okay. Do you have a current appraisal on the property?"

"No…I hate to sell it. The tenants aren't too happy, but I can't take care of it like I used to."

"I'll tell you what. I'll arrange for the appraisal. Then we can talk about the purchase price and financial arrangements. That way you won't need a real estate agent or have to pay a commission. What do you think?"

"Well, I don't know—"

"Do you have any other offers?"

"No—but real estate transactions can be so confusing. Is Josie coming with you?"

"Sure."

"Then I'll hold off on the real estate agent until we

talk. I do have an older appraisal from a few years ago." He paused. "Will that help?"

"It's a place to start. How about we meet you—"

Devlin glanced at his watch, then at Summer, who held up three fingers then waffled her hand back and forth.

"Say around three this afternoon?"

"Sounds good. Want to meet at the carriage house? I need to meet with the young man who's moving out and get the keys."

"We'll see you then." He touched the screen and ended the call. "So what are we thinking? Joint venture?"

"How much can you afford to invest?" Devlin raised a brow.

"I can meet whatever you invest, it'll just take me time to get it. As I told Summer, I have to return home to handle business matters and pick up my truck and trailer, but it shouldn't take more than a few days. I can have the funds wired to your bank."

"Hey! This is my home you're talking about. I have savings I could add," Josie said. "That way I'd have a stake in the place."

"Keep it. You may want to redecorate the carriage house. If we get this venture off the ground, you'll be the resident manager. If everyone agrees, we could draw up a contract giving you a percentage of ownership in lieu of monetary compensation." Devlin ambled toward the fireplace.

"Sounds good," Josie said as the others nodded. The old grandfather clock in the studio chimed eight. "Do you need me for anything else? I need to get ready for class."

"I'll toss a couple more logs in the fireplace, get this placed warmed up." Devlin stopped beside the wood box, then snapped his fingers. "By the way, I have an appraiser friend who might be able to help us get a quick appraisal. Want me to make the call?" He hoisted a couple of logs into the fireplace, wadded up newspaper, and struck a match, touching it to the corners of the paper.

"Sounds good," Daylan said.

Behind her back, Summer flicked her wrist, and the fire came to life, engulfing the newspaper and roaring up the edge of the aspen logs.

Josie's eyes widened. "Wow, you are some fire starter. It'll be warm in here in no time." She rubbed her hands together, then bounded up the stairs.

Devlin smiled at Summer and gave her a thumbs up.

"Can I have a word, Daylan?" Summer picked up a soft-sided briefcase from beside the door and motioned for him to follow her.

"I'll give you two." He snickered. "Feeling generous today."

She frowned at him, then proceeded through the studio, down the hallway, and out the back door.

He'd never noticed the patio extended the full length of the building. At the far end, a round glass-top table and several wrought iron chairs sat next to a large built-in grill. A rolling cabinet fit neatly between the grill and a matching swing. A beautifully carved wooden bench sat off to the left side.

Summer opened the bench seat and pulled out pastel-printed cushions, placing them on the chairs around the table. She slipped into one of the chairs and motioned him to the other across the table. Swinging the briefcase onto her lap, she pulled out an old black-and-white drawing of a man and woman dressed in wedding attire and placed it on the glass top.

Next, she set on the table a cream leather diary, worn on the corners and pages yellowed with age. Finally, she took out several sheets of paper with writing on them, the ink faded so the words were barely readable. Spreading them out, she made a sweeping gesture over the table. "I believe these hold the key to part of your situation."

He scrubbed his hand over his face, then picked up the drawing. The face staring back at him was his own, or at least it sure looked like him. "Who are these people?" He handed the drawing back to her.

"Our several greats-grandfather, Daylan Ian Allaway, and grandmother, Tautha Fairbairn Duff." She paused. "Born in the seventeen hundreds in the highlands of Scotland to Fearghas Allaway and Beatress Blair Allaway."

He sucked in a breath. "You do have all the family records. I didn't mean for you to spend your weekend working on this rather than your wedding."

"Originally my intention was to hand this all over to you. Let you figure it out on your own. But I thought better of it after my temper cooled." She paused, drumming her fingertips on the tabletop. "And at Devlin's suggestion. Strangely enough, he found all this family history fascinating."

"Probably to avoid all the wedding dresses, flowers, invitations…"

"Don't talk about things you don't know about or are none of your business. Get to know him before you claim to know his preferences. He's a good man and is happy to help plan our wedding."

The heat rose from his neck to the tips of his ears. "Sorry. He's such a rugged—big—"

"Stop digging a hole before I let you bury yourself." Summers stern expression faded to a smile and a nod. "Back to business."

"Dropping the shovel." He grinned. "They are—were—a beautiful couple."

"Yes. But darkness followed them from the beginning. Rumor has it that Tautha was named after a Fae princess—Fae blood ran in her veins. The story goes that her father was a powerful Fae warrior who was enamored with her mother, a Scottish lass, and she with him. Their union was forbidden."

"Oh, of course, it was," he scoffed, leaning back in his chair. "Wasn't everything back then?"

"Do you want to hear the tale or poke fun? It's your life hanging in the balance," she retorted.

"Sorry. No offense. I find this all a bit intimidating and snark is my coping mechanism."

"I suggest strongly that you keep it under control." She shook her head and sent him a withering glance. "The lass was with child when the Fae warrior was killed in battle. Her mother attempted to raise Tautha as a mortal child, but at a young age, she began to wield magic. From that point on, she and her mother were outcasts.

"The Fae swooped in and took the child. At her mother's pleading, they allowed her to accompany her young daughter. Tautha was promised to Khellan, a Fae prince, but she had other ideas as she grew into a young woman. She fell in love with a warlock, Daylan Ian

Allawy. He spirited her away and married her. Khellan was furious, but Daylan's power far exceeded the Fae's, at the time."

"Wow, this sounds like one of those faerie tales Mom told us at bedtime."

"Actually, she did, but you were too busy poking fun, as you are now, to listen and learn. I believe she was trying to warn us."

"Oh…"

"May I continue?"

He nodded. "By all means."

"As time went on, Khellan came into his magic and power. He became the most feared leader of the dark Fae warriors. Though he dallied with many women, he remained obsessed with Tautha. Determined to have her as his own, he called on dark magic to lure her away. When that didn't work, he ordered his warriors to help him kidnap her, but there was a traitor among his warriors and Daylan was warned."

"Whew…what a mess. And Mom and Dad named me after him knowing all this? No wonder…"

She cut him off with a stern glance. "He secreted Tautha away in a safe location and waited, armed with a sword he'd forged embedded with white magic and ancient Fae magic from Tautha in preparation of this day. The battle was fierce, but in the end, Daylan mortally wounded Khellan. Before the Fae warrior died, he cursed them both. They'd have no peace in life or death, as he'd had none."

He raised his hand. "Can I say something?"

"Of course. Unless it's snark again." Summer narrowed her eyes.

"Is this the curse the ghost is talking about?"

"I believe so. This is where it gets wonky. According to Tautha's diary"—Summer held up the tan book—"blood burbled out of Khellan's mouth on what they thought was his dying breath. Instead, he raised his arm, murmured something, and poof!" Summer made a starburst motion with her hand. "Disappeared."

He let out a low whistle. "Did he return to the Fae realm? How did Tautha know what happened during the battle? She wasn't there. Was she?"

"Don't have answers to those questions. All I know is during that time magic ruled the realms and anything was possible. The Fae were, uh, *are* supposed to be the guardians of the mortal world. When Khellan went rogue, he was disgraced and banished. With that in mind, I'd say he couldn't return to the Fae realm. But that's only a guess."

His eyes grew wide. "I agree. Am I the recipient of an eighteenth-century faerie's revenge for a perceived wrong to a relative from that same century because we share the name? That's a bit farfetched."

"Don't forget you share the same profession as well. And have ownership of enchanted tools of the trade which you've left unprotected. And you're the one with the ghost following you around." She paused and blew out a breath. "Since you've arrived, magic is running amuck all over the place, affecting my life, security, and business. Not to mention I can't plan a wedding with all this going on." She waved her hands wildly at her sides and above her head. The pieces of loose papers fluttered to the floor. She picked them up and tucked the documents into the briefcase.

"I'm sorry. I had no idea. What a tangled mess." He paused for a long moment, drew in a breath, and let it out slowly. "I didn't know—about your wedding, either. But since I have to return home, I'll try to take my problems and solve them there." Daylan's shoulders slumped, and he stared at the ground.

The back door creaked as Devlin eased outside. With Piper trotting beside him, he ambled over to Summer. "I've got to go. There's still no answer at Moon Ridge. Walk me out?" When she pushed up from the chair, he wrapped an arm around her waist and kissed her. Turning his attention to Daylan for a beat, he said, "We'll see you and Josie at her place around three? I'm waiting for a call back from my friend. I also may have some ideas regarding your forge."

"Yeah?" He straightened, a grin tugging at the corners of his mouth. "We'll see you there."

Summer's lips formed a thin line as she quirked a reddish-blonde brow at her fiancé. "Without talking to me?"

"Yep." Devlin guided her around the building toward the parking lot. "But I'll tell you for a price." He grinned seductively.

Chapter Thirteen

A Demand for Explanation Would Remain Unanswered

Summer and Devlin disappeared around the corner of the house, her voice reaching a fevered pitch a couple of times before they were out of earshot.

Though Daylan tried, he couldn't quite make out what was being said. He smiled, easing down on the bench. His headstrong sister could be difficult, to say the least. She inherited the power and temper to match, but Devlin handled her with amazing expertise. He leaned back. Certainly better than his parents did. *They were a good match.*

He sat there mulling over the situation with his forge, the ghost, the Fae, and his sister's wedding. If this whole thing blew up and ruined Summer's wedding, there'd be no way to mend their relationship—ever. Twins or not.

A gentle breeze ruffled his hair just as the door banged open. Heart racing, he jumped up and twisted around to see Josie sashaying toward him. *I must be more on edge than I thought.* He blew out a breath, and his pulse slowed. "Hey, girl."

She reached out and brushed the stray strands of hair from his forehead. "A bit jumpy?"

"Naw, deep in thought. How was class?"

"Good. Gained two new students, and they're

bringing more friends next time. Chi-ching. Gotta love those college students." Josie pumped her hand as if playing a slot machine. "Where'd Summer and Devlin go?"

"Devlin had to go to the gun club. Summer—"

"Is right here." Summer rounded the corner of the building adjacent to the parking lot, Piper in tow. "Better get my paperwork done, if I'm going to attend the meeting this afternoon." She yanked open the back door.

Tail wagging, Piper bounced over to Josie to be petted, eying Daylan with suspicion. He reached into his pocket and pulled out a treat before he knelt, saying, "Piper, look what I've got," and waggling the treat in front of the dog. Yesterday, he'd snatched several treats from the jar in Summer's office, hoping to convince Piper he was okay. The dog sidled up to him, sniffed, then carefully took the treat and backed off, never letting him out of her line of sight nor allowing him to pet her.

"Huh, it appears Piper may accept you after all." Summer shrugged. "Traitorous dog." She scratched Piper's ears affectionately and gave her a quick pat on the head.

He stood up and wiggled his fingers. "Yep, still have all five digits. That's a start. And you better put a wiggle on, dear sister. You've got less than an hour. How long is Devlin going to be gone?"

"Not long—hopefully." Summer held the door open for Piper, then followed her inside.

Josie eased onto the bench and patted the seat beside her. "You don't have to buy the property—for me. I'll just find somewhere else to live if the new owners create a problem."

He sat and stretched his long legs out in front of him. "We aren't. It's a good investment. Knowing you're there making sure the property is taken care of is a win-win for us."

"And me." She pointed a thumb at her chest.

"You wouldn't happen to know how much land that building and the carriage house is sitting on, would you?"

"I'm guessing two to three acres, at least. The property stretches behind to the next block. Huge paved area for parking, then a wide expanse of grass, or at least what used to be grass. It didn't get enough water and most of it died." She grimaced. "We should have helped Jim out more, but we never noticed he was slowing down."

"Might be able to be saved if it has a good root system. We'll take a look this afternoon."

"When are you going to tell me what the heck is going on?" Josie asked.

"What? I don't know what you mean."

"Oh, I don't know. Carrying on a conversation with someone when there's no one in your room. Things being rearranged in your room and the apartment when you didn't have time to do it. I saw your face at Hanging Lake. Whatever happened up there was not a freak of nature.

"If I had to guess, I'd say more supernatural—if there is such a thing. Not to mention the atmospheric difference from one room in the studio to the other. Case in point, last night, the apartment was freezing. I could see my breath when the rest of the place was warm and cozy as usual. None of these things happened before you arrived."

At a loss for words or an explanation that wouldn't get him in all kinds of trouble, he simply shrugged. "Overactive imagination?"

She punched him in the arm and flounced toward the back door. Stopping midway, she turned. "And there is always a feeling of someone watching me lately. I'm not talking about Kurt. I think he's given up."

"I wouldn't bet on it." A feeling of foreboding washed over him. "When did Kurt start coming here?"

She worried her bottom lip. "Oh…no more than a couple of weeks before you arrived."

Silence settled around them as Daylan tried to figure out his next move and what the hell was Kurt's deal… Lack of sleep was distorting his perception. He tented his fingers and peered at Josie. *Was it time to tell her?* No…not without talking to Summer first. *Best if I go back home and take care of business there and let the dust settle here.*

He turned to Josie.

"Hey Josie, want me to take the afternoon class?" Mandy stood in the doorway. "Still having trouble with Kurt?"

"Yeah, sort of."

"Then I'll call my boyfriend and have him hang around here while I teach class." At Josie's puzzled expression, Mandy grinned. "Summer called this morning and asked me to cover a private lesson and stay around the studio till you all get back."

"Thanks. I thought we were going to close—never mind." A rumbling engine had her glancing toward the parking lot.

Devlin's truck drove into the parking lot. He jumped out and strode to the front of the studio.

A few minutes later, Summer stepped out of the back door with Devlin behind her. "We're ready to go."

Devlin held the door open for Piper, who bolted out and ran for the truck. "Lead the way. We'll follow you in the truck. Piper doesn't share her back seat well." He chuckled. "Unless you want to leave her here to guard the place with Mandy. Then we'd all fit in the truck."

Mandy, phone to her ear shook her head, held up her index finger. "See you in a few." She disconnected the call. "Mick is joining me to play bodyguard." She giggled. "Seriously, can't the police put a kibosh on Kurt?"

"Not so far. Can't find him to serve a restraining order on," Summer said. "We've made a perimeter check, and no sign of Kurt." She followed Piper to the truck and opened the back door to the vehicle. Piper jumped in. Three cars pulled into the parking lot. Summer smiled and waved. "Go on in. Mandy will be there in a minute."

Mandy shot two thumbs up at Summer and sprinted into Earthbound.

\*\*\*\*

When Josie pulled into the parking lot, Jim was sitting on a chair on the porch of the apartment building. Devlin parked beside her. They got out of the vehicles. Summer told Piper to stay in the truck before walking up the sidewalk hand in hand with Devlin. Josie joined the group as Daylan made sure the SUV was locked. He did a quick survey of the area and hurried to catch up.

The old man smiled as the group converged on him. "Brought reinforcements, I see."

Josie nodded, grinning. She pointed to each individual as she said their name. "This is my boss, Summer, her fiancé, Devlin, and her brother Daylan."

"Glad to meet you. I've talked to most of you via phone." He stood and clasped hands with Devlin, Daylan, and Summer. He gave Josie a hug, sending a shrewd glance at the men. "So you're interested in buying my building."

"Possibly. Why don't you give us the tour?" Devlin surveyed the area. "How much property do you have here?"

Jim shoved up from the chair and moseyed toward the carriage house. "Two or three acres give or take. The back lawn is going to need some work. It belongs with the carriage house, but the tenant didn't keep up his end of the bargain, as you can see." He motioned toward the dried-up grass that spread out beyond the carriage house. He tossed a set of keys to Josie. "I'm afraid the tenant left the place a mess."

Summer and Josie lingered in the carriage house with a checklist while Daylan, Jim, and Devlin walked to the main house converted to apartments. Jim led the way inside the apartment house and knocked on Lizzy's door. She was home and let them in to look around.

While Jim lingered talking to Lizzy, Devlin and Daylan stepped outside into the hall to wait.

"If you're interested, I have a solution to your forge dilemma." Devlin tucked his thumbs in the front pockets of his jeans and leaned against the wall.

"I'm all ears. But I don't want my problem to cause a rift between you and Summer."

"Understood. Your sister wants what's best for you, and my solution will benefit all parties. I have a vacant supply building on the land adjacent to the Moon Ridge. Had problems with transients camping out in there. Leasing the building to you for the forge could be the answer. What do you think?"

"Sounds great. I'd like to take a look at the place. We could work out the details after I return from Martha's Vineyard. I've got so many irons in the fire right now, I can hardly think straight."

"No problem. Take your time."

Jim sauntered out of Liz's door. "Ready to see the rest of the property and hammer out a deal?"

"Yep." Daylan and Devlin chorused.

After the tour was finished, Summer and Josie joined the guys in the small office on the bottom floor of the converted building to work out the details. Jim had old appraisal and maintenance records going back for years, including tenants' contracts. He spread all the documents out on the table. Daylan and Devlin sifted through the paperwork.

Josie insisted on having the appliances in the carriage house replaced. Jim agreed. Devlin handed him the appraisal his friend had worked up. They negotiated a price that all parties could live with.

All the while, Daylan kept an eye on the sky. Something was brewing; he could feel it. Shifting from one foot to the other, he was anxious to get to a less public place. His fidgeting brought a stern glance from Summer and a puzzled one from Josie.

"I'll have my lawyer draw up the papers, and you can have your legal representative take a look. Should be able to button this all up by the end of next week."

Devlin stood.

"Perfect. I've sold my house, and my son is coming down from Montana to help me move my stuff up there. Gotta go house hunting. He's picked out a few he thinks I might like, but we'll see. I told him no stairs."

"My dad and stepmom live in northwestern Montana, as well as my sister and her family. Small world." Devlin extended his hand to Jim.

He took the offered hand and smiled. "It sure is. That's the area my younger son and his family live in. My older son and daughter live in southern Montana near Yellowstone National Park."

Jim extended his hand to Daylan. "Been a pleasure." Daylan's phone chimed in his pocket. He yanked it out and stared at the screen. "I gotta take this. Josie, I'll meet you in the truck. Dev, are we all set?"

"Sure, go ahead."

Touching the icon, he put the phone to his ear. "Hang on a minute." Out of earshot of the others, Daylan leaned against Josie's SUV. "Hi, Dad, what's up?"

"I thought you were coming out here. The police want to wrap up their report."

"I had business to attend to here first. I'll be on the first plane out tomorrow morning. But I can't stay. Summer was able to shed light on the ghost situation. It's an unbelievable tangle."

"Okay, see you when you get here. Let me know when to pick you up."

"Thanks." Watching Devlin and Summer amble to their truck, where Piper was waiting none too patiently, Daylan disconnected his call before his dad could reference Summer or her location. Josie was still talking with Jim, so Daylan tucked the phone into his pocket and strode toward the truck. He didn't mean to eavesdrop, really he didn't. But…

As they let the dog out of the truck, Devlin brought Summer up to speed on the offer he'd made on the forge. She was none to happy about it, but reluctantly agreed to it on a trial basis.

He gave a little fist pump then waited a beat and joined their group. "Hey, Devlin. After talking to my dad, I'd like to take you up on your offer to move my forge to the empty building on your gun club lot. I've got several orders to fill, and the completion date is not far off."

"Sure, but your sister is none too happy about it. Finally, I brought her around to my way of thinking." A Cheshire Cat grin curved the corners of his mouth.

"On a temporary basis only," Summer interjected, scowling at her brother. 'Piper, get back here." She strode toward the patch of grass where the dog was sniffing.

He glanced from Devlin to his sister. "I appreciate it. Just talked to dad. I've orders that need to get done and property that needs to be protected. With the break-in, I don't trust it will be safe in Martha's Vineyard with no one there. I'm going to leave tomorrow to get things settled and transfer funds for my share of the apartment purchase."

Devlin's eyebrows rose nearly to his hairline. "So that's where you two are from. Summer never mentioned… It takes a lot of coin to live there."

"Yeah, I suppose." Daylan snorted. Pausing for a moment, he snapped his fingers, then said sheepishly, "One more thing, if I'm going to get my business off the ground here, I'm going to need to bring my fifth-wheel trailer so I can attend some of the Scottish games around here to drum up business. Would I be able to park it at your gun club too?"

"Sure, you can park it next to your forge. The building doesn't have an active alarm, but I can arrange for service." Devlin hesitated for a beat. "But I imagine you'll create your own kind of security."

"Not nearly enough," he said under his breath.

"What's that?" Devlin asked.

"Oh, nothing. Talking to myself."

Devlin raised a brow as Summer and Piper came trotting toward the truck.

"I'll pay three months' rent in advance, along with the cost of the alarm monitoring for the forge."

"We'll work out the details when you get back," Devlin said hurriedly as he opened the truck doors for Summer and Piper.

"Thanks. I appreciate it." He turned his attention to Summer. "Did you feel that?"

"If you are referring to the buildup of magic, I do." She gave him an eat-shit-and-die look. "Any idea what is going on?"

"None. We'd better return to the studio to avoid a public spectacle, though." Out of the corner of his eye, he saw Josie sprinting toward them. "We're going to have to tell Josie. She's already suspicious and confronted me on the patio this morning."

"I'll handle Josie," Summer said. "But I'll wait until you return."

"Well, about that…"

She sent him a warning glance. "I told you not to get involved with her. I'll not have you play with her, break her heart, and discard her as you do the women in your life," she hissed in a low voice.

"Give me a break—people change."

She shook her head vehemently.

"I'm off. Got a plane to catch. Told Dad I'd be there tomorrow morning. Thanks for letting me set up my forge in Devlin's spare building. He wouldn't have offered if you'd objected."

Summer fisted her hand at her waist. "Truth be told, he offered without talking to me. He makes his own decisions and I couldn't talk him out of it. So don't screw this up. No more secrets. Or I'll send you and your magical tools back home so fast you won't know what happened. Clear?"

"Crystal. I could use a little help with the strength of the protection spells. Not good with ancient Fae magic."

"Apparently neither am I. But now that we know what we are up against, together we should be able to weave a protection spell that will keep 'em out."

"Hope so." *I'm not so sure, but will deal with that when I return with my tools, including the anvil and hammer, and I'll verify the chain.* A chill shot up his spine. He shook it off and hoped it wasn't a harbinger of things to come.

Out of breath, Josie hoisted herself into her SUV and fastened her seatbelt. "How long will you be gone?" She fiddled with the window switch.

Before he could answer, Devlin and Summer jumped into their truck. Summer rolled down the window. "See you when you get back. Don't give out my location. Understood?"

"Right. Won't be there long enough for Mom to

wheedle that info out of me. Not really comfortable leaving under the current circumstances, but it can't be helped."

Summer waved as Devlin backed the truck up and took off toward Earthbound.

"So you'll be back Monday," Josie echoed.

"Yep." He reached over and tilted her chin up and brushed a lingering kiss across her lips. "I'd like to explore this thing between us, attraction or something more, but I don't want to do it behind Summer's back. I've been on her bad side long enough. We've got to be upfront with her, since she made it quite clear that you were off limits to me."

"Yeah, we kinda broke that rule from the get-go. At least I did. When I saw you, something sparked inside me. I didn't want to admit it for fear you didn't feel the same way. And I didn't want to get fired. I love my job." She paused for a beat. "I like the way you make me feel like I'm special. Never felt like this before."

"I couldn't agree more." Sliding his arm around her, he pulled her close, recaptured her lips, more demanding this time as his tongue slipped inside, touching and teasing. She stirred his blood like no other. What a relief to discover she felt the same way. Raising his mouth from hers, he gazed into her eyes for a long moment and sighed. "I'd better get going, or I may never leave. Reluctantly, he started the SUV and wound his way through traffic to the airport. He took his bags out of the back seat and closed the door as Josie scooted over into the driver's seat. He leaned in the window and kissed her again. "Until Monday."

"Until Monday." She touched her finger to her lips

as he crossed the sidewalk, looking back at her, then waved before he disappeared through the automatic doors with a whoosh.

Chapter Fourteen
They Who Wield the Magic May Be a Force to Be
Reckoned With

A week later, Summer and Daylan sat, heads together, on the patio at Earthbound. Josie skittered to a halt beside Daylan, grabbing his arm to steady herself. "What are you two fussing about now? I swear you're like oil and water. I thought twins were supposed to be closer even than normal siblings."

"Says the woman who hasn't spoken to her parents or siblings for—how long?" Summer challenged.

"That's different." Josie fisted her hands on her hips.

"How?" Summer gave her brother one final scathing look before returning her attention to Josie.

"Do you see my siblings or parents trying to get in touch with me?" She paused, her eyebrow winged up. "No, you don't. Because they don't care. Yet your brother has gone out of his way to make amends for whatever drove a huge wedge between you two and— you won't let go—give him a chance."

Summer's face contorted, then relaxed as if coming to a hard decision. "And I told you not to get involved with him." Her eyes shimmered with something Josie thought was just a little scary.

Summoning up her courage, she blurted, "I didn't—I mean, we didn't—" Josie sucked in a breath, counted to ten and began again. "Summer, we're both consenting adults. Your brother is an entertaining breath of fresh air compared to the men I've dated," Josie said in a defiant voice. "We've done nothing wrong. Hell, he hasn't even really tried to kiss me." *Not counting the touch of his lips on mine at Hanging Lake and the goodbye kisses at the airport.* "Even when I gave him the chance." *Oops, said too much.*

Daylan blew out a breath and rolled his eyes skyward. "Jossiee." He drew out her name in warning.

Glancing from Josie to Daylan, Summer's lips set in a thin line. "I torched his vampire girlfriend as she was draining the life from him. Unfortunately, I was forced to take that drastic action in front of our coven. That's the wedge between us. And I warned you off him."

Josie took another cleansing breath, her gaze shifting from one to the other. Then she snickered. "A little early for Halloween. You're kidding, right? Speaking metaphorically. There's no such thing as vampires. Unless you are talking about blood-sucking lawyers. Now, *that* I would know about. My family is full of them." Her grin started to fade. The fury on Daylan's face and the grim expression on Summer's face told her this was no joke.

Devlin bolted across the yard from the parking lot and grabbed hold of his fiancée's shoulders.

Josie's pounding heart crashed to her stomach as she clamped a hand over her mouth. *Why can't I keep my damn mouth shut?* Babbling when she was nervous had always been a problem. One of the worst recurring nightmares she'd had as a teen was standing before a jury, babbling uncontrollably in court like an idiot.

Consequently, she'd defied the career path set forth by her parents and promptly changed her major to liberal arts.

"Summer—what in the hell are you doing? Tell Josie you're kidding. You're scaring her." Devlin gave her a little shake.

She closed her eyes for a moment, then drew in a breath. "No. My brother wanted to get everything out in the open. Best to start at the beginning, don't you think?" Summer pursed her lips and stared at Daylan. "Brother, take it from here."

A trickle of sweat rolled from his temple down the side of his face. "If you don't mind, Sis, I'd like to talk to Josie alone," he hissed through clenched teeth, then took Josie's hands in his.

She jerked her hands away as her mouth fell open. Her breath hitched in her throat. *This can't be happening. What have I gotten myself into?* Finally able to draw a full breath, she straightened her shoulders. "If this is some kind of joke, I'm not laughing."

Summer stood still for a minute, and then Devlin whispered in her ear and tugged her toward the back door. He whistled for Piper.

"What just happened?" Josie's forehead creased in confusion as she watched Devlin, Summer, and Piper disappear into the studio. "I never saw Summer so—"

"Yeah, well, your oil and water description is about right—now. When we were kids, we were inseparable." He eased down on the swing and patted the space beside him, angling toward her. "Josie, you might want to have a seat."

The bright sun gave way to shadows shifting across the lawn. She glanced to the sky and shuddered.

Suddenly the wind increased and changed direction, bringing a cold chill to the warm day. She tugged her sweater close around her as a thin maroon line formed along the flat bottom of a dark, boiling cloud spreading across the sky. Moments before, there'd been only an occasional fluffy white cloud floating in the bright blue sky. *Oh, no, not again.*

The line slowly drifted to vertical and spread open to reveal a sparkling interior. Four striking creatures appeared, bearing sharp-angled features with fierce expressions on their inhumanly handsome faces. Gleaming swords hung at their sides as they slipped out of the cloud and stepped onto the ground not more than fifty feet from her and Daylan along the tree line of the property. *Holy shit. This can't be happening.*

She rubbed her eyes, but when she opened them the men were still there. Dressed in heavy boots, jeans, and formfitting leather vests, shimmering silver bands adorned their muscular upper arms. Two of them had thick, shoulder-length blond hair; the others had jet black hair hanging in waves past their shoulders.

She jumped up and opened her mouth to scream, but Daylan reacted faster, clapping his hand over her mouth while still facing the advancing creatures. To her surprise, a soft giggle escaped from her lips. *They look like a group of medieval bikers.* Their apparent leader, his reddish sable hair hanging well beyond his shoulders in waves, paused a few yards in front of them.

The others flanked the leader in a V formation. Her heart beat a tattoo against her chest. The vision taking place in front of her wavered and spun. *I will not pass out. I will not faint. I absolutely will not.* She pried

Daylan's hand away and sucked in a deep breath, then blew it out slowly.

The wind settled down to a light breeze that flipped strands of her hair over her face and eyes. Raising a hand, she brushed the hair out of her face and licked her lips nervously.

In the distance, a door banged, a dog growled, and then eerie silence prevailed.

"You can see the Fae, the cloud, and feel the change in temperature?" Daylan whispered, his voice tinged with surprise.

Everything snapped into focus, and she nodded, her eyes wide. "Fae?" *I've lost it. This isn't happening. For god sakes one of them has a pointed ear sticking through his hair.* Catching movement out of the corner of her eye, she saw Devlin, Summer, and Piper joining them. Piper remained behind Summer, voicing her displeasure in low menacing growls.

"Shhhh," Summer commanded.

"Don't be afraid. I don't feel any malice." He sent her a warning glance. "Don't say anything. I'll explain everything later." Still, he pushed her behind him as the Fae approached.

"Where's Khellan?" The leader asked, his piercing blue eyes taking in his surroundings as he took another step forward.

"Good question. No idea. I've a better question. Who the hell is Khellan?" Daylan stood with his feet in a wide stance, shoulders straight, and head held high.

"I'm Shay. We mean no harm. Khellan is a rogue Fae warrior, and his trail leads here."

"Your business here must be urgent, to reveal yourselves in front of a mortal," Summer said, taking a step forward, her shoulders squared, and feet firmly planted. She bounced a small ball of fire snapping and popping in her hand.

Shay's sharp gaze surveyed the group, hesitating on Josie for a beat then moving warily to Summer. "You're in no danger from us. Please put out the witchfire." A puzzled expression crossed his face. "Witches, werewolf—" he paused "—Fae. There are no mortals here."

"Think again. Shay." Summer shifted the fireball from one hand to the other then extinguished it.

"I speak the truth," the Fae insisted.

Daylan twisted around, his forehead creased, sent a wan smile to Josie, then returned his attention to the Fae. "We'll get back to that. Why would Khellan be here?"

In a tired voice, Shay said, "It is a long story." He pointed at Summer. "One she knows well. Except he is now looking for revenge and will take what you have to even the score."

"There's nothing here of his," Daylan said defiantly.

"Oh, do not be so sure."

A tendril of mist snaked out the door left partially open, crawled along the ground, growing thicker by the minute, then wound around a tree next to the patio and took shape.

Josie swallowed hard and blinked.

Out of the mist, in full Scottish regalia, a ghost stood, his transparent red-and-green belted plaid blowing in the breeze.

She shook her head, closed her eyes, scrubbed her hands over her eyes, and blinked them open. "What the hell?" burst from her lips before she could control herself. "It's some kind of bad dream. Right?" She rubbed her eyes again, opening only one this time. "Shit, you're all still here." She dropped her arms to her sides and glared at Daylan and then Summer. "Someone better tell me what's going on—right now." Her hands fisted and unfisted at her sides.

Daylan returned her scathing look. "Later."

"We meet again, Shay," the ghost said. "What kind of attire are ye wearing?"

"Never mind. Ye are the cause of the problem, Daylan." The leader glared at the ghost.

"Oh, no—not this time," Ghost Daylan said.

Daylan stood straight. "No way. I'm not taking the blame for this."

Shay grinned. "Oh, now things are falling in place." He pointed a finger at Daylan. "You are his namesake, and that is why Khellan has returned." He flicked a finger at the ghost. "And you have attached to your namesake hoping he or his twin can break the curse. What a tangle." Shifting his gaze to Josie, he continued, "This young lass is caught in the middle, with naught of power to protect herself."

"For god sakes. She's mortal. How can she be caught in the middle?" Daylan shouted. "She shouldn't even be able to see what's happening."

"Yet she does. Something to think about." Shay shrugged one shoulder. "She is besotted with you, as you are with her. The lass's blood may be diluted, but it's there. The cycle begins again."

Gravel crunched on the driveway as a car turned into the parking lot and stopped. Several young people clambered out.

Shay glanced at the new arrivals. "This is not the end. Have a care. Khellan has been rogue for hundreds of years after he cursed you. Now—he's quite possibly out of his mind and deemed dangerous to all, which is why we have come to collect him. We will not be far." With that dire warning, the Fae warriors disappeared. The ghost faded to mist before disappearing altogether.

"Why now?" Daylan said, blowing out a breath in frustration. "Where'd they go?"

"Where do you think?" Summer snapped.

Voices echoed around the front of the house.

Mandy stepped out of the back door. "Do you need me to take the next class too?"

"No, Mandy. Thanks for your help today. Go on home. I'll take the next class." Summer paused for a beat. "Mandy, are you interested in working more hours?"

"Sure." She shifted a worried glance at Josie. "You're not quitting?"

"Nooo," she said still a bit dazed.

"I'm cutting back my hours so I can get everything ready for the wedding," Summer said. "So much to do. And no time." She waved a hand in a dismissive gesture. "Josie will take part of my office responsibilities too."

"I will?" she asked, wondering where Mandy had been all the time the Fae were here. *How could I have not noticed what was going on?*

"Yes, I hope you will. I made these decisions while at the cabin over the weekend." She smiled at Devlin, took Mandy by the arm, and the three of them walked into Earthbound, leaving Daylan and Josie alone in the back yard.

"Daylan, you've got a whole lot of 'splaining to do." She yanked him down beside her.

"Where do you want me to start?" He lifted his gaze from the ground and peered at her for a moment.

"At the beginning. Torched your vampire girlfriend?—And I thought Kurt was a problem."

"If what I suspect is true, he's more than a problem, and he's not mortal, to boot." He heaved a heavy sigh and leaned back against the swing.

She jerked up straight, grabbed his chin, and turned his face to her. "What in the hell are you talking about? Kurt was in the picture long before you appeared and—what are you?"

"A witch, warlock, being of magical power. So is my sister, my parents, the Fae and Khellan. Yep, my sister torched my vampire—yes, they exist—girlfriend, or I wouldn't be alive today. But she did it in front of a coven gathering during our Samhain, uh—Halloween celebration. All the elders were present. Witchfire is not a common talent, and it shocked the other witches in our coven."

"That's what she was bouncing in her hand during the conversation with Shay."

He nodded. "A partial demonstration. Our parents always insisted that we keep our unusual talents under wraps. We were allowed to display the normal abilities for adolescent witches, but that's where it ended." He paused a shadow of uncertainty crossed his features.

"Not sure whether it was the fact she could wield witchfire or the way she used it, but the coven shunned her. Well, not officially, but the actions of a few cut Summer to the core. Most of their reaction was due to jealousy. Our parents had told us to keep our many talents under wraps—I wish they'd told us why. Witches can be an envious bunch. Not all—but some. And those cause the trouble."

"Wait, what...? Witches? I'm crazy... That's it...just crazy." She covered her face with her hands, hoping when she lowered them all of this would be a bad dream.

He gently brushed her hands from her face. "Look at me. That doesn't change who I am or who Summer is. But at the moment, we've got a huge magical problem to deal with, and hiding from it won't help anyone. We have to figure out how you...can see what you shouldn't have been able to..." He paused and looked into her eyes.

Silence hung in the air between them. She met his gaze and parted her lips...

Chapter Fifteen
The Truth Will Set You Free—Or Crush Your Heart

Daylan swooped in and took her mouth with his. The tip of his tongue slipped between her full lips, touching, tasting, and exploring, something he'd dreamed of doing ever since he brushed his lips over hers at Hanging Lake and the kiss the airport. After his confession, he may never get the chance again. *So I have nothing to lose.*

She was so warm, soft, her mouth so sweet, he could be lost in her forever. He feathered his fingertips along her ribs and up the side of her breast. Then he saw stars. Through the sexual haze, he caught her hand to stop her from hitting him again with whatever she had in it.

"What do you think you are doing?" she shrieked, jumping out of the swing, but she did touch a finger to her lips for a beat.

Maybe all was not lost. "I'm sorry. I got carried away."

For several moments an uncomfortable silence hung between them. "I'm sorry too. My reactions are off-kilter after learning all the things that go bump in the night and make up my worst nightmares walk among us. I'm not sure how to feel about any of this." She paused for a couple of beats and brushed her bangs out of her eyes. "That's not entirely true. It scares the shit out of me. Not to mention that you're a warlock, witch or whatever you are. Can you spell me to make me do your bidding, or fall for you?"

"No…well, it can be done—but not by ethical witches. We have rules and regulations just like the mortal world and breaking them can have dire consequences."

"So hypothetically, if you did use a love potion or spell, and were caught, what could happen?"

"First, my sister would end me." He scrunched up his face, then relaxed it into a sober expression.

She crossed her arms over her chest and tilted her head to the left, eyes narrowed. "Seriously."

"Oh, yes. Okay, if it wasn't me. The magic user would be hauled before the council, charges read, witnesses testify, and a decision reached. If guilty, the penalties range from being spellbound for months or years or even life." At her puzzled expression, he stopped to explain. "Spellbound means your magic powers are taken away. Anyway, if the charge is serious enough, your life could be forfeit."

Her soft, full lips formed an O. "Kinda like our legal system. Let the punishment fit the crime?"

"Only ours is swift. No appeals, no extenuating circumstances. It's swift and final."

"But if you sister really torched a vampire—wasn't it self-defense? So there were no consequences?"

"She did. Summer did nothing wrong because the vampire committed the crimes. My sister stepped in and handled the situation. There were no mortals involved. The penalties are severe if you use magic in front of mortals. Still, she paid dearly for her actions. Taking a life is a terrible thing to live with even though she didn't have any other choice."

"So your sister is a witch. Is Devlin a—"

"That's Devlin's tale to tell. I don't know much about him. Only that as far as he's concerned the sun rises and sets in Summer. They're a lucky pair." He placed his hand on her thigh.

She brushed it aside. "What happens now?"

A jolt of sexual awareness zinged to his crotch. He shifted in his seat and crossed his leg to hide the impending reaction. *What is it about this woman that has me reacting like a horny teenager?* "How about dinner and a movie tonight? No sneaking around, we'll tell Summer our plans. I could use a distraction."

"Is it safe? That warrior—Shay said…"

He shrugged. "We'll put a plan together, then live our lives."

"Maybe we could invite Summer and Devlin to go with us. Kind of a double date? Safety in numbers kind of thing."

"Not exactly what I had in mind, but we could do that." *Take it slow. She's had enough shocks today to last a lifetime…with more to come. Kurt is the next order of business.* Daylan hesitated for a moment, twisting in his seat. A tall, willowy woman and a muscular man sauntered to the edge of the parking lot, then stopped. They spotted him and started toward them. "Now what?" He nudged Josie, bringing her attention to the couple.

"Probably new students." She stood and greeted the couple. "Looking for the yoga class?"

The woman laughed. "Not today, though I've participated in Summer's classes before."

"Oh, you're looking for Summer." Josie studied the woman's features. "She in class right now. Can I give her a message?"

"No actually, I'm looking for my brother. We stopped at Moon Ridge, and they said we'd find him here."

"No wonder you look so familiar. You're Koda. Took a couple classes here with Summer a while back. Right? Up close the family resemblance is remarkable." She reached out and hugged her. "This handsome man must be your husband?"

"Sure is. I don't know where my manners are. I should have introduced myself and Wyatt."

"Is Devlin expecting you?"

"Of course not. I never give him any warning, or he'll run for the hills." She snickered. Wyatt looked uncomfortable.

"Babe, why don't we leave these nice folks alone and wait for Summer and Devlin at the Moon Ridge apartment. It's a weekday, so they'll probably be staying there, rather than heading for the cabin."

Her face crumpled. "I wanted to surprise them."

A booming voice came from the back door. "What are you doing here, Sis?" Devlin smiled wide as Koda sprinted toward him, braced himself, and caught her in midair. "You are going to have to quit doing this. One of these days you're going to knock us both over. We're not kids anymore." Laughing, he kissed her on the cheek and set her on the ground.

"Aww...you'll always be my big, strong, Navy SEAL brother."

*Well, that clears up a lot of things.* Daylan relaxed and wrapped an arm around Josie. She pushed his arm away and took a step.

"Wyatt, how's it going?" Devlin grabbed his hand, then pulled him into a bear hug.

Wyatt shook his head. "Sorry about this. You know your sister. Things are good. And you?"

"Never better. Living the dream. Or nightmare, if we're talking about wedding plans." Devlin grimaced for only a moment. Then his lips twitched, motioning toward the other couple. "You know Josie."

Koda nodded. "She's one of Summer's instructors. Right? Anyway, I'm here to help," Koda said. "Dad and his new wife, Rita, took the twins to Glacier, camping for a week. So we decided to come down here and see what mischief we could scare up." At Devlin's look of horror, Koda laughed. "Dad knew what he was getting into, and Rita—she's on her own." Koda glanced around. "You and Summer have this place looking good. Love the new flower boxes at the edge of the patio. Those are new?"

"Yep. Going to the garden center in the next couple of days to get whatever plants Summer wants. She's got it all sketched out." He shrugged. "I'm just transportation in that endeavor. As far as Rita is concerned, she'll learn. I'm glad Dad's got someone now," Devlin said.

"Yeah, she fits well. You and Summer need to come up and visit when you're not so rushed. I'm so glad you were able to attend their wedding and Dad got to meet Summer. He's thrilled for you, you know. The twins can't wait for your next visit."

"They'd gotten so big I hardly recognized them."

"That's what happens when you spend all your time on covert missions. I'm glad you retired." She wrapped her arms around his neck and squeezed. "Of course, the twins will be here for the wedding. By the way, I was only kidding about the mischief. Figured Summer could use a little help with the wedding since it's only a few weeks away."

"About that."

"What?! You didn't call off the wedding? Did you?" Koda's eyes widened.

"No, no. Nothing like that." Devlin paused, then jerked his chin toward Daylan. "This is Summer's twin brother, Daylan."

"Talk about family resemblance." Koda chortled. "Should have known. Great to meet you."

"Likewise." He nodded to her and shook Wyatt's offered hand.

Koda's gaze wandered from Wyatt to Devlin and then paused on Daylan. "Hey, there are sure a lot of twins in our family. Devlin, you and Summer could have a set of your own." She giggled.

He huffed out a breath. "Don't even say that in jest. Summer should be done in about fifteen. Can I get you something to drink? I bet I can scare up a couple donuts or bagels while we wait."

"Sounds good," Wyatt and Koda chorused, following Devlin into Earthbound.

He took Josie by the shoulders and turned her toward him, trying to determine what was going on behind those beautiful turquoise eyes. "What's wrong?"

She shrugged out of his hold. "Where do you want me to start?" Pausing, she dragged her top lip through her bottom teeth. "I think I need some time alone to…"

He gave her an apologetic look. "You can't really do that. It's not safe."

"So you said." She strode toward Earthbound, yanked open the door, and let it bang closed behind her.

He rushed in after her, only to be blocked by Devlin and a snarling Piper. "Don't start anything here, especially in front of my sister, or get your sister riled. Let Josie have some space. If Kurt is Khellan, it's not a good idea to let him see you're in love with her."

"I'm not." He stepped sideways, putting Devlin between him and Piper.

"Whatever you say." Devlin shrugged. "How was she able to see the Fae? That's a question that needs answering."

Summer joined the group. "Last student just left, and I locked the front door. What's up?" Her glance shifted from Daylan to Devlin and a grumbling Piper. "What'd you do to irritate my dog?"

"Nothing. I thought we were getting along better. Guess I was wrong."

Calling the dog over to her, Summer reached down and scratched her ears. "If I have to put up with him, so do you. Now leave it." Piper circled behind her and plopped down at her left side with a huff.

Devlin grinned at the two. "Koda and Wyatt are in the office enjoying a few of the donuts we brought in earlier."

Summer smiled. "I thought I heard Koda's voice. Popped in for a visit? She has an uncanny way of showing up at the worst times."

"Yeah, they want to help with the wedding." Devlin rolled his eyes. "Grandpa has the twins for a week or so, and then they're all coming here for the wedding."

"Great. With everything that's going on, we could

use their help. But I'm not sure they want to be dragged into this mess with Daylan." She looked at her brother. "How'd Josie take it?"

"At first she seemed okay with it all, but now, not so much."

"If I have to postpone the wedding because of you…" Summer threatened, jabbing a finger at her brother.

Devlin held his hand out in front of him. "Whoa, wait a minute. There will be no postponing the wedding."

Summer whirled on him. "We can't subject anyone to magic forces we don't understand and can't control."

"Then I suggest you figure out what is going on and get control," Devlin roared, then quickly lowered his voice. "Sorry. I've had about enough today."

"Enough of what?" Koda stepped out of the office, a half-eaten donut in one hand, a napkin in the other. "Where'd you get these? They're great."

Blowing out a breath, Summer appeared to compose herself, then hugged Koda and Wyatt. "Good to see you. You've met my brother?" She motioned to Daylan.

"Briefly. Didn't mean to just barge in," Koda said, batting her eyes at her brother.

"The heck you didn't." Summer laughed. "I know your modus operandi. My brother shares the same one. Why don't you two and Devlin head on over to the apartment at Moon Ridge? I'll wrap things up here and join you in a few." She glanced around. "Where's Josie?"

"I think she went upstairs. I heard the apartment door close a few minutes ago," Devlin said. "You might

want to have a few words with her. Given her abilities."
He raised an eyebrow and shot her a knowing look.

Daylan glanced at the floor and shifted from foot to foot. *The last thing I need to be is left alone with my sister and Josie.*

"Did we interrupt something?" Koda asked. "Sorry, if we did."

"No, you're not." Devlin grinned at her. "You love to be in the thick of things. This time you might have bitten off more than you can chew. Come on. I'll fill you in on the way to Moon Ridge." He reached out and wrapped his arm around Summer's waist, and nuzzling into her neck, he breathed a lingering kiss between neck and shoulder. "Miss you." He straightened and started for the door.

Laying a hand on his arm, she stopped his progress. "Miss you too." She stood on tiptoes and pressed her lips to his. "I'll be along shortly."

Chapter Sixteen
The Sh** Hits the Fan and Common Sense Goes Out the Window

The voices downstairs dwindled, and the front door closed. Josie relaxed a little and eased back on the couch. How had her world spun so far out of control? Vampires, witches, warlocks, Fae warriors—and she was in the middle. *How?* Her parents blamed her wanderlust on her father's branch of the family tree with native American ancestors. Now a Fae warrior insinuated that she had diluted Fae blood. *Not possible. I'm from a long line of tough trial lawyers. Nothing magical about that.*

A soft knock sounded on the door. "May I come in," Summer asked in a melodic voice.

"Sure, why not. It's your..." She padded over to the door and flung it open then caught the sharp edge to her voice and added, "Sorry, Summer. Didn't mean to sound so abrupt."

Summer slipped inside, with Piper trotting along behind her, and patted Josie on the shoulder. "Been quite a day, huh?"

"That's an understatement." She closed the door and flipped the lock. *The last thing I need is Daylan barging in.*

"I won't stay long. You and Daylan have some things to straighten out. But I wanted to know, if you don't mind, how much of your heritage are you familiar with?"

"I've been rolling that around in my mind too. My mother is from Scotland, and the bedtime stories she told us were of faeries and magic. But she also made it quite clear…" She paused for a moment, remembering the wistful expression on her mother's face as she had firmly told them those were tales for young children. *Now I'm not so sure.*

"Josie, you all right?"

"Sure just a memory of better days with my mother. My parents tended to blame each other for what they considered my shortcomings. Wanderlust from my father's American Indian heritage many generations back and dreamer from my mother's Scottish background. I often wondered how I could be so different from my siblings and my parents." A half smile turned up one corner of her mouth. "One of the reasons I never felt like I belonged. I feel more at home here than I have anywhere, and now…" She plopped down on the couch.

"Family dynamics are tough sometimes when only half-truths are told." Summer followed her and eased down beside her. "I'm sure you got the gist of what Shay was alluding to."

"That there is magic in my background. Not possible."

"That's the only explanation for your ability to see the events this afternoon." Summer suggested mildly. "May also be why Kurt was drawn to you. Whatever the reason, you could be in grave danger."

"Super. I don't mean to be rude, but I've had about all I can handle today. All I want is peace and quiet to figure this out."

"As long as you promise to stay in this apartment, I'll leave you to your musings. But as a favor to me, please don't leave without protection." Summer rolled her eyes and a little snicker slipped out. "I didn't mean that the way it came out."

Josie giggled. "I understand. And I promise. But I need to go to the carriage house to make it livable, sometime after this situation has blown over."

"Understood, and we'll make those arrangements as soon as I can piece all this together. Believe me, I want this settled as quickly as you do. I have a wedding that Devlin refuses to postpone in three weeks."

"Not good. Anything I can do to help with the wedding?"

"Stay put and be patient. Don't take any chances. I have to go over to Devlin's apartment and explain this all to Koda and Wyatt, and enlist their help, if possible."

She nodded solemnly and opened the door for Summer and Piper, only to find Daylan standing there, hand raised as if to knock. "How long have you been standing there—eavesdropping?"

Summer sidled out the door between them. "I'll leave you to it." She stopped and gave Daylan a scathing stare. Piper took the opportunity to growl low in her throat, curling her lip. "Leave it, Pip. Daylan, don't you stir up any more trouble." With that, she and the pup scurried down the stairs.

Josie closed the door with a bang. "Don't you think…"

"Look I came to apologize—about everything. I had no idea my ghost was connected to such a sordid and dangerous affair that would affect my sister and her new life or someone I just met." He blew out a breath, shaking his head slowly. "Seems my adult life has been nothing but one screw-up after another. At least since her."

"You are responsible for making your own place in this world." Her words were harsh, but she wasn't going to be part of his pity party. "Where are we as far as the purchase of Jim's place?"

He ran his fingers through his hair. "Waiting on a formal appraisal, title search, and closing date. I wired funds to Devlin and Summer when I picked up the tools, truck, and stuff from my forge back home. Any day we should be able to close."

"Wonderful. I'll need to go over and clean out the carriage house so I can move in. Any chance you'll go with me now to do it?"

He rocked back on his heels and jammed his hands into his pockets. "Not a chance. You're not going anywhere. Summer said to stay put in the apartment, where her protection spell should at least give us a warning of impending trouble."

Hands fisted on her hips, she glared at him. "You can't tell me what to do," she shot back. "If I hadn't gotten involved with you, none of this would be happening."

"If I remember correctly, you were already having trouble with Kurt before I arrived."

"But he wasn't some rogue creature that bad-asses were after."

Daylan sighed. "I'm not sure why he was in the picture before I was? You heard what Shay said, that Khellan was always a rogue Fae Warrior. If my suspicions are correct, Khellan and Kurt are one and the same."

"No. No. No. Life was normal—even boring—until you arrived." Her chin jutted out, as she stared at him defiantly.

"No...you were an innocent. My sister has always been a witch. You just didn't know. Now you do," his voice rose with frustration.

"Because you showed up." She stomped to the door and flung it open. "Out. I should've heeded Summer's warning."

"Wouldn't have made any difference." He snapped his fingers and trudged toward the door. "Kurt was after Summer first. Right?"

She pointed to the door. "Out."

"Just answer my question," he growled.

Her lips set in a thin line as she gritted her teeth. "Yes. All right, yes." She paused for a beat. "Until he got a look at Devlin. Now go."

Stepping outside the door, he stuck his boot in the way before she could slam the door. "Somehow, Kurt ascertained that Summer wasn't who he wanted...and then it was you. Even before I arrived. But how?"

She kicked his boot, dislodging it, and slammed the door. "I don't care," she shouted. "I want my ordinary life back."

"I hate to tell you, but it doesn't work that way. You were his target before I arrived. Not my fault." He threw his hands up in the air and turned on his heel. His heavy footfalls pounded down the stairs and hallway to his room.

She released her breath and leaned against the wall, waiting for him to close the door to his room. But he didn't. *Shit*. She padded over to the window and opened it a crack. The fresh air on her skin was cool. It relieved the smothering feeling that came over her the minute Daylan left the room. Taking a cleansing breath, she braced her hands against the window frame and took another deep calming breath.

Moonlight flooded inside with a light breeze. There it was again, that pull. Something was drawing her outside. Warning bells went off inside her head. *Don't do it. Don't do it.* Despite her fear, the desire to go outside was overwhelming.

The security alarm started counting down and she quickly closed the window. *Shit. No way out. Unless...There it was again. She had to get outside.* Shoving the window open again, she called Summer, who picked up after only one ring. "There's something wrong with the window. I opened it to get some fresh air—forgot about the alarm until it started counting down. I pulled it closed, but it won't stay, and the alarm keeps going off now."

"Where's Daylan?

"In his room." She paused for a beat. "We kinda had a disagreement."

"Figures. You'll have to suck it up, kiddo, and go get him to come fix it. Meanwhile, I'll try to bypass the window remotely. I'll wait while you go get him. If he can't fix it, Devlin and I will be there shortly."

"Okay. Be right back." She put the phone on the counter. The powerful urge had her pick up her backpack, slip out the window, skitter across the roof to the corner of the building, and shimmy down. It was like she had no control over her own movements. Her brain screamed for control—to no avail. Then she was sprinting to her vehicle in the parking lot. Carefully she opened the door, climbed in, started the engine, and slowly pulled out of the parking lot onto the street before she floored it.

Suddenly a cold clammy hand closed around her throat. Nails dug into her neck. "Take a right here. Pull into the driveway and stop. Don't turn around."

Finally, self-preservation took over. Releasing the steering wheel, she clawed at the hand closing off her oxygen and opened her mouth to scream. Nothing came out. Then everything went black.

Chapter Seventeen
The Search is On, Using All Resources Available

Daylan looked at the screen on his vibrating phone. *Great, what does she want now?* "What's up?"

"Is Josie with you?" Summer demanded.

"Noooo…we had a little disagreement. She's in the apartment. I'm in…"

"I need you to go get her *now*."

"Why? What's going on?" He slipped on his boots and sprinted upstairs to the apartment and twisted the door handle. It was locked. Waving his hand over the lock, he pushed the door open. "Josie? Josie! Summer wants to talk to you." Silence. He walked into the kitchen and stuck his head out the open window. "Summer, Josie's gone, and so is her SUV. "

"Find her. We're on our way."

He surveyed the area from the window, then disappeared, reappearing at the edge of the driveway, and sniffed. "Magic." He whirled around, but there was no sign of Josie, and the early fall evening had a bite to it. Leaves rustled in the light breeze. He bent over to touch the tire tracks in the gravel where Josie's SUV had been parked and where the magic trail faded away.

"Shit." He kicked at the gravel.

Summer and Devlin appeared next to him with a pop. "Well?"

"She's not here." He shoved his fingers through his

hair and paced back and forth. "Appears she escaped the house out the window to her SUV, where Kurt was waiting for her inside her vehicle. He must have used magic to spirit her away. Even as angry as she was with me, she wouldn't have left the safety of EarthBound. I sensed dark magic when I arrived here." Pointing to the tire tracks, he said, "It's gone now, with the vehicle." He paused to glance around uneasily. "Where's Piper?"

"In the apartment at Moon Ridge." Devlin leveled his gaze at Daylan. "So where would he take her?"

He threw his hands up in the air in a "I give up" gesture. "Hell if I'd know. I should have stayed with her. There was a strange ambiance inside the apartment. I chalked it up to her fury at me. But…"

"Back to where this all began." The ghost appeared next to Summer.

She jumped and glared at the ghost. "I wish you'd quit doing that."

"Sorry."

"Not possible." Shay and two of his warriors joined the growing crowd behind EarthBound.

Summer jabbed at the ghost. Her finger went right through his filmy outline. "This is all your fault." She turned her anger on her brother. "And yours." She fisted her hands at her waist. "Now what are you two going to do about it— Wait…why is it not possible?"

"If he attempts to hide in the Fae realm, or use the veils to travel through time, he'll be arrested, his powers forfeit as well as his life. He's spent eons plotting his revenge, so he's not going to give it up without a fight." Shay paused and shook his head. "If he's got the lass, he plans to spirit her away and wed her, as he believes ghost Daylan did to Tautha."

"Using magic?" Summer asked incredulously.

"Possibly," Shay said.

Summer raised an eyebrow and stared at him. "Really." She hesitated for a moment, slipping her bottom lip through her front teeth.

He scowled at her. Her childhood habit of chewing on her lip was alive and well when she was formulating a plan. *She better come up with a good one, 'cause I've got nothing. How could I let this happen?* Scrubbing his hand across his face, he turned his attention to Shay.

"That much use of magic in the mortal world should be easily traceable. If he can't hide in the Fae realm or use the Veils of Time to disappear, we can find him." Summer turned at the sound of paws pounding the earth. Two huge wolves appeared in the pools of light cast in the parking lot.

Following her gaze, Shay took a step back, sending a wary glance at his warriors. "Who called in the wolves?"

"I did," said Devlin, who'd stood silently by as the others speculated. "Someone had to do something. The longer we stand here discussing the what-ifs, the lesser the chance we find Josie before it's too late."

The wolves paced the area where the SUV had been, noses to the ground and tails swishing. Suddenly, the darker of the two started off toward the street.

"Hey, Wyatt, this is the city. A wolf can't stalk the streets without drawing attention. You and Koda make yourselves presentable and tell us what you've discovered. We'll go from there."

The smaller wolf nudged the bigger wolf, her fangs bared. The larger wolf shook his massive head, chuffed, and let out a mournful howl, racing to the end of the parking lot. The smaller wolf took up the chase.

Devlin ran his fingers through his hair. "None of that either. Koda, get back here."

Both wolves skidded to a stop, trotting back to the place the SUV was parked beneath the parking lot light.

In amazement, he watched what appeared at first a trick of light as they moved into the shadows, their silhouettes changing shape with the movement between shadow and light. They disappeared momentarily into the darkness and emerged on two legs, a bit disheveled but human and dressed.

"You know it's easier to track in wolf form," Wyatt huffed, straightening his shirt.

"I wouldn't know. Koda always had all that fun," Devlin deadpanned. "Need I remind you a woman's life is at stake? Come on, you two. Time is of the essence. Do you know where they went or not?"

"Not far." Wyatt sprinted across the parking lot and turned right, with Koda following.

Without hesitation, Daylan, Summer, and Devlin hurried after them. Shay and his group were slower.

Summer glanced back with an impatient wave of her hand. "What the hell are you waiting for?"

Shay frowned but picked up the pace. "Don't want to tip our hand. He may sense we are here, but the element of surprise…"

"Gotcha." Summer raced to catch up with the others.

Two blocks south, the SUV was abandoned in a circular driveway in front of a large unoccupied turn-of-the-century home. The driver's and passenger's doors stood wide open, the key still in the ignition with an alarm sounding. Josie's backpack lay on the ground, the contents strewn below the open door.

"This place reeks of magic." He bent down to examine the pack and discovered one shoe and her collapsible baton under the vehicle. He crawled under the car and retrieved the shoe and baton. Stuck in one of the sections of the telescoping baton were skin and several strands of hair. "Well, she didn't go without a fight." He sifted through her stuff. "Anyone see her phone?"

Summer and Devlin searched the area and checked under the bushes. "No phone. But the magic is dissipating quickly. We weren't far behind them until..."

Gathering up the contents, Summer stuffed the items in the pack, tossed it into the SUV, and surveyed the area once again. "Better get her vehicle back to Earthbound."

"Shouldn't we call the police?" Devlin suggested.

"And tell them what? 'Our yoga instructor was abducted in her SUV by a rogue Fae warrior seeking revenge. Two huge werewolves tracked the vehicle here, where obvious signs of a struggle ensued,' claimed two witches, a handful of Fae warriors, a half werewolf, and a ghost." She threw her hands up and blew out a breath.

"Hey, we were in human form before we tracked them here," Koda protested, still antsy and pacing.

Summer sent Koda the stink eye and continued, "The trace magic indicates that he tried to force his will upon her, but—" She hesitated for several seconds, then spoke slowly. "Why didn't he simply subdue her with magic?"

"When you put it that way, involving the police

isn't such a good idea. But that's a good question." Devlin closed the passenger door and walked around to where Summer stood next to the driver's side. He reached in and jerked something out. Josie's keys dangled at the end of his finger. "Let's discuss this back at EarthBound before we attract gawkers."

Koda grabbed Wyatt's arm and announced, "We're going to see if we can pick up their scent or his magic trail."

Before Summer could voice an objection, they were gone. She looked to Devlin, who raised his hands in a gesture of surrender.

"You know I've no control over my sister. Besides, it's not a bad idea."

Shay interrupted. "He didn't subdue her with magic for the same reason she could see us earlier." He hesitated for a beat. "No matter what the lass says, magic pulses through her veins. Otherwise, there'd have been no struggle."

"Good point." Summer raised her arm over the vehicle.

Devlin put a hand on her arm mid-wave. "Better to drive the SUV back to Earthbound. We'll draw less attention." The words were no sooner out of his mouth when the air crackled with magic and more Fae warriors arrived. Another loud pop as the air sucked in around them and the Fae disappeared. "What the hell was that all about?"

"I believe Shay summoned reinforcements," The ghostly Daylan whispered and faded away.

By the time he trudged into Earthbound, head hung low, and shoulders slumped, Summer and Devlin had already returned with the SUV and were inside the studio. "I can't believe this is happening...again."

"Shake it off. Gotta find Josie." Summer turned to Devlin. "I'm going to call Mandy to fill in for classes tomorrow and maybe the next day, depending on how our search goes."

Devlin grimaced with a slight shake of his head. "Wouldn't it be safer to cancel classes?"

"No, he's got what he wants. I doubt Kurt— Khellan will be back here."

Daylan shoved his hands into his jeans pockets and joined his sister and Devlin in the middle of the studio. "I'm going to check the cottage. I can't just stand here, talk about it, and do nothing."

"You're not going anywhere alone." Summer scooted in front of him, her hands on hips. "You came here looking for help. If you still want my help, you'll do things my way."

"I'll go with him." The ghost materialized.

Summer glowered at the Scotsman. "A lot of good you'll be. In fact, you're responsible for this whole damn mess."

The air expanded in the studio. With a loud pop, ten Fae warriors formed a semicircle around them.

Summer shuddered. "Geeesh, I wish you'd quit doing that." She glared at Shay. "Why are you here? Shouldn't you be chasing that wayward brethren of yours?"

Shay held up his hand, palm out. "No need to be insulting. We've come to help. If you don't want our assistance..." His voice trailed off, and he shrugged.

"Where would he take her? If he can't return to the Fae realm or his own time, where would he go?" She stared pointedly at him, waiting for an answer.

"He's smart, sly, and spent eons avoiding capture and becoming more delusional. So it's hard to say for sure."

Summer's shoulders slumped as she worried her bottom lip between her teeth.

"But in the past, he's avoided being caught by hiding in plain sight."

Wyatt and Koda burst in through the door. "The magic trail from the driveway where the SUV was left led up the pass toward Devlin's cabin, but veered off at a place marked Cave of the Winds."

"A tourist trap," Wyatt clarified. "When we questioned the whispering wind spirits of the cave, they confirmed he no longer inhabits the far-reaching caverns of the cave." He scrubbed his hand over his jaw. "It's almost as if Khellan set a deliberate diversion inside the cave. Except he didn't have time."

"He is capable of manipulating time," Shay said thoughtfully. "Though attempting to subdue the lass and control time would be a strain on his magic. Not to mention disguising his signature so we couldn't follow him. No, I don't think he's far…yet."

Daylan straightened and snapped his fingers.

Chapter Eighteen
The Chains That Bind

"Take your filthy hands off me, you muscle-bound magical jerk." Josie struggled against the chains that bound her to some type of cold heavy metal object barely wide enough to sit on, with no back support. Slivers of moonlight cut through the dirty windows, but it was still too dark to ascertain what type of building she was being held in. One thing she was certain of was the building hadn't been used in quite a while.

She coughed and sneezed in the dust-infused air that irritated her throat and her sinuses as he commanded the chains bind her. The links shimmered a muted gold as they wound around her, stopping once before he grabbed the end and forced the chain around her neck, securing it with conjured heat. Once she'd thought she heard voices, car tires on pavement, maybe a door slamming in the far-off distance. But she couldn't be sure.

When she screamed, he slapped his hand over her mouth. She sank her teeth deep into his palm, but it wasn't enough. He continued muttering words she couldn't understand, and now she wasn't able to utter a sound. Stepping away from her, he rotated slowly in the middle of the floor, still muttering, his arms outstretched. Apparently, his efforts blocked the moonlight from the windows and silenced any outside sounds. *I gotta get out of here.*

A lot of good those police dramas she watched on TV did her now. The victim usually talked her way out of the situation or distracted the kidnapper and escaped. She could barely move without the chain cutting off her oxygen. *Talking. Yeah, that was a moot point.*

When his back was turned, the chains warmed and pulsed occasionally as if they were trying to tell her something. What, she couldn't fathom, and it was all probably her imagination anyway. In her mind, she replayed the incident in the back yard of the Studio.

*The leader—whatever he was—Fae, I think—suggested there was magic in my veins or I wouldn't be able to see them. I saw them clear as day. Or maybe it was a group hallucination. Hell, maybe this whole thing is a hallucination.* She tried to straighten. The links tightened, and she choked. *Nope, these chains are real.*

For a couple of beats, the links heated, pulsed, then loosened. She struggled and the chains loosened even more. With the slack, she was able to move her arms a bit, and one hand passed over the phone in her pocket. As she tried to manipulate it out of her pocket, the links suddenly snapped tighter as Kurt strode toward her.

He stroked her cheek with his knuckles. "It doesn't have to be this way. I can give you more than you can imagine. You'd never want for anything as my..." He hesitated, then whispered, "...wife."

Bile rose in her throat. She sucked in a breath. His stench was overwhelming as she closed her eyes tight. *A plan...I need a plan.* Opening her eyes, she blinked up at him adoringly. At least she hoped there was some glimmer of adoration. Never being much of an actor or able to hide her feelings, she was on shaky ground. If there was ever a time to turn in the performance of her life, it was now.

Rather than the desired effect, her actions enraged him. "Do you think me a fool?" He yanked on the chains, causing her to shift, and the phone fell to the ground. His eyes narrowed. "What's this?" Still holding onto the chains, he bent over and retrieved the phone and turned it over in his hand, then slammed it to the ground and stomped on it.

She gasped as the links cut into her neck. Then she lowered her head as much as possible, and stared at the floor. A single tear rolled down her cheek.

He jerked her chin up and glowered at her. "Your tricks won't work on me. However, you will consent to be my wife, or I'll destroy everything and everyone you hold dear. Starting with Daylan and your little yoga family." He trailed a finger across her cheek and along her jawline. "Tautha was never allowed to experience my gifts. She was spirited away by the conniving warlock, but...things will be different with us."

Revulsion welled up inside her. It was all she could do to keep it tamped down and raise her gaze to him, playing the part. *You gotta sleep sometime, bastard.*

He bent over, caressing her cheek with his lips, lingering for a beat. She leaned into his caress, her hands fisted behind her back. He turned an uncertain gaze on her. "It won't be so bad. You'll see." Turning, he strode across the floor, yanked open a door, and let it slam behind him. His footsteps echoed loudly in the building at first, then faded away until she could no longer hear them. *Was he gone? For how long?*

The links heated and loosened as she struggled to get free. The chains clanked to the floor. She froze.

*Could he hear her?* Seconds ticked by…still no sign of his return. She got stiffly to her feet. Shuffling her feet in an effort not to trip over anything, she kept her hands out in front of her as she made her way across the floor. The inky blackness made it impossible to navigate.

*It must be some type of abandoned warehouse.* Her foot struck a solid object. Reaching out with her hands, she felt around the item. There was more than one, and they were stacked on top of each other. *Cardboard boxes. But I don't feel any dust or dirt. Maybe it's not abandoned, and the owner will return. Sooner rather than later.* Her hopes for rescue soared until she heard his deep chuckle. *He's playing with me.*

"There's no way out. So you're wasting your time." He cursed. "Figured those chains would betray me. Good thing I took extra precautions."

A ball of light flashed in the air. Momentarily she was blinded, but a second later she located him on the back side of the boxes. His arm snaked around to grab her. She jerked in the opposite direction, took several steps backward, and rushed at the stack of boxes, jumped up, and shoved several top boxes on top of him.

The light winked out. Sprinting across the floor toward the group of boxes lined along the wall, she squeezed between the boxes and the wall. *Now what?* She worried her bottom lip with her teeth and listened. A groan came from the vicinity of the toppled boxes. The wall behind her vibrated. He'd managed to soundproof and darken the building, but vibrations got through. There was something big outside—a truck, maybe. Someone would have to be driving the vehicle.

If she'd felt the vibration, maybe she could draw the attention of whoever was out there. But she'd give away her hiding place. Her choice was clear, she had to chance it. Bracing her back against the boxes, she kicked and pounded on the wall with all the strength she had left. The wall shivered and the windows rattled. *What the hell?*

She paused listening. Light was seeping in. Apparently, he wasn't well enough to maintain his spell. A key scraped in a lock several feet from her. Shifting, she placed a hand against the box. A faint orange glow reflected on the box. Jerking her hand back, she stared at the box. The glow was gone, but when she turned her hand over, her palm was glowing the same orange. She muffled a scream and shook her hand. Another moan and shuffling came from across the room. *He was alive and apparently mobile. Not good.*

Chapter Nineteen
Magic, Werewolves, and Witches to the Rescue

The group exited Summer's SUV, closing the doors quietly. "Oh no," Summer breathed.

The carriage house door stood wide open. Daylan approached with caution, followed by Summer. Devlin brought up the rear. Wyatt and Koda circled around the back. He stepped inside and his shoulders slumped. Nothing. A faint trace of Kurt—Kheelen's magic—lingered, but he hadn't been here in a while. Koda charged around the corner. "The Fae is long gone. Good news, his scent wasn't mingled with Josie's. Khellan was here, but he was alone."

"You sure?" Devlin held a hand up to impede her forward momentum.

"Positive." Wyatt joined the group. "Don't think it was even intentional, like the cave. He was looking for her, but she wasn't here."

"Great. Where next? We're running out of time." Daylan shoved his fingers through his hair, then rubbed the back of his neck. The tension was so thick he could cut it with a knife. *This is all my fault.* His cell phone's popular tune broke the silence. Yanking it out of his pocket, he stared at the screen, then put the phone to his ear. "What?" he bellowed into the phone.

"Didn't you say this building was supposed to be empty?" A rough male voice shot back.

Irritation dripping from his voice, he yanked his temper back. "Yes. Of course it's empty. Your instructions were to stop at Moon Ridge gun club's office, pick up a key, and unload my equipment in the center of the building."

"I understand that. No need to get testy. I followed the instructions exactly. But when I backed up to the door and got out of the truck. A loud banging on the walls commenced. I heard faint voices or a voice. A woman's voice." He paused. "So I called you."

"Pull the truck back around to the front of the gun club office and wait for me."

"I'm on a time crunch. I can't be wasting my time—"

"You'll be paid well for your time. Just do as I say—NOW."

"Yes, sir," the man said in a surly voice. "A strange odor, kinda like sulfur, is pretty strong around here. You don't have explosives in here, do you?"

"Of course not. Just do as I say. I'll be there momentarily." He disconnected the call, shoved the phone back in his pocket, and turned on his heel, heading for the door.

"What's going on?" Devlin grabbed him by the shoulder.

"The delivery driver says there's someone inside the forge building at Moon Ridge. Bet Khellan is holding Josie there." He tried to jerk free of Devlin's hold.

Devlin's fingers dug in and gave him a little shake. "Don't go off all half-cocked. Summer, can you and Daylan port all of us there?" No sooner were the words out of his mouth than they all were sprawled in the trees behind the buildings at Moon Ridge.

"Guess so." Devlin smirked.

Daylan was the first on his feet, running toward the building.

Without warning, Shay and his Fae warriors materialized beside the group. An eyebrow raised, he nodded. "We'll take it from here."

"Not with Josie inside," he protested.

A loud boom shook the ground, and the side wall of the building collapsed. Purple smoke billowed up, and Shay cursed. "Get him! Don't let him get away." The warriors rushed forward toward the building. A column of the purple haze rose upward and spread across the sky, dimming to lilac. Shay and the warriors disappeared with the haze.

Josie stumbled out, coughing and choking. He rushed to her side as she collapsed in his arms, holding her hands out, palms up. The group formed a circle around them as he eased her to the ground.

Summer's eyes widened as she pointed to the subtle orange glow rising from Josie's palms. "I believe her latent magic must have saved her."

A big burly man with thighs the size of tree trunks and biceps that bulged beneath the material of his T-shirt lumbered toward them. He yanked his baseball cap off his head, slapped it against his worn jeans, and shook his head. "What the hell kinda place are you running here?"

Devlin strode over to the man with a hand extended. "I'm Devlin Sawyer, owner of Moon Ridge Gun Club."

"Good to meet you." The man grasped Devlin's hand. "Tex. I own this rig." The man waved in the direction of a shiny black-and-silver haul truck.

"This building was empty for an extended period of time. It appears transients embedded themselves inside without my knowledge or permission. Mr. Rylie recently rented the space from me and has been moving in. He's a great bladesmith, you know." Devlin pointed to a squat building to the north of the gun club's office. "Let me direct you to my supply building, and we'll unload the machinery there. Then you can be on your way."

The man slapped his cap back on his head and shifted his gaze from Devlin to the smoking building, then in the direction Devlin was pointing. "Ooookay."

Customers and employees flowed out the main doors of Moon Ridge and milled around in the front. Wyatt sprinted to the group of people. "Nothing to see here." He herded them all back inside.

Daylan helped Josie to her feet. Summer placed a hand on her arm. "You okay? Did he hurt you?"

"No. no. Just scared ten years off my life. I'm okay."

Summer eyed her carefully. "You're better off resting here for a few minutes and catching your breath. As soon as you feel able, we'll move you to Devlin's apartment behind the gun club, and you can tell us what happened." She dug a set of keys out of her backpack and tossed them to Koda. "Would you mind unlocking the apartment and staying with her?"

"No problem." Koda caught the keys in midair and sauntered toward the building.

Daylan brushed the hair from Josie's forehead. "You feel like standing on your own?"

"I think so."

He steadied her, then released one hand, and she wobbled a bit and grabbed for his arm. Scooping her up in his arms, he carried her several yards toward the apartment.

Red patches bloomed on her cheeks. "Put me down. I'm not an invalid," she squealed while trying to squirm out of his arms.

He lowered her feet to the ground. She swayed for a moment. This time she got her bearings, then held onto him for support.

Josie relayed what had happened from the time she went outside to her SUV until the time she felt the truck's rumble beside the building. "The rest is pretty fuzzy. The trucker apparently heard me and must have called someone when I pounded and kicked the wall. Then Kurt, uh, I mean Khellan, made a grab for me as the building filled with purple smoke. Obviously, he missed, but when he whispered some kind of incantation it felt like all the air was being sucked out of the space. He was sucked upward, and the wall blew out sideways, taking me with it." She looked at her hands, turning them over and over. "Funny thing—when I was beating on the wall, I paused for a moment, leaned against a box, and the palms of my hands glowed orange. Little tendrils formed and then subsided back into my hand. Or maybe I was dreaming." Her forehead creased in puzzlement as she shrugged. "The way things have been going, who knows."

Daylan and Summer exchanged glances and looked back at Josie.

"Is there something you're not telling me?" Josie narrowed her eyes at him.

He shifted from foot to foot. "Not exactly. It can

wait."

She stared at him suspiciously but said nothing.

"Well, I've had enough excitement for one day." Devlin surveyed the damage to the wall. "Better get my contractor out here to assess the damage and begin repairs ASAP. Daylan, do you want to secure your boxes in my warehouse for the time being?"

"Yeah, probably a good idea." He scrubbed his hand over his jaw. "I've a couple of customers wanting their projects." He paused again and slid a glance over to his sister. "Or since magic was the cause of the damage—maybe magic should be the fix?"

"Absolutely not," Summer said flatly.

"Not sure how I'd explain that to my employees." Devlin grimaced. "I imagine they're wondering what the hell is going on as it is. Got a creative explanation, Summer?"

"I like your transient story." Summer wrapped an arm around his shoulder.

"I've an idea." Wyatt surveyed the wall before switching his gaze to his brother-in-law. "It wouldn't take you, Daylan, and me long to get a temporary wall erected. Daylan could work his magic out of sight of the employees and be operational by the weekend. A few forged magical instruments couldn't hurt our situation."

"We still don't know if Khellan is really gone. Do you think Shay will report back to us?" Josie rubbed her hands nervously on her jeans.

"Doubt we'll see Shay again unless he brings bad news." Summer glared at her brother. "Where's your ghost?"

He shrugged. "Don't know. Possibly still at your

Tena Stetler

yoga place."

"Where we'd best be going anyway. Mandy is probably wondering what is going on too." She shook her head, drawing her bottom lip through her teeth. "We'd better postpone the wedding."

"No. Don't get me wrong. I proposed knowing magic snafus could occur. But in my wildest dreams...I couldn't imagine. Never mind. Unless you can guarantee this particular situation is at an end or something like this will never happen again, I suggest we arrange to take our vows in front of a justice of the peace in Divide. A few close friends and family could attend, and we could hold the wedding celebration later. When I said sooner rather than later on Valentine's Day, I meant it. I've been patient, but..." Devlin enveloped Summer in his arms, pulled her close and nuzzled her neck, whispering in her ear.

She stared at him adoringly. "I know you have. However, I may have a better idea. Why don't you and Wyatt do damage control here? Koda can stay with Josie. Daylan and I will go back to Earthbound, settle things there, and talk with the ghost." She shot her brother the stink eye. "We can assess the situation tonight."

"Is Mandy alone at the studio?" Devlin asked.

Summer shook her head. "No. Her boyfriend is there, and Shay left a guard on the property. He was instructed to stay out of sight. No need to let the whole mortal world know there's a lunatic who wields magic on the loose."

"Don't you think Mandy should be brought into the loop?" Devlin's raised eyebrow formed a question mark.

"On an as-needed basis. Right now, she doesn't need to know." Summer said firmly. "One wazzed out semi-mortal is enough at the moment. Don't you think?" Summer's hand flew to her mouth as she glanced in Josie's direction.

"Hey, the wazzed out semi-mortal is standing right here." Josie straightened and fisted a hand on her hip, giving Daylan a little shove.

"I didn't say it." He frowned.

Summer grinned at Josie. "Sorry. Don't take it personally. You've seen and had a lot happen to you in recent days." Her gaze returned to Devlin.

"I see your point." Devlin held up one finger. "Listen."

Several plaintive howls rose from the direction of Devlin's apartment. Summer grinned. "Someone is unhappy." She planted a smacking kiss on Devlin's lips and started toward the sound. "I'll let her out and take her with me to Earthbound. Meet me back there later tonight?"

"No, I don't think so. Wyatt and I will be working on getting a temporary wall up so Daylan can work his magic when he returns. I've got leftover building supplies in the warehouse. Might be enough to erect a temporary wall."

Summer shrugged one shoulder, looking dubious. "Okay, are we all staying in your apartment tonight? It'll be a bit crowded."

"Safety in numbers, depending on what your brother's ghost has to say. Besides, Wyatt, Daylan, and I will be working in his soon-to-be forge most of the night. So you girls make yourselves at home when you get back."

As Summer walked toward the apartment, Devlin jangled his truck keys. "Need a vehicle?"

"Yeah, that'd be helpful." Summer held her hand out. The howling stopped, replaced by thundering paws as Piper raced in their direction.

"She wasn't having any more of staying here," Koda hollered out the open door to the apartment. "Since you were here and headed this way, I figured it was safe to let her out."

"That's fine. She's coming with us anyway. Be back soon," Summer waved.

Daylan eyed the dog nervously. "Or we could just..." He hesitated at the stern glance Summer shot his way. "Guess not."

"Been enough of that here today." Devlin tossed the keys to her. "You might want to stop by Josie's carriage house and pick up your SUV."

"Good idea." She caught the keys, blew him a kiss, and sprinted to the truck.

Chapter Twenty
Now What? Decisions and Ghostly Advice

Summer pulled the truck into the parking lot of Earthbound, turned off the engine and started to exit the truck.

Daylan rested his hand on her arm. "Hold on a minute. I've been thinking."

"Now that's a first," she snarked.

"Hear me out before you veto my suggestion." He shifted in the seat to face her.

"About what?" She eyed him suspiciously.

"As Devlin says, there's safety in numbers. Consider inviting Mom and Dad to the wedding—"

Summer opened her mouth, but he held up an index finger. "Wait. If he is hell-bent on going ahead with the wedding, why not stack the odds in your favor? Hopefully, Khellan will be apprehended by then. But what if he isn't? Having two more experienced magic wielders on hand can't hurt. Dad and Mom are somewhat aware of the situation. We could bring them up to speed on the possibilities."

He waved his hand as she started to protest again. "No—"

"So you're willing to risk the possibility of Khellan showing up and raining hell-fire down on us as he attempts to abduct Josie again, not to mention spoiling your wedding day? All this in front of your mortal friends and family?"

"Devlin and his family are werewolves, not mortals."

"And don't stand a chance against a Fae that's hundreds if not thousands of years old. We couldn't hold our own either without the assistance of Shay and his warriors."

"If…Khellan isn't captured by the wedding date, Shay will be on his trail. If the fugitive shows up here, I'm sure Shay or some of his warriors will be waiting," Summer shot back.

"Don't bet on it. Shay has better things to do than provide security for your wedding."

"It's his fault Khellan is on the loose to begin with," she huffed indignantly. "If he'd done his job, none of this would be happening. If you'd stayed in Martha's Vineyard, my life wouldn't be upended and everyone I care about in danger." Jerking her arm out from under his hand, she jumped out of the truck and slammed the door.

*That went well. Not.* He climbed out of the truck and planted himself right in front of her. "I'm sorry about all that, but playing the blame game won't help anyone. I'm trying to come up with alternatives that will keep everyone safe and mend our family, especially since, there again, I'm the one who drove a wedge in it.

Summer raised a brow. "True."

"Mom and Dad haven't been the same since you left, and that's a damn heavy load to carry around." Turning on his heel, he strode up the path, shoved open the door to Earthbound, and let it bang against the wall. No one was inside, and he went directly to his room.

The ghost materialized as soon as he closed the door.

"And you! Get the hell away from me. This whole situation can be laid at your feet. Hopefully, Khellan is no longer a threat, and you can be on your way."

Shaking his head sadly, the ghost put a hand on Daylan's shoulder. "Ever consider fate is playing a part in all of this? Siblings, especially twins, shouldn't be at each other's throats like you and Summer. Family should have each other's back."

"Yeah, that's where you've been? Got my back, do you?"

"Sadly, no. I only wanted to spend the hereafter with the love of my life, Tautha. Had no idea how you and your family's life would be affected. Had I known..." Ghost Daylan faded away.

"Wait! I need to talk to you. Summer needs answers before planning her wedding. Daylan...Ghost Daylan..." There was no answer, and he jammed his fingers through his hair, then slammed his fist into the wall.

"You're going to repair that hole." His sister stood in the door frame, glaring at him, with Piper at her side. The dog's lip curled back in a snarl. "What did you do, piss the ghost off?"

He whirled around. "Don't you knock?" Shaking his fist, he grabbed a roll of paper towels and wrapped his bleeding hand.

"Not when it's my property. You'd better ice that." She held out her hand and a small bag of ice appeared. Tossing the bag to him, she eased down on the bed. "I didn't mean all the things I said. It seems if there is trouble...you're involved."

"Not by my own making. Wrong place, wrong time." Daylan held his injured hand up to stop the bleeding, stuffed his other hand into his front pocket, and rocked back on his heels. "With the exception of the vamp."

"No, it's the company you keep. But not this time. This time you're the innocent bystander involved only because you're Ghost Daylan's namesake. I guess we could lay that at Mom and Dad's feet. Let me see that." She took his injured hand in hers and a blue glow emitted between their hands. When she released her hold, she observed, "There that's better."

He unwound the paper towel and flexed his hand. "Thanks, Sis."

"No problem. Might want to get control of your temper, though." A wet towel materialized in front of her, and she wiped the blood from her hands and handed the towel to her brother. "Now, how do we get the ghost back?"

He shrugged. "Don't know. He appears at will and has a habit of showing up at the worst times possible. Usually."

A sudden chill fell over the room. Mist trailed around the room until, finally, the ghost materialized. "My fair lady, I am so sorry to have brought all these problems on our family. "Had I known—" The ghost paused for a couple of beats. "I still would have married Tautha. I love her with all my being." He sighed. "Now what can I do for you?"

"Is Khellan really gone? Have you heard from Shay?" Daylan demanded.

"Sadly, no, I have not. There is no way to know if Khellan has met his end. Sorry. I can tell you this. If

Khellan was caught, Shay would not return until after the proceedings are concluded and the sentence commenced. His attendance would be required. If he escaped, Shay will continue to hunt him.

"Either way, you cannot put your lives on hold or wait for a resolution to feel safe. Shay and his warriors are an elite group of Fae tasked to keep balance in the mortal world, assisting humans where necessary. Draw comfort from that, if ye can."

"If that's true, how did this situation go on so long and get so out of control?" Summer got to her feet. "Where were they when Josie was abducted?"

"No one is perfect. Not even Fae warriors." The ghost shrugged, a half smile tugging at one corner of his mouth. "I nae believe they were aware of Khellan's motivation. Shay may have had an inkling when he first saw the two of ye together, but until he took the mortal woman—" He raised his hands. "Khellan went rogue, broke Fae laws, and failed his assignments. That's the reason they hunted him. The Fae council was unaware he was a danger to mortals. Now it's different. At least that is me humble opinion. There is a presence here. A Fae warrior still stands guard over this establishment. Ye won't see him unless there's trouble."

"That's just great." She paced the small room. "Come on, Daylan, we gotta get back to Moon Ridge. I'll call Mandy from there, since it appears she's gone home for the day."

****

The SUV slowed in front of the apartment at Moon Ridge. Daylan hopped out and sprinted to the door, where Josie had rushed to greet him. Wrapping her arms around him, she planted a smacking kiss on his lips, then held him tight.

"If I'm going to get that kind of greeting every time I leave and return…" He pretended to turn and walk out the door.

She grabbed his arm and kissed him. "So what did the ghost have to say?"

"About what we figured." He relayed the conversation as Summer and Piper veered off in the direction of his soon-to-be forge. "Gonna let me in, or am I to stand outside all night?"

She laughed and moved to allow him to pass. "Devlin and Wyatt are working on the wall. You're supposed to join them." She tilted her head up and gave him a mischievous smile. "Unless you want to assist in Summer's wedding plans." Spread over the couch, coffee table, and flowing onto the floor were wedding planner books, catalogs of gowns, and samples of decorations.

Ambling through the living room, he paused. "As inviting as that sounds, I'll pass. If you'll steer me to the fridge, I'll grab a cold drink and join the guys."

The sound of a refrigerator opening and closing came from an adjoining room. Koda appeared with a cold drink in hand and tossed it to him. "There you go, you're all set."

Eying her with suspicion, he reached out and caught the can carefully. "I don't suppose you shook the can before tossing it?"

Koda's face crumpled. "You don't even know me. Why would I do that?"

It was all Josie could do to keep a straight face at the feigned hurt and innocent expression on Koda's face. *The girl is a great actor.*

He slid a nail under the tab, then hesitated. "I'll open this outside."

The girls collapsed into fits of laughter after the door closed. "Didn't think he'd fall for that," Josie said trying to catch her breath, then shrugged. "It was worth a try."

The boards on the porch creaked, and the girls glanced toward the sound. Summer pushed open the door and surveyed the wide-eyed women as Piper shoved her way into the apartment. "What?"

Josie blew out a breath. "Thought you might be Daylan or…"

"Nope, just me." Summer settled on the couch beside Josie. "How are you doing?"

"Fine, a little shaken at first, but better now. So what's the plan? Heard from Shay?"

"No, and according to the ghost, we may not for some time. So it's business as usual. Speaking of business, I need to call Mandy and see if she can work full time for a while."

"Are you cutting my hours? This situation isn't entirely my fault," Josie objected.

Summer shot her a dubious look. "I told you not to get involved with my brother."

"But Kurt—I mean Khellan—was hanging around before Daylan arrived."

"Slow down, Josie. I'm not cutting anyone's hours. I need time to get my wedding put together, entertain the out-of-town guests that have arrived and will be arriving. And…never mind that. I'll need you to oversee more of the administrative side of the business for a while. Are you okay with that?"

Heat flushed her cheeks. "Sure." She glanced

around. "Looks like a wedding planner blew up in here. Need any help?"

"I'm glad you asked." Summer leaned over, shuffled a few magazines, and yanked a piece of paper out from under one of the books and handed it to her. "This is the guest list, and the check marks indicate the ones who have RSVPed they will attend. We need to be sure arrangements are made for all of them, and all the information you need is in the box under the coffee table."

"So you are going ahead with the wedding without knowing the status of Khellan?"

"Yep. Devlin is of the opinion that if our world is going up in a ball of flames at the hands of a rogue warrior, so be it. He's spent his life serving his country and protecting others, to the detriment of his family. He was on assignment when his mother passed away. They couldn't get word to him before she was gone. It changed him. Changed his priorities."

"Wow. Is that why he retired from the Navy SEALs and bought the gun club?"

"Yep. He's even suggested we get married by the justice of the peace in Divide. Tomorrow. That's not going to happen."

Josie looked over the list, switched her glance to Summer and again back at the list. "Are you really going to get married without inviting your parents?"

"I am." Summer scooped the magazines and papers off the floor and piled them in the middle of the coffee table. "Don't look so surprised. If you were in my shoes, would you invite your parents?"

"That's different. I'm a disappointment to my family. Besides, my family doesn't wield power like yours apparently does. You and Daylan must have inherited it from someone. Seems to me the more magic protection we…uh…*you* have, the better chance of the wedding going off without a hitch." Her hand flew to her mouth, eyes wide. "I didn't mean to overstep my bounds."

"It's all right. I've heard the same thing from a couple of other people today."

"Maybe you should think on it." She reached under the coffee table, pulled out the box Summer had indicated, and moved to the kitchen table, grabbing her phone on the way. "I'll get these rooms settled so we're ready to greet everyone and know they have a place to stay."

"Thanks," Summer said, absently pulling her own phone out of her bag.

Chapter Twenty-One
Magic Reconstruction & Wedding Plans to Include a Family Reunion?

"What happened to you?" Devlin asked as Daylan shoved aside a couple of scorched boards to gain entrance to the building.

"Your sister." One corner of his mouth kicked up in a half grin. He took a final swig of his soda and tossed the can onto the trash pile.

"Oh. Sorry about that." Devlin eyed the brown stain on his blue shirt. "She never outgrew practical jokes or popping in on people." Devlin opened a cooler and offered him another can of soda. Moisture and ice chunks slipped down the container and dripped onto the floor. "Or I have bottles of water." Stifling a yawn, he pointed to the cooler.

"I'll take the water."

Devlin reached into the cooler and tossed a bottle of ice-cold water to him. "So how's Josie? What'd the other Daylan have to say?"

"Josie is one tough cookie. She claims to be fine, but…as soon as things settle down, she'll have more questions that I have answers." He went on to fill Devlin in on the ghost's thoughts. Then he rubbed his hands together. "Let's get this party started. How can I help?"

"If you'll hold the boards in place for Wyatt at the

other end of this wall, then help us hoist it into place, I'll nail it down, and then it's up to you. While you work your magic, Wyatt and I'll go get your equipment out of the supply building."

"But I can just—" He waved his arm.

"Not while there is any chance my employees can witness something they shouldn't." At the sound of approaching footsteps on gravel, Devlin paused and held a finger to his lips. Kevin stuck his head around the corner where the wall was missing. "Everyone is gone. The club is all locked up. Will you be working tomorrow, or do I need to fill in?"

"We need to have this wall up tonight in order to secure the building." Sweat trickled across his forehead, and Devlin wiped it away with the back of his shirt sleeve. "Would you mind opening tomorrow?"

"Not a problem." Kevin tilted his head and scoped out the place. "Need help tonight?"

"No…well, if you want to stick around, we could use help hoisting the wall up as soon as we get the braces nailed in place."

"Sure." Kevin pulled leather gloves out of his back pocket. "I'll pick up the rest of the debris and put it in the dumpster while I wait. Trash pickup comes in the morning."

"Great idea. Thanks." Devlin went back to work on his section of the wall, while Wyatt instructed Daylan where he wanted the two-by-fours placed. A few hours later, with Kevin on one end of the wall, Wyatt on the other, Devlin and Daylan at the top, they hoisted the wall up. The three of them held the wall steady while Devlin nailed it in place.

Resting the nail gun on a nearby box, Devlin

grasped Kevin's hand. "Thanks for your help, Kevin."

\*\*\*\*

Before dawn, with the wall up, they emptied most of the boxes, arranged the display cases, power equipment, grinder, and propane forge. He placed a magic ward over the enchanted sledgehammer, anvil, and chain. *Won't leave those unprotected again. Wish I'd known. Maybe this whole debacle could've been avoided.*

Wyatt and Devlin wearily leaned against the wall, sipping at bottles of water as Daylan turned the empty building into a working blacksmith shop. "I can arrange the rest later." He glanced around the room, pleased at the progress. *I should be able to get some of my orders completed this week.*

Picking up his order book from the floor, he thumbed through the pages until he reached "Recent Orders." The Scottish games were in a few months, and he had orders for three claymore swords, two with baskets. The eight dirks—three to be jewel-encrusted—plus the leather scabbards for the four thirteen-inch blades were going to take a while to complete. Six months of work in three, plus a wedding and protection detail that according to Devlin could last however long the uncertainty surrounding Khellan would exist. "Whew."

Of course his sister would be engaged to a former Navy SEAL. He shook his head as something touched his shoulder. Whirling around, fists braced in front of him, he stopped short of throwing a punch as he peered into Devlin's eyes, which crinkled at the corners with amusement.

"Whoa there, boyo. I'm a friend, not a foe, and it's

time to get a little shuteye before the women are up with more for us to do. One of us has to take the first shift at Earthbound with the women." Devlin stretched his arms above his head. "Josie has the first class this morning, so that makes it your job, Daylan. Not sure how Summer has the week planned, but I'm sure she'll tell us."

Piper gave a soft woof as Devlin unlocked the door to the apartment and stepped over her. "Shhh, girl. It's okay." The rooms were dark except for the slices of moonlight filtering through the curtains. The sleeper sofa had been made up with fresh sheets. Arranged in the middle of the room were two air mattresses with blankets and pillows. Devlin crashed onto the bed, rolled over, pointing to the two air mattresses and then to Wyatt and Daylan.

"My place, my choice," Devlin whispered.

Not bothering to throw back the blanket, he eased down on the mattress and was fast asleep the minute his head hit the pillow.

The delicious aroma of freshly brewed coffee wafting through the room awoke Daylan as his stomach growled loudly. For a moment he lay still, listening to the silence broken only by occasional soft snores of the two men in the room. The sunlight streamed through the skylights in the ceiling.

He rolled over, got to his feet, and padded into the bathroom, thankful the women weren't up yet. It would be a fight for that room soon. After a quick shower and shave, he followed the coffee scent into the kitchen and poured a mug of coffee. He pulled a chair away from the small wooden table and sat. The rest of the inhabitants of the apartment stirred, and the battle for the bathroom began.

Devlin won the first battle, as he volunteered to cook breakfast. Clean and fed, the group crowded around the little kitchen table, with Summer and Devlin setting out the agenda for the week. Josie would take the morning classes and do the admin work in the afternoon, while Mandy took the afternoon and one evening class. Daylan would accompany Josie to Earthbound and remain until she was ready to leave. Devlin and Summer were heading to the cabin to finish getting it ready for the wedding and prepare the guest rooms there with the help of Koda and Wyatt.

"I hate to be the thorn in your side, Sis, but I have a backlog of blades and swords to finish, and that won't get done hanging out at yoga."

Summer's eyes glittered with mayhem. She opened her mouth to respond and snapped it shut at Devlin's warning glance.

"Hey, Koda and I can relieve Daylan and return Josie back here when she's done for the day. Then we'll head up the pass and join you two at the cabin."

"That'll work," Devlin said, gently pushing Summer toward the door until his phone rang. "Hello? Oh, hi, Jim. Hold that thought while I put you on speaker phone." Devlin touched the screen and put the phone in the center of the table. "Go ahead, Jim."

"Have you heard from the title company on a closing date for my property?"

"No...but I haven't checked my voice mail since yesterday morning. Been a bit chaotic around here, with family coming in for the wedding and all. I'll give them a call and let you know where we are."

"Thanks. I'd appreciate that. My son and his wife

are coming down to pick me up next week. They've found a property they claim is perfect for me and want to make arrangements to transport my stuff to Montana."

"No problem. I know our funds have cleared, and if the title to your property is clear, then I see no reason we can't close in a few days."

Summer rolled her eyes and waved her arms to get Devlin's attention. He ignored her.

"Okay, thank you," Jim said in a relieved voice.

"I'll be in touch as soon as I hear from the title company." Devlin disconnected the call and switched his attention to Summer. "You have a problem?"

"Yes. You. Don't you think we have enough irons in the fire right now without adding a walk-through, a real estate closing, and whatever else that entails?"

Devlin drew in a breath and let it out slowly. "Summer, you are a magic creature. Living as if you aren't hasn't gained you anything. It's time you acknowledge your heritage and start acting like a witch. Don't look now, but you've been outed to all your friends, with the exception of Mandy. For her own safety, you need to fill her in."

Summer opened her mouth to protest, but Devlin held his hand up.

"Let me finish. I know the rules. Magic cannot be used for self gain. But you can't tell me that using a little magic to ready the cabin so we can help others— Jim, for example, and Josie—will be frowned on." Devlin shoved his hands into the pockets of his jeans.

"Sis, he's right and you know it. Now chill, before you drive us all bat-shit crazy." He grinned and released a breath he didn't realize he was holding as his phone vibrated in his pocket. Yanking it out, he stared at the screen. "Oh, now what?" He put the phone to his ear. "Everything all right, Dad?"

"Yep. Just checking to make sure all your equipment arrived without damage. You know that moving company charged an arm and a leg, and complained the whole time they were loading the equipment."

"Yes, it arrived and has been set up. Now I really need to…"

"Good, because I'm fielding calls on a daily basis from that Scottish group. You need to transfer your phone to the new location. Your mom and I won't be here to answer our landline while we're traveling or attending your sister's wedding. And, sure as heck, I'm not forwarding it to our cell phone."

"Wait…What?"

"She didn't tell you?" His dad chuckled into the phone. "Last night, out of the blue, Summer called, brought us up-to-date on the situation, told us she was getting married, and invited us to her wedding. Your mom is running around here like a chicken with its head cut off trying to get ready to go. Apparently, we have nothing to wear and no one to care for the plants and the cat while we're gone." His dad snickered again. "But we'll be there, one way or the other, a few days before the wedding and possibly naked, if what your mom says is true."

"Oh, I don't believe appearing naked at the wedding would be a good idea." He laughed at the expression of horror on his sister's face. "I'm glad she called you. Now, I really have to go. We have business to attend to. See you when you get here." Ending the call, he grinned at his sister.

"What do you mean 'naked'?" she blustered.

"Oh, nothing." He filled her in on the conversation. "You did the right thing, you know, inviting Mom and Dad. They've missed you something fierce. Of course, you always were their favorite." Attempting to move out of reach, he wasn't fast enough. She landed a blow to his shoulder that knocked him back a couple of feet.

"You never learn." She snickered.

"It's been a while. But you still hit like a girl." This time he disappeared and reappeared across the room next to Josie, slung an arm around her shoulder and squeezed.

"If you two are through..." Devlin paused for a beat, shifting his gaze between Summer and her brother. "I talked to the title company while you were on the phone. The closing for Jim's property is tomorrow afternoon. I let him know. He agreed to a walk-through on the property this afternoon. That way I can hire a contractor to bring Josie's carriage house up to her standards and make the minor repairs to the other apartments we discussed." Devlin glanced in Josie's direction. "Gonna have to cut your workday short today."

Josie nodded. "If it's all right with the boss."

"Sure. Why not." Summer glared in Devlin's direction. "We've nothing else to do."

"Honey, everything will turn out fine. You'll see. Everyone will pitch in, and the wedding will be everything you dreamed. Wrapping up the real estate transaction before the guests arrive and the wedding preparations are in full swing makes sense. Don't you think?" Devlin wrapped an arm around her waist and pulled her to him, brushing his lips across hers. Then, pulling away, he let a wide grin spread across his face. "Change of plans and schedules. Everyone rendezvous at the cabin tonight for a big feast. We can all use a little downtime." He tossed a set of keys to Koda. "Head on up to the cabin. We'll meet you there after the walk-through."

"Okay. If you sure."

Wyatt reached over her head and caught the keys. "See you there."

Hands on hips, Summer stared wide-eyed at him. "Who's going to prepare this feast?"

"Jenny, the new housekeeper and cook I just hired to help get us through the wedding and beyond. She comes highly recommended."

Summer's mouth opened and closed a couple of times before she found her voice. "When did you have time to do this?"

"When Shay and his group appeared at Earthbound, I had a feeling things weren't going to go as planned. Besides, with Dad, his new wife, and the twins arriving in a few days, I knew you wouldn't have time to cook, clean up after them, and finish the wedding prep too."

"Now I remember why I agreed to marry you." She beamed up at him.

Chapter Twenty-Two
Will It Be Business as Usual?

Sitting, legs crossed, in the middle of the empty practice room, Josie tried to quiet her mind. *How am I ever going to teach a class when my mind is racing and my muscles feel like bowstrings? Come on, you can do this.* She closed her eyes, willed her mind to settle, and took several cleansing breaths. Murmurs from Summer's office floated through the room. Her body began to relax, and she moved through several full body stretches for pain and flexibility. After forty minutes, nearly twice as long as usual, she was ready and got to her feet as the first students began arriving. "Spread out your mats and get settled. I'll be back in a minute."

Padding into the office, she was surprised to find it was empty. She grabbed a water bottle from the fridge and glanced out the window. Daylan was lounging against the fender of her vehicle in the parking lot, intent on something out of her view. As if he felt her watching him, he turned to face her, and smiled, and made his way toward the building. To her surprise, he didn't come in the front door but continued his trek around the building. A whiff of lilacs came in with the light breeze as the back door opened and shut quietly. For a minute she froze.

"Miss me?" Daylan appeared in the office doorway, sauntered over to her and wrapped an arm around her waist. Pulling her to him, he nuzzled her neck and trailed soft kisses along her jawline and across her cheek. When he brushed his lips over hers, pausing to trace her lips with the tip of his tongue, her body melted against him as she lingered in his embrace, deepening the kiss. Someone cleared their throat and she jerked away.

The girl's face was flushed crimson from her neck to the tips of her ears. "Sorry to interrupt, but I'm new and was looking for the water fountain."

"No worries. We don't have a water fountain." She pointed to a bottled water dispenser, with a sleeve of paper cups mounted to the side, positioned in the corner of the office. "Help yourself. Class will begin in a moment."

The girl hurried over, filled a cup, and drank deeply. "Sorry for the intrusion." She backed away out of the office.

"Caught in the act. The story of my life." Daylan chuckled, caressing the small of her back. "I'll have a seat on the corner couch while you conduct the class. I've orders not to let you out of my sight. You know."

She considered asking him what he was doing outside when he was supposed to have her in sight at all times. But she'd decided to pick her battles, and this one didn't warrant her attention. "You could join the class."

"Naw…I'm not flexible."

"Don't I know it." She giggled. "A little flexibility in mind and body might not be a bad thing for you."

"So I've been told more times than I can count. But I'll pass for now. Rain check later." He wiggled his eyebrows, then took the water bottle out of her hand, took a sip and gave it back with a wink. "Thanks." With a light touch to her arm, he shifted her toward the door and swatted her ass. 'The sooner you get started, the sooner we can get out of here."

"I'm in no hurry," she teased. "I enjoy teaching yoga."

"I'm sure you do…" He raised an eyebrow. "But I have other enjoyable activities planned, if we ever get a moment alone."

"Not likely, with the current state of affairs. "She snickered and flounced out to join the class.

After class, the building cleared, and she bolted out the door, pausing momentarily to wave to Mandy as she arrived to take over. A few early students congregated in Earthbound's parking lot, and she exchanged greetings with them before climbing into the back seat of Summer's SUV. Daylan clambered in after her and closed the door. Piper sat in the front seat between Summer and Devlin. The dog gave him a hard stare but didn't curl her upper lip or snarl.

"Gee, looks like you and Piper are making progress," Josie teased.

He slipped a piece of beef jerky out of his pocket and offered it carefully to Piper, who sniffed at it, glanced at Summer, then carefully took the treat from him. He leaned back against the seat and wiggled his fingers. "Yep, we're making progress—sometimes. Summer controls that dog with telepathy. I'm sure of it. If she's displeased with me, so is the dog."

"Piper's well trained and picks up on body language." Summer turned around in her seat and pointed a finger at him. "And your body language screams troublemaker."

"Aw, come on, do we have to go there again? At some point, you are going to have to forgive me and move on."

Summer flipped around in her seat to face forward. "Devlin convinced me to forgive you months ago for my own wellbeing. But forgetting? Not a chance, it comes in handy for leverage."

Josie snickered. "This family reunion should be interesting." *Oh dear, did I say that out loud?* By the look on Summer's and her brother's faces, it was apparent she had. *Open mouth, insert foot.*

Devlin slowed the truck in front of the apartment building. "We're here. Everybody out. First item of business, the walk-through." He handed out clipboards with pads to each. "List anything you notice that needs to be repaired. Then Summer and I'll talk to the remaining tenants."

"Piper, you stay. I'll let you out later." Summer made sure the window was down a few inches and closed the door.

Daylan jumped out of the SUV and met her behind the vehicle. "After the walk-through, Josie and I'll head over to her carriage house."

"Good enough." Devlin led the group through the walk-through.

Jimmy was waiting in the front, leaning on his cane, as they exited the door. "After packing up my house, I just didn't have the energy to walk the property with you. Anything I should know?"

"Nope. Same as before. Josie and Daylan are going over to check out the carriage house."

"Funny thing about that. Last night around midnight, one of the tenants saw a light in the building.

When he went to check it out, the light went out, and the door was locked. So the tenant called me after walking around the house. I texted Josie but didn't get a response. Didn't check it out since I knew you all would be here this morning."

All eyes shifted to her. "My phone had a mishap and I haven't had a chance to replace it." She shrugged. "Number will be the same."

"If something like that happens again, call me." Devlin handed him a business card. "We've given my card to all the tenants, with instructions to call if there's a problem or anyone sees anything out of the ordinary until Josie gets moved into the carriage house. She will be our resident manager."

Jimmy nodded thoughtfully. "Gonna fix it up before you move out of the apartment?"

"Yes. I'm staying over at Earthbound for the time being—uh—watching Summer's apartment." She opened her mouth to continue but thought better of it. The less he knew the better. She'd probably said too much already.

Daylan grabbed her hand and tugged her toward the carriage house. "We'll let you know if anything is amiss."

They circled the carriage house, peering in all the windows, before slipping the key in the lock and opening the door. Faint traces of magic wafted out. He put his hand in front of her to stop her forward momentum. "Let me check it out first."

She frowned but remained in place. After a few minutes, he returned to the door and gave the all clear. In the corner of the kitchen, the refrigerator hummed merrily. When she opened the door, the foul odor of rotting food or worse assaulted her senses, and she gagged at the sight of the huge rat flayed open from throat to hind legs resting on the middle shelf among rotting meat and veggies. A light green mist floated over it. She screamed and slammed the door shut, but a tendril of mist escaped. Daylan peered over her shoulder, shoved her to the side, and waved his arm. The tendril and the old refrigerator disappeared.

"What the hell?" She turned her head to look at him.

He flung open the windows and doors as he pushed her out the back door, all the while murmuring words she didn't understand. He followed her outside and slammed the door.

Summer sprinted over to them, Piper on her heels. "What's going on?"

Daylan eyed Piper for a moment, then turned his attention to his sister. "Someone left us a present in the old refrigerator. It'd been there for a while, and whatever type of spell it contained had nearly lost its abilities. Thank the Goddess." He blew out a breath. "I've cast a cleaning spell, along with a protection spell, inside and around the perimeter. It should be safe to go inside now."

Piper sniffed at the door, then barked. "Leave it, Piper." Summer turned back to Daylan. "Didn't you check it out before letting Josie go inside?"

"Of course I did. Didn't occur to me to check the fridge. My bad," he shot back. "I removed all the curtains, rugs and other things left over from the last tenant—just in case."

Jimmy trudged over with Devlin at his side. "Anything wrong?"

"No…Josie found a dead rat. That's all."

The landlord scratched the top of his balding head. "Never had a pest problem before. I'll get someone out here right away."

Devlin clapped the old man on the shoulder. "Don't worry about it. We'll handle it."

"Oh…okay. By the way, I have a new tenant that wants to rent Josie's old apartment." He handed Devlin a completed rental application. "I checked him out and he's got great references. Just came here from California—got a job promotion. Company is moving him out here. Willing to sign a two-year lease. He's a friend of Lizzie's." The old man glanced at Josie. "And you know how picky she is."

"Oh, yeah. Should be a good tenant."

Devlin's gaze switched from Summer and Daylan to Josie. "Great. We'll get your stuff moved out this afternoon."

"Yeah, I don't have much," she said, trying to keep the tremor out of her voice.

"And get a cleaning crew in there tomorrow. When does he want to move in? I'd like to paint the place and put new carpeting in before he arrives." Devlin reached in his pocket and took out his phone.

"In the next week or two, whenever his furniture gets here."

"That'll work. Let's get her moved so we can head up the pass. Only a few hours before dinner will be served." Devlin grinned. "We can all enjoy a relaxing evening. Want to join us, Jimmy?"

Jim paused for a minute, then sighed. "I'd like to, but I am plum wore out. Maybe another time."

"Sure." Devlin accompanied him to his vehicle.

"Are you sure you're okay?"

"Yep. Going to stop, get a bite to eat, watch a little TV, and turn in." Devlin closed the vehicle door behind Jim as the group gathered around and watched him slowly pull out into traffic.

"Josie, lead the way." Daylan slung an arm around her shoulder.

"You sure my stuff will be all right in the carriage house?" She looked dubiously over her shoulder to the building.

"Yep. Positive." He guided her toward the main apartment building.

She unlocked the door and walked in, stopping to survey the room. Piper bounded into the room, sniffing at every corner. "I don't remember leaving everything in such a mess." She bent over and picked up papers scattered over the floor, then glanced at the open window and back to the intricately carved wooden secretary her grandmother had bequeathed to her. It had been in the family for generations. Her mom and dad were furious when what they deemed was such a valuable antique was left to her. They suggested she should leave it with her sister for safe keeping. But something made her refuse, which angered her parents even more. "The wind must have blown my paperwork—Wait a minute. I'm sure…" She glanced at Summer. "I'm sure we didn't leave that window open."

"Certainly did not." Summer frowned. "Piper, come away from the window." The dog returned to her side with a low grumble.

"Oh, no." Josie plopped down on the floor, slid under the secretary, reached up and pushed a button. A secret drawer dropped down, and an old leather-bound book fell into her lap. Breathing a sigh of relief, she hugged the book to her chest and scooted out from under the small desk. All eyes were on her, with varying degrees of curiosity. "It belonged to my great-grandmother. I think." She caressed the book. A soft golden glow wound its way around the edges and then was gone, like a trick of light. Daylan and Summer exchanged glances.

"What?" She glanced from Daylan to her boss.

"I thought I saw something. Must have been mistaken." Summer nudged her brother.

"Oh." Josie opened the front cover carefully and took out a yellowed envelope with her name scrawled in faded red ink across it. "I discovered the drawer during one of my frequent moves, after I'd had the secretary for several years." The silence in the room was deafening except for the crinkling as she unfolded the worn letter and read out loud. "My darling Josie. Wish I could be there to explain, but your parents wouldn't allow it. You're not so different as you think. One day it will be imperative that you understand your heritage and hidden talents. Keep this little desk and its contents with you always. Sharing the information may not be in your best interest. Love, Grammy." She slid the letter into its envelope and tucked it inside the book. "Would you like to see it?"

Summer reached out her hand, grasped the book, and gently turned a few pages. "It seems to have a weak magic signature of its own. That's probably what Khellan was looking for. Let's put it back for now. We've enough irons in the fire right now."

Josie leaned over and returned the book to its hiding place with a click. Getting to her feet, she surveyed the group. "If he couldn't find it the first time, it should be safe."

"What's written in the book?" Daylan asked.

"I don't know. Part of it looks like stories and others like a list of recipes. From what little research I've done, it appears to be written in ancient Scottish Gaelic. I hesitated to find someone to translate, due to the last sentence of Gram's letter."

"I'd say that's a good guess." Summer nodded. "I may know someone we can trust to take a look. But for the moment, let's just leave it be."

"Under the circumstances, should we take the little desk with us, or leave it here in the carriage house with the rest of her stuff? If it was Khellan who went through her apartment, he didn't find what he was looking for and probably won't be back." Daylan stared at the desk, then at Josie. "Anything missing?"

She leafed through the paintings lined up around the walls, pulled open the drawers in the secretary, and shook her head. "Not that I notice." A box of paints, brushes, and other art supplies were untouched in the corner of the room on a small table. "There isn't much in the kitchen, as I rarely cook. I don't have a lot of valuable belongings except the secretary."

"Or we can temporarily store it at Earthbound or Moon Ridge, where someone will be around most of the time," Summer interjected.

"How about we let her decide while we move the rest of her furniture to the carriage house?" Daylan picked up a carton and began to fill it with kitchen items.

An hour later, her stuff was arranged in the carriage house. "Wow, I've lots more room here."

"And several more windows. I'll have an alarm system installed before you move in. Won't help with the magic wielders, but it's a deterrent to the mortals. You can check the video via your phone when you drive up, before you open the door." Devlin scribbled a note on his pad.

Summer wandered over to the new refrigerator standing in place of the old one. "I see you took care of the fridge problem, Daylan." She reached around behind the appliance and plugged it in. Then she grinned at him. "Works better when you plug it in."

He shrugged and turned his attention to Josie. "Yeah, you can get a real bed." Daylan teased pointing to her white aspen wood day bed. The headboard was covered with delicate paintings of faeries frolicking in a green meadow surrounded by aspen trees, with a babbling brook flowing over rocks.

"I painted that myself," she shot back, crossing her arms over her chest. "I like it just fine."

"It's beautiful." Summer moved to the bed, reached out, and touched the headboard. "You are so talented."

"Aww, thanks. Actually, it's my way of relieving stress." She picked up the box of art supplies and turned into the arms of Daylan.

He grinned and whispered in her ear, "For only you—but not for two." He waggled his eyebrows and jerked his chin in the direction of the bed. Heat rose in her cheeks.

"Okay you two, time to head up to the cabin. I'm starved," Devlin declared then whistled for Piper to follow. "Josie, have you made a decision?"

Chapter Twenty-Three
A Decision, a Discussion, and Finally a Relaxing Evening

"I have." She chewed on her bottom lip lowering the art supplies onto the floor beside her easel and clean canvases. "I want to leave the secretary at Earthbound until I move into the carriage house permanently. Ghost Daylan seems to be stationed there. I'll be there most mornings teaching class, and then however long the administration stuff takes. Mandy will be there in the afternoon and for a couple of evening classes. Unless you are going to cancel those until things are settled." She glanced inquiringly at Summer.

Summer peered at Devlin, who shrugged. "We'll leave the class schedule intact at the moment. The evening classes are quite popular. I can't let this situation impact my—*our*—livelihoods. Devlin and Wyatt can take turns playing bodyguard in the evening until Daylan gets the forge operational and finishes his back orders." She paused. "Didn't Shay say he'd have warriors stationed discreetly at Moon Ridge, Earthbound, and our cabin until Khellan was apprehended?"

"I believe that is what he said, though we haven't seen him for a while." Daylan frowned.

"The same magic enchantments and protections are in place at Earthbound as the carriage house. Correct?"

Josie gave Summer a hopeful look.

"Yep. Good choice. Load it up, boys, and we'll be on our way." Summer waved her hand toward the antique secretary.

"The boss is back." Devlin and Daylan did a quick eye roll and sauntered over to the desk, hoisted it up, and shuffled toward the door. "It should fit in the back of the SUV, with the third seat folded down."

"Of course it will. We can drop it off on our way to the cabin. Position it against the far wall of the studio not far from Daylan's room. What do you think, Josie?"

"Great." She held the door open while Summer and Piper rushed out ahead of the guys to fold down the third seat. "Are we ready to lock up?"

"Yep." Devlin crossed the threshold with his end of the desk. She followed them out, closed and locked the door.

After a quick stop at Earthbound to drop off the desk, and an impromptu conversation with Ghost Daylan, they headed up Ute Pass to the cabin. When Devlin opened the door, the most delicious aromas wafted out. "Jenny, everything smells wonderful."

A smiling, middle-aged woman with sparkling blue eyes and dark brown hair pulled back in a messy bun rounded the corner from the kitchen. "Good evening, and thanks. Your timing is perfect. I pulled the pot roast out of the oven a few minutes ago. Homemade rolls are in the warmer. Green beans and garlic mashed potatoes are in warming trays in the center of the table. A Dutch apple pie is on the counter, and vanilla bean ice cream in the freezer. Koda and Wyatt are upstairs cleaning up for dinner. If that's all, I'll be on my way. See you tomorrow around nine?"

"Yes. That's perfect. Thank you so much."

"My pleasure." Jenny slipped on her jacket and passed by Daylan as she made her way out the door.

His stomach growled as he entered the cabin, his arm slung around Josie's shoulders. "Wow, nice place you got here." A cheerful fire warmed the family room as he passed it to slip into the formal dining area, where place settings for six were arranged on a polished octagonal wooden table. Only a few more steps and he could see bottles of wine chilling on the kitchen counter beside crystal wine glasses. A coffee maker and full pot of coffee sat on the opposite counter with mugs. *Sis picked a good one. The gun club must do well.*

Summer pointed down the hallway. "Powder room is on your right. You can wash up there." She paused to make sure Piper had food and water at her feeding station next to the back door. Piper sniffed around for a bit, then grabbed a mouthful of food and started toward upstairs. Summer leaned down and scratched the pup behind the ears. "Looking for Koda and Wyatt? Huh?" She laughed, stopped at the kitchen sink, and washed her hands. "Now, what can I get everyone to drink? We have wine." She motioned to the bottles on the counter. "Or soft drinks, iced tea, coffee, milk, and hot chocolate. The evenings up here are cool, even in the summertime."

Devlin grinned, wrapped his arm around Summer's waist, and brushed a kiss over her lips. "I'm going to start the deck heater to chase off the chill so we can enjoy our pie outside and watch the wildlife. If that's all right with everyone?"

Murmurs of agreement filled the room. Koda came bounding down the stairs from the open second level, with Wyatt close behind, and Piper at his heels. "What'd we miss?"

"Lots of heavy lifting when we moved Josie's stuff from the apartment to her carriage house." Devlin gave them a quick rundown on the condition of her apartment, antique desk, and the letter.

"Hey, you're the one that told us to come up here." Wyatt joked.

"Excuses, excuses." Devlin grinned. "Grab a plate and serve yourselves. Summer's getting drinks."

"Can I help?" Josie and Koda chorused.

"Sure. Tumblers are to the left of the stove in the upper cabinet. Fill them with ice. I believe we need glasses for two soft drinks and two iced teas. I have wine for Devlin and me." Josie filled the tumblers with ice. Koda helped Summer with the drinks and placed them on the table. Once everyone was seated and plates filled, the only sounds were silverware scraping the china plates. As they finished up, the conversation turned to Josie's secretary, worn leather book, her Grammy's letter, and plans for the rest of the week.

Devlin stood. "Anyone ready for pie? It's Dutch apple and can be a la mode."

Everyone nodded.

"Through the sliding glass doors is the deck. It should be nice and warm. Pick up your pie in the kitchen, and we'll meet you out there." Moving easily through the state-of-the-art kitchen, Devlin sliced the pie, scooped ice cream, and served the tasty treat on the china plates Summer had gotten down from the cupboard. She handed each guest a piece of the pie and they meandered out onto the huge deck.

With her fork, Josie scraped up the last bite of pie

from her plate and scooped up a tiny bite of melting ice cream and slipped it into her mouth. "Mmm, this is delicious." A jaw-popping yawn took her by surprise, and her attempt to stifle it failed miserably. "Guess the day has caught up with me." A soft giggle escaped her lips.

"Know the feeling." Summer covered her mouth as she too yawned.

"We better let these lightweights head to bed under their own steam before we have to carry them," Daylan teased. "We need to borrow a vehicle to get back to the Springs."

"You two can stay here for the night, and Devlin will take you to Earthbound midmorning." Summer stretched her arms over her head.

"That won't work. I have a full early morning class tomorrow for college kids, you know—before their academic classes convene."

"And I'd like to get an early start at the forge."

Summer glanced at Devlin. "When is the rest of your family arriving?"

Devlin scrubbed his hand over his face. "Not sure. Tomorrow or the next day. They wanted time for Koda and Wyatt to show them around the town before the wedding. I'll give them a call tomorrow. Then we can rework the schedule to accommodate the new arrivals."

"Do you see a problem with Josie and my brother staying in the Springs?"

"Like you said, we can't put our lives on hold. More convenient at Earthbound than at Moon Ridge. There's security at Earthbound for both magical and mortal. It should be relatively safe. Besides, if something goes wrong, you can get us there in seconds, if necessary. Right?"

"Yes, I can port us there."

"We'll then have the element of surprise rather than all being trapped in one location." Devlin paused for a beat. "Yeah, that'll work."

"Tomorrow, I'll relieve Daylan early to work at the forge as planned. That way Josie isn't alone and Koda can stay here to help Summer."

"Great plan." Daylan opened the door to the cabin. "See you all tomorrow."

Summer walked over to her backpack resting on the arm of the couch. She dug around in her pack for a second, retrieved her SUV keys, and tossed them to Daylan. "Take my vehicle. I'll be here most of the day tomorrow working on the wedding. Koda can bring me down later to retrieve the vehicle." Grabbing a sweater from the peg by the door, she handed it to Josie. "You're going to need this tonight."

"Thanks." She put the sweater on. "The list of tasks that need to be done is on the computer. Right?"

"Yep. You've covered for me before. Don't forget to date stamp the mail. Any questions, call me."

"Will do."

Inside the vehicle, Josie turned to Daylan. "Why do you think all these strange magically things are happening to me now?"

"Best guess, you need to be protected from what could possibly be your own people. Namely, Khellan. Your magic first surfaced when you were captured and inside my forge trying to get out. The chains did their best to protect you. When you pounded on the wall and were in danger from Khellan, magic appeared in your hands."

"I had no idea what to do with it." She slumped in the seat. "At first, magic scared me. Now it frustrates me."

"Understandable. It's new to you." He started the engine and pulled out onto the street. Giving her a quick sideways glance, he cleared his throat. "Did you happen to notice the glow from the edges of your book in the secretary while you were holding it?"

"No… It glowed? Well, kinda, but I thought it was my imagination."

"Yep. Started at the bottom and ran right around the edge. I know Sis and Devlin saw it." He turned onto Highway 24. The road was deserted. Only an occasional set of headlights bobbed on the road, headed in the opposite direction. He glanced at his watch. *Nearly midnight. Where has the night gone?*

"Really?" She hesitated for a beat or two. "Maybe we should contact someone who can translate the book for us—after the wedding."

"May want to do it sooner rather than later. Mom or Dad may possibly be able to help when they get here. If it's all right with you?" Suddenly, he snapped his fingers. "Why didn't I think of it before? The ghost may be able to help as well. After all, he is old and Scottish."

"But we would be trusting him with whatever family secrets that book contains," she said uncertainly.

"I wouldn't worry about that. Who's he going to tell? He's dependent upon us to unravel his situation. Don't think he's going jeopardize that. Do you?" He stole a quick glance at her.

She picked at the hem of the sweater.

"It's going to be all right. I can feel it." It was a lie,

but he hoped to ease her mind, at least for the moment. In truth, he had no idea what the future held.

Chapter Twenty-Four
Her Book, His Ghost, a Surprise

Slowing the SUV in front of Earthbound, he surveyed the property. Everything seemed normal. Mandy had left the night security light on. The tension he'd felt ebbed away as he turned into the parking lot. "Let's walk around the building before you unlock and disarm the alarm."

"Okay. Wish we'd brought Piper with us."

"Why? That dog doesn't like me." He jumped out of the SUV, and gravel crunched under his feet as he met Josie in front of the vehicle.

The grass in front of the studio was drenched with dew and she left footprints when she walked across it. "She just doesn't know you. But she has a sense for trouble. Summer always let her run through the building before we entered." She shrugged. "That was before Devlin."

"Oh, Devlin took Piper's job?" He chuckled.

"No, silly." She couldn't help but giggle. "Things changed when Devlin entered the picture. He is so protective of Summer. They are so cute together. It was a whirlwind romance. You can tell they're perfect for each other." She sighed. "He is so romantic. Made a special trip over here to bring her hot chocolate when it was snowing. Romantic lunches. Except the one Koda and Wyatt crashed. That was a fiasco." She giggled again. "Whisking her away to his cabin for cross-country ski lessons and a Valentine's Day proposal." She followed him around the building.

"Wow, he doesn't seem that type."

"That's what is so cute. Mandy and I teased her endlessly when she claimed they were just friends. Now he's all take charge and protective of everyone around her. It's a Navy SEAL thing."

"I'd believe that. I'm happy for her." The breeze tousled his hair as they finished the circuit around the building. Everything normal, he grabbed her hand and walked to the porch, where they climbed the stairs together. Pulling the keys out of her bag, she unlocked the door, stepped inside behind him, deactivated the alarm, and waited while he checked the rooms.

"Nothing's changed since we dropped off the desk." He flipped on the light. The studio was bathed in soft light. Shadows danced on the walls from the breeze blowing the trees near the windows. The colorful yoga mats were all stacked in the corner and the secretary remained against the far wall.

"About time." A voice called from the hallway. "Naught a thing happened since ye left."

"Thank you for sticking around and keeping an eye on it. But we'll take it from here." Daylan made shooing motions with his hands.

"What about?" Her forehead scrunched up, she looked quizzically at him.

"We'll wait for Mom and Dad. It's a better choice," Daylan said firmly.

"Nite." She followed him upstairs, unlocked the apartment, pushed the door open, and deactivated its alarm.

"Naught a soul has been up there either," the ghost called from the bottom of the landing.

"Great. Good night." Daylan closed the door behind him and motioned her to stay put as he walked through the little apartment. When he returned, he flipped the light on. "All clear. Geez, you'd think this was Fort Knox rather than a yoga studio and a mostly empty apartment."

"Security is extremely important to Summer." She hesitated a moment. "I sometimes wondered if she was running from something. But she was so kind and stable—after the old owner flipped out. I was relieved when she sold the building and business to Summer, then left town. Now—it makes sense."

"You really had no idea?" he asked incredulously.

"Nope. None. Why would I? Things that went bump in the night were only faerie tales to me until recently." She shook her head.

"Good point." He glanced at the little fireplace and snapped his fingers. With a whoosh, flames danced over the logs in the hearth. "Nothing like a romantic fire on a chilly evening."

She rolled her eyes. "Competing with Devlin?"

"Nope, making sure you're warm." He crossed to her and caressed her cheek, feathering his fingers along her jawline to her chin. Lifting her chin a bit, he brushed his lips over hers, then murmured, "Alone at last."

"I believe we are."

His hands slipped to her waist, pulling her tight against him. Heat and desire swirled through her. This time she wouldn't pull back. This time she didn't care what anyone thought. She'd never in her whole life felt like this with anyone. This was meant to be. It had to be right. He had to be the one. Giving herself up to the moment, she snaked her arms around his neck, her fingers caressed the baby-fine hair at the nape of his neck, then wandered up through the back of his hair. Like him, it was strong, masculine, and soft all at the same time. Standing on tiptoes, she deepened the kiss, pressing into his body, eager for his touch.

His tongue probed gently between her parted lips. The soft stroking and exploring created a sizzling trail of fire and want through her body. She needed more. Her arms slipped down his sides, and reaching under his shirt, she ran her fingers over the sinewy muscles of his chest and abs, then followed the soft V of hair to his waist. He eased away as a sensual smile curved his full lips. Her heart thundered in her chest. Butterflies careened through her belly.

"Playing with fire, you could be burnt." Pausing, he fingered the buttons on her shirt. "Are you sure this is what you want?" Before she could answer, he nibbled along her jawline. His tongue licked to the junction of her neck and collarbone, then trailed lower. She moaned, tilting her head to allow him further exploration.

Looking up, his eyes locked on hers as he unbuttoned her shirt one button at a time and pushed it off her shoulders. Slipping her arms out of her blouse, she grasped his biceps, feeling his muscles bunch and contract beneath her fingers. She reveled in his strength.

"I guess that would be a yes." He reached around behind her and released the clasp of her bra, cupping her breasts as they spilled into his hands. The rough pads of his thumbs caressed her nipples until they were hard berries sending jolts of lust through her. When he covered her nipples with his warm mouth, sucking gently, she moaned and arched toward him.

"Too many clothes." She tugged at the back of his shirt and pulled it over his head, tossing it onto the floor. Suddenly, her back was against the wall, his legs between hers, and he slid his hands around her thighs, easily lifting her up. She wrapped her legs around his waist and his arousal pressed against her. The heat was intense even through their clothes. She bowed back, causing him to take a step backward. Using that opportunity, she reached for the button on his jeans and flipped it open. "What are you hiding in there?" Grinning, she wiggled her fingers inside the band of his briefs.

As he shifted her in his arms, his seductive smile returned. "I think it's time we take this to the bedroom, where I can take you in all the wicked ways I can imagine."

She giggled. "I couldn't agree more." Her arms came up around his neck, where she breathed a kiss at the hollow, then nipped, and soothed the bites with the tip of her tongue. His scent of spice, pine, and citrus filled her nostrils, and she inhaled deeply, enjoying the masculine feel and taste of him.

He made his way to the bed but paused, his gaze scorching. "This won't do." With a jerk of his head, the remainder of their clothes disappeared.

She squealed as his hand under one leg slid to her thigh and then to her center, fingers teasing, stroking, and lightly penetrating. *Oh God, if he doesn't stop, I'm going to...*

He bent down, laying her gently on the bed.

Leaving her legs dangling, he knelt between them, spreading her wide and kissing his way from ankle to her hot, moist center. Pausing, he stared at her, blowing gently across her bared flesh. "You're absolutely beautiful." Caressing the little bundle of nerves with his tongue, he slipped a long finger, then two, inside her.

*Oh God...nothing had ever...how could he...* She couldn't think, couldn't breathe, and then she screamed his name and arched against him, crashing over the edge into pure ecstasy. Searing heat shot through her veins as she writhed under his ministrations, riding the waves of sensation pounding through her body in long, pulsating tremors. Her fists clenched in the comforter as she enjoyed each quaking explosion. Never had anyone brought her to such a climax. "Wow," she breathed as her body went limp. "Just wow." Their entire relationship recently had been a balancing act on the edge of this. *What the hell was I waiting for?*

Rising to his feet, he crawled up beside her, a smug expression spread across his face. He rested on his side and caressed his fingers over her cheek, his smoldering gaze holding hers. "And I'm nowhere near finished with you." His hand slipped down between her thighs, fingers teasing again.

Suddenly, thunder crashed, shaking the building, and long branches of lightning illuminated the night. Trees outside cast frenzied shadows on the walls while the lightning flashed. She froze. Her eyes went wide. "Oh God, now what?" She tried to push him away.

He lifted his head and smiled reassuringly. "It's only a thunderstorm. Nothing more." As if hearing his words, the storm released sheets of pounding rain on the roof and pelted the windowpanes. Shifting his leg between hers, he brought his mouth down over hers, hungry and demanding. Of their own volition, her lips parted, and his tongue thrust inside to entwine with hers in a sinuous dance. His body moved over her. Thunder exploded overhead again, and lightning streaked across the sky.

She relaxed and her legs spread, welcoming him. *He was right. Only a rainstorm.* Then he was inside her, moving slowly at first, filling her with his warmth. "Oh God," she moaned. She arched up to meet him. Together they found the rhythm that bound their bodies in exquisite harmony. A groan escaped his lips as he increased the rocking of his hips. "I want you, but first…" His breath coming in short, quick bursts, he shifted inside her, and she shrieked. His hardness electrified her, and her own breath came in long surrendering moans as her body began to vibrate. A tremor flowed inside her like molten lava, heating her thighs and center as she soared to another shuddering climax. A moment later, he followed her over the edge into ecstasy. Their bodies naked, legs entwined, still moist from lovemaking, he touched her breast, and then his fingers walked down between her legs. "Ready for round three?"

\*\*\*\*

In the morning she woke to the rich aroma of coffee and the sound of splashing water. Someone was in the shower. The water stopped and the door opened. Daylan stood, water droplets falling from his hair, a towel tied loosely around his hips. "Good morning, my love."

The words flowed smoothly off his tongue, and she blinked. *Did he just say love? Did he mean it?* She rolled over and sat up, a bit stiff and sore from their marathon lovemaking last night. Smiling, she swung her feet to the floor and got up, unabashed by her nakedness. He'd seen, touched, explored, and tasted her in every way imaginable exactly as he'd promised. At the memories, desire zinged through her. "Good morning to you." She padded over to him and tugged at the towel. It fell in a heap on the floor. *Blessed be, he was ready, willing, and able.*

He grinned. "Making up for lost time? Unfortunately, you've only got forty-five minutes before your first class. Now, I can help you stretch before you get dressed…"

"Why didn't you wake me?" She tossed him a scathing look, then scurried to the closet, where she yanked out purple yoga pants and a matching striped top.

"Because you looked so peaceful and content. Besides, you kept kicking the covers off, so the view was mesmerizing." He shrugged. "Couldn't help myself."

Outside, a truck engine rumbled as it pulled into the parking lot. "That would be Devlin. He texted a little while ago to say he was on his way. Wyatt's been sent on other errands."

"You brat." She grabbed a bra and panties from the dresser drawer and bent to slip her foot into the panties. He moved behind her, cupping her breast and pressing against her. "Daylan," she shrieked. "Stop it!"

"Then don't tempt me with that cute little ass of yours. He kissed her long and hard. She returned the kiss with reckless abandonment, then slithered against him. *I'm going to be late.*

He snapped his fingers, and she was fully dressed. "Breakfast is on the table." Waggling his eyebrows, he patted her bottom and winked. "We'll continue this interlude tonight." The alarm beep told them Devlin was in the studio.

"Crap."

"Relax. After all, we are consenting adults." He grabbed her hand. "Take a deep breath. I'll invite him to breakfast." She blew out a breath and walked into the kitchen as he opened the door. "Hey, Devlin, up here. Care for a bit of breakfast?"

"Thought you'd be ready to go to the forge by now."

"Running a bit late. Was really tired last night." He held the door open for Devlin.

"Yeah, I bet you were." Devlin gave him a sly grin. "The night was uneventful, I assume. Magically speaking."

"Yep. How about your household?"

"Same. Summer is planning a family dinner in lieu of a rehearsal dinner next week." He turned his attention to Josie. "Said you'll need to put up signs at Earthbound to cancel next Friday's evening classes and all of Saturday's. Then Mandy is free to attend the wedding on Saturday." He handed her a list and rolled his eyes. "This is Summer's revised list of tasks that need to be taken care of this week and next. With the wedding, things are changing minute by minute." He blew out a breath.

While looking over the list, she took another bite of blueberry bagel and washed it down with chocolate milk. "Will do. I gotta get downstairs and stretch out before the students arrive. See ya later."

Daylan caught her arm and kissed her affectionately. "Meet me at the forge late afternoon?"

She glanced at Devlin, who nodded. "Yes, I guess so, after I finish my work."

In the studio, she rolled out a yoga mat and settled down. Clearing her mind and relaxing her muscles was harder than she expected. But keeping her attention on the class was nearly impossible. Either thoughts of Daylan or recent events kept derailing her lesson plan. This was a first for her. The students trickled in, and despite her misgivings, the class went off without a hitch. Finally, the class was over, and she said her goodbyes. Mandy came in and took the afternoon classes. In the office, Josie checked off the tasks as they were completed. She walked to the front and posted the signs with the Saturday closure and the new hours for next week on the front door.

"Hey, girl, you about ready to close up?" Mandy came in, followed by her boyfriend, Clay.

Josie looked up over the computer monitor. "Yep. Did Summer talk to you about next week?"

"She did. I think we're all set." Mandy grinned. "She sounded a little frazzled on the phone."

"I imagine. Her in-laws should be here soon, and her mom and dad will be here at week's end."

****

Devlin dropped Josie off at the forge and drove on up to the cabin.

When she pulled the door open to the forge, a shiver ran up her spine and a bell tinkled overhead. The well-lit building was nothing like the place where she'd been held hostage. It smelled of heat and metals. The building had been partitioned, with a showroom located in the front. Lightly, she ran her fingers over the glass cases, and she stopped to look at the knives, swords, and various weapons displayed inside. "Hey, Daylan, you here?"

The loud pounding stopped. "Sure am." He pushed open a swinging door, wiping his hands on a cloth and grinning. "I felt you come in." There was a sweatband tied around his forehead and a black smudge across his cheek. His T-shirt, wet from sweat, glistened in the fluorescent lighting as he held a flattened piece of metal in his hand and motioned her farther in.

"Looks like you're busy." She wrinkled her nose at the unusual scents in the building.

"Never too busy for you. Want a tour?"

She surveyed what she could see. "Sure," she said hesitantly.

Holding the swinging door open for her, he said, "This is where all the work gets done. Power hammer is what was running when you called out." He pointed to the center of the room. "This is my propane forge. You're personally familiar with the anvil, hammer, and chain beside it. Around the walls are settling tanks and the other supplies for my craft." Pointing to the door in the corner of the room he said. "That's the bathroom, complete with shower. So what do you think?"

"I think it's dirty and hot in here." She snickered, wiping the sweat from her forehead with her arm. "But the weapons out in the showcase are beautiful." With her fingers, she lightly touched the edge of the bench lined with finished knives, daggers, and swords. "Is this the order for the Scottish group?"

He nodded, taking a clean cloth out of his pocket and wiping his hands. "Yes. I made good headway today. By the end of the week, I should have most of the order done."

Turning her attention to the bench adjacent, she noticed several partially formed swords and daggers, unlike the others on the previous table. Reaching for the cloth in his hand, she wiped the black off her fingers and pointed. "What are these for?" She waved the cloth in the second table's direction.

"I'm experimenting with a few new ideas." Grinning, he snatched the cloth from her hand, untied his leather bibbed apron, pulled it over his head, and tossed it and the cloth on the bench. "Let me get cleaned up and I'll take you out to dinner. Any preferences?" He shoved the swinging door open and held it.

"Steak and baked potato would be great. I'm starved. Forgot to eat lunch."

"How was your day? Did you get everything Summer wanted done and conduct a fabulous yoga class?" His eyes glittered with amusement.

"Of course." She grinned.

"Have a seat on one of the benches while I make myself presentable. I'll be right back."

She wandered back through the showroom, taking a better look at what was on display.

After about fifteen minutes, he appeared, dressed in jeans, blue sport shirt, and polished black boots, then held his arms out. "Better?"

"Cleaner," she clarified, then ran her fingers through his still damp hair. "I think you are the best I've ever had." She snorted a laugh.

Chapter Twenty-Five
Family Sightseeing Days Before the Wedding

The week flew by without incident. With the arrival of Devlin's family, Josie and Daylan were invited to join the fun outings when they were off work. She liked playing tourist, especially with the twins. They were so exuberant about everything.

The view at the summit of Pikes Peak was breathtaking. A recent spring storm had left patches of snow behind rocks and in shady areas. Rain in the lower regions sometimes translated to snow on the peak. The summit house offered the best donuts ever, and she'd eaten more than she should have.

On the way down the mountain, Devlin's dad and his wife wanted to stop and shop in Manitou Springs. Then it was on to the next attraction.

While the family gathered at Cave of the Winds, she heard whispers inside the cave as the hair on the back of her neck stood on end. *Am I imagining this?* She'd been here numerous times but never experienced such a phenomenon. She paused. *Sure enough. I can't quite make out what they are saying.* The rest of the group had moved on, and she hurried to catch up, then tugged on Daylan's arm. "Do you hear that?"

He put his hand over hers, quirking a brow. "Yeah, it's the whispering spirits Koda and Wyatt were talking about." He kept his voice low so as not to disturb the spirits further nor have the others overhear their conversation.

"Can you understand them?" Her forehead creased in concentration.

"Sure." He regarded her with interest. "Can't you?"

"No. I hear sounds, like partial words being formed, but they're not clear—too breathy."

"They are warning the ancient one has been here. Others looking for him swept through the deep caverns but left some time ago."

Her eyes widened, and her pulse raced. "That means he's not been captured?"

"I don't know. A week, a month, a year or ten are all the same to the spirits—unless it was yesterday or today."

She tilted her head to look at the ceiling of the cave and lost her footing. Her squeal echoed through the cave as her shoulder slammed into the stone wall. Still gripping Daylan's arm, she yanked him off balance. He toppled toward her but managed a quick turn and braced his hands on the wall on either side of her. "You okay?"

"I think so." She rotated her shoulder and winced, sucking in a breath. "It's sore, but nothing serious. Wasn't watching where my feet were going." She gave a little laugh. "There are so many unique formations in here."

Summer and Devlin hurried over. "You two all right?"

"Yes, we're good. Think this will be our last adventure for the day." He wrapped an arm around Josie's waist and gently pulled her to him, kissing the top of her head. "I've work to finish at the forge, and then we'll head back to the Earthbound apartment."

"Remember the family dinner will be tomorrow evening. Hopefully, your parents will be here by then." Summer quirked a brow and an uncertain smile turned up one corner of her mouth.

"Don't give me that crap. They're your parents too. It will be good to be a united family again. You'll see." He lowered his hand to the small of Josie's back and guided her toward the cave's entrance.

Summer bumped her hip against Daylan's. "Hey, take my SUV today. I'll take Josie's. Devlin doesn't want her vehicle parked at the studio overnight, advertising she may be there alone. She won't be, but... And don't forget to disguise magic signatures when you get out of the SUV, on the off chance he's still..." She wiggled her eyebrows. "You know."

Despite her shoulder, Josie giggled, then clamped her hand over her mouth and glanced around a bit self-consciously, lowering her voice when she said, "It feels a little like we're dealing with 'the evil wizard who isn't named' from the boy wizard movie."

Summer rolled her eyes and shook her head. Daylan and Devlin snickered. "Maybe it does, just a little," Daylan conceded.

The rest of the entourage joined them at the mouth of the cave, looking a little worse for wear, in her opinion. Loren and his wife had dark circles under their eyes. The twins were picking at each other. Koda had one by the shoulder and Wyatt had the other one by the arm, separating them. "I think we'll head back to the cabin. Dad and Rita are beat, and the twins may not live to see tomorrow if things don't change immediately." Wyatt slid a warning glance to his children.

"Wait. I'd like to peek into the gift shop before we leave." Rita glanced over pleadingly at Loren. "It'll only take a minute."

"Take your time." Wyatt motioned toward the touristy shop. "I'll take the kids to the vehicle and discuss manners." He pointed toward the parking lot, and two subdued kiddos trudged in the direction of the car.

"We'll see you up there?" Koda nudged her brother in the ribs.

"Yep. Want to swing by Earthbound. Then we'll be along." Devlin glanced at Summer. She nodded. He turned his attention to Daylan. "You're going to Moon Ridge first, right?"

"Sure am. Want to finish up a couple of projects before the wedding festivities and family arrive."

Josie rolled her eyes, stifling a yawn. "Can't it wait until tomorrow?"

"Shouldn't take long." He leaned over and whispered, "May have more family to entertain tomorrow."

Devlin nodded. "If anything looks suspicious—"

"You'll be the third to know," Daylan interrupted with a chuckle. Josie rubbed her shoulder and leaned heavily against him. "You know what—on second thought, we'll go straight to Earthbound," he said. "She needs to rest or she'll be grumpy tomorrow."

"That's a terrible thing to say." She straightened, planted her hands on hips, then winced and rubbed her shoulder.

"I don't hear you denying it," he baited further.

She shot him a scathing glance, then walked toward the vehicle.

Devlin grinned. "Better abandon the shovel before you bury yourself, bro. Probably best anyway. Summer and I'll go by Moon Ridge and then to the cabin."

****

Once inside the vehicle, her demeanor softened, and she shoved up the console and slid next to Daylan. "Thanks for skipping the forge. I want to go to bed. Bright and early tomorrow will be soon enough to take care of your projects." She rested her head on his shoulder, dozing on the way to the apartment.

He slowed the SUV in the block where Earthbound was located. A streetlight flickered on and off across from the studio as he turned into the parking lot and stopped. An unfamiliar car was parked under one of the parking lot lights. Two people appeared to be inside. "Now what?" he grumbled.

She sat up and blinked. "Who's here?" She rubbed her eyes and leaned over to open the vehicle door.

He put his hand in front of her. "Don't. Stay here. Let me find out what's going on." His door squeaked as he pushed it open.

The occupants in the other car moved around inside. Josie held her breath. *The last thing I need tonight is a confrontation.* A few months back, they'd had a problem with people parking in the lot and sleeping there. Devlin had put a stop to that. *Were they back?* She pulled out her keys to the studio, then fingered her cell phone inside her backpack. *Maybe I should call Summer.*

The doors of the strange vehicle opened and two people emerged.

"What are you doing here?" Daylan's voice was loud and friendly. She yanked the door handle and jumped out. Landing on the ground jarred her shoulder. She winced and stood still for a couple beats, waiting for the pain to subside.

"We just got in, and this is the only address Summer gave us." A tall man stood under the light, his dark hair sprinkled with silver. A light-haired woman almost as tall as the man joined him. Daylan caught them both up in a bear hug. "This is Summer's yoga studio, Earthbound. She has an apartment on the second level. But she lives in Divide with Devlin most of the time." He whirled around and motioned Josie over.

Carefully, she picked her way over to them, her good arm holding her injured arm against her body.

Concern creased his forehead as his gaze searched her face. "You okay?"

"Yes." She waved her good arm around. "Jarred my shoulder when I jumped out of the SUV. No biggie."

He slid an arm around her waist. "Josie, these are Summer's and my parents. Brody and Vera. Mom, Dad, this is my girlfriend, Josie. She works with Summer."

She extended her good hand to them, intending to shake their hands. Instead, they enveloped her in a careful hug.

"So glad to meet you. We knew something was keeping Daylan here besides his sister." His dad chuckled. "Now I understand." He winked at her.

"Oh, stop it, Brody, you're embarrassing her." Vera patted her shoulder, and she winced. His mother jerked back.

"Earlier today she had a run in with a rock wall at the Cave of the Winds." Daylan paused, his lips twitching. "The wall won. She injured her shoulder."

Grinning, he pointed in the direction of the studio. "Let's get inside and I'll call Summer. She may still be in town. Devlin, her fiancé, owns a state-of-the-art gun club east of town, and they were going to make sure all was well out there before heading up the mountain." Daylan shrugged. "He's a retired Navy SEAL, so…he needs to be on top of everything."

She unlocked the door, turned off the alarm, and flipped the lights on. "Come on in. Can I get you something to drink? Summer usually has soft drinks and iced tea on hand, and Devlin keeps a few bottles of beer in the fridge. What's your poison?" She hesitated to invite them up to the apartment without Summer's permission.

"Oh, no, dear, we just ate a little while ago at the quaint little Italian restaurant two streets over." Vera motioned down the street, paused, and glanced at her husband, who jerked his chin in the opposite direction. "Well, it wasn't far from here."

Daylan slid his phone out of its holder on his belt, punched Summer's number, and waited. "Gee, you answered on the first ring. Mom and Dad are here at Earthbound. Where are you?" He paused for a couple beats, listening. "Do you want to meet them here? Or shall I give them directions to…" Pausing again, he chuckled. "Okay see you in a few." Ending the call, he turned to the fireplace, snapped his fingers, and flames roared to life. "These old buildings can be a bit cool, especially in the summer evenings. No matter how warm it is during the day, it always cools off when the sun goes down."

"Noticed that, son." Brody turned in a full circle. "Nice place she has here. Look at that carved banister.

Don't see workmanship like that anymore."

"You say this is her business? Does she own the building too?" Vera surveyed the room.

"Yes, she bought the building and the business from Jasmine a year or so ago. Jasmine had some personal problems, wasn't a good money manager, and wanted to leave Colorado. Summer made her an offer for both and..." She put her hands to her heated face. *Geez, I'm babbling again. Don't know what Summer wants them to know and what she doesn't.* "Well, anyway, here we are." Absently, she padded over to the little secretary and ran her fingers over the smooth wood, a way of reassuring herself all was well. Swaying a little, she leaned on the desk and glanced up the stairs.

Vera followed her. "What a beautiful antique secretary. Does it have secret compartments? You know, many of these little desks did, back in the day."

"Mother," Daylan said in an exasperated voice.

"What?" Vera glanced from her son to her husband. "Well, they did." She smiled at Josie and returned to her husband's side. "Only making conversation," she said quietly, more to herself than to anyone else, Josie suspected.

"Yes, as a matter of fact, it does. It was my great-grandmother's. I inherited it from my grandmother when she passed. I've always loved it." She cleared her throat and stared at Daylan, then stole a glance below the desk.

"Excuse us for a moment." He put his arm around her waist and steered her toward the office. "Do you want to show Mom the book?"

"Seems like as good a time as any, while we wait

for Summer and Devlin. After today, there's only a couple of very busy days before the wedding."

He shrugged one shoulder. "You're right. I'll ask. What harm can it do?"

"Less than if you don't know what it says and all hell breaks loose at the cabin." A shiver shot up her spine, and the feeling of foreboding that had followed her for days returned. *I'm probably just tired.*

They came out of the office with two bottles of water, an iced tea, and a bottle of cola. He handed a bottle of water to his mom. "We have a favor to ask. If you don't want to do it, say so. Don't mean to put you on the spot."

Vera tilted her head. "Of course. What is it?"

Josie sat down on the couch and let Daylan retrieve the leather-bound book. She relayed the story of the desk, the book, and trying to find someone to translate it and her grandmother's words. "Daylan thought you might be able to decipher the writing. It's written in old Gaelic."

He brought over the book, sat down beside her, and brought them up to speed with the recent events, the ghost, Khellan, and Shay, then handed his mom the book.

Vera tried to open it, but it wouldn't budge. Josie took the book, and a golden glow raced around the edges and the book flopped open. She handed it back to Daylan's mom.

Carefully, Vera turned page after page, delicately running her finger down a page. "My Gaelic is a bit rusty…but there's no doubt." His mom glanced up from the book to Josie. "It's a written family ancestry and contains powerful magic, incantations handed down from generation to generation. Are you—or rather your family—" Vera hesitated only a moment before staring directly into her eyes "—of Fae heritage?"

"If someone had asked me that a few months ago, I'd have thought you were crazy. Since that time, I've learned that magical creatures do exist, and I could be one of them." Glancing down at her hands folded in her lap, she relayed the information gleaned from her parents, which wasn't much, and how different she was from her siblings.

"Wow, what an honor! If you're descended from the individuals who wrote this book, you're Fae royalty. By any chance is your mother Olivia Adee? That's the last complete entry made. Then, in different handwriting, there is the name Josie but no last name or information."

"Olivia Mackenzie. Oh, wait, my grandmother's maiden name was Adee."

"You mentioned siblings. Are you the oldest?" Vera jumped at the sound of a car door closing.

"No. The youngest." At the sound of footsteps, she turned and looked at the door expectantly. Her heartbeat picked up the pace.

The old wooden door *creaked* open. Devlin and Summer strode inside. Devlin gave Summer a little nudge forward. "Sorry we're late to the party, but we didn't know when you'd be here." Devlin grinned. "Glad you made it. I'm Devlin, the lucky man to wed this beautiful creature." He glanced at Summer, winding his arm around her and kissing her cheek.

Summer ambled forward, more subdued that Josie had ever seen her. "Mom, Dad, you're looking good."

Vera and Brody exchanged glances. Vera made the

first move, enveloping her daughter in a tight hug. "I've missed you."

Her father joined in, his arms around both Vera and Summer. "It's been a long time, Mag."

Josie's heartbeat returned to normal, and her forehead creased as she switched her attention from the family reunion to Daylan, who was standing back. "Mag?"

He snickered, then gave in to a full-on laugh. "Dad used to call her Mag—short for 'magic'—because he never knew what magic she'd conjure when she was a kid. Never had a fire witch in our family before, and when a flaming bow appeared in her hands at the age of eight, she pulled back the fiery arrow and let it fly. I thought Mom was going to have a heart attack. Dad stood there beaming." He jerked his head toward the group. "You guys remember that?"

His mother released her hold on Summer and put her hand to her chest. "That was only the beginning."

"Hell yes, I remember. Had to get the garden hose and put out the fire racing up the outside wall of the house." His father put his hand on his hips. "Then you tried to help." He shook his head. "Put a spell on the hose and it went wild, soaking everything within several yards but the flames. It's a wonder we ever got the fire put out."

The red crept up Daylan's neck and spread across his face. She was beginning to enjoy this family reunion. The strained atmosphere relaxed, and it was then Ghost Daylan made his entrance. She held her breath, hoping his appearance wouldn't ruin the newly found camaraderie.

"It wasn't my fault. If Daylan hadn't turned Flopsy

into a toad, I wouldn't have been so angry." Summer smiled. "You always were trouble. But to be fair, apparently you came by it honestly. Mom, Dad, ever wonder how he would have turned out if you'd named him Bob?" She eyed the ghost. "Speaking of trouble." She spread her arms wide and motioned toward the ghost. "He's baaack."

Ghost Daylan waved his hand in the air. "Don't want to interrupt, but…" He hesitated for a couple of beats. "It may be nothing, but I would be amiss if I did not bring it to your attention."

Daylan crossed his arms over his chest, the muscle in his jaw twitching as he rubbed his brow. "Spill it and be quick about it."

"The magic is restless, as if waiting for—I don't know—something to happen. While I don't feel Khellan's magic signature or a masking spell, an unsettled feeling is surrounding me regardless of where I am or who's around me." He paced slowly, leaving a wispy trail in his wake. "I guess what I'm saying is that you should be extra vigilant. Shay has left warriors here to protect, but they be spread thin, guarding and searching. On a positive note, it's possible Khellan's state of mind is disrupting the magic." A slight smile curbed the specter's lips.

"Have you considered setting a trap?" his dad suggested.

"Yes, but Summer's wedding is the day after tomorrow," Daylan growled, giving a quick, disgusted snort. "I won't be held responsible for wrecking her wedding."

"All the more reason to put a plan in place in case you need one." His dad steepled his fingers and touched the tips to each other repeatedly.

For the next hour, various ideas were bounced around among the group until a majority vote settled on an action.

Chapter Twenty-Six
He's Back & the Sh** Hits the Fan

"I don't like it," Daylan bellowed.

"You don't have to like it." Josie put her hand on his arm. "But it makes the most sense. If he wants to get to me and put on a show to disrupt your family, it's going to happen at the cabin. Since his behavior has been erratic, we stand a better chance to catch him off guard. With your mom and dad, Summer and Devlin, Koda and Wyatt, not to mention Devlin's dad and the Fae, we have a magic army of varying depths to call upon. If he's even still running loose."

"But you're the one with the least amount of magic to pull from." He shook his head vehemently. "Khellan's slipped through the fingers of powerful, ancient Fae warriors for eons. How can we expect to…"

"They didn't have what he wants." She spread her arms wide. "Me. Apparently, his plan preceded your appearance here. Stands to reason there's more at play than meets the eye. What if—"

He opened his mouth to protest. But closed it as she held her hand up.

"Let me finish. What if he is a seer or has limited abilities in that arena. It would explain why he harassed Summer and me long before you arrived. It would seem he knew or suspected who or what I was before any of us did."

Summer snapped her fingers. "During my research, I ran across an interesting phenomenon. Apparently, if a witch blessed with the sight desires a certain outcome in their own life, they can actually see what they want, but the vision to get there will be skewed because the desire is so strong. Couldn't the same be possible with the Fae abilities? Especially if he is a few ingredients shy of a full spell?" Summer snorted a laugh.

The others groaned. "That was really, really bad, Daughter. However..." Her dad rubbed his chin thoughtfully. "It could be a possibility. Where's this leader of the Fae you keep talking about?"

"Participating in the search or prosecution of Khellan. Who the hell knows. First, he's appearing all over the place spouting possibilities. Then when you really need him, he's nowhere to be found." Devlin shoved his fingers through his hair, leaving little furrows.

"If you insist on taking this path, it's imperative that I finish projects at my forge which should assist in our success. If it comes to that."

Several pairs of questioning glances settled on him. Summer was the first to speak. "Do tell."

"Not until I'm finished. Even discussing...might— Anyway, I have to get back to the forge. Josie is coming with me. After I'm done, we'll meet you at the cabin. Early morning?"

"Not a good idea for you and Josie to be alone or involving innocents, meaning my employees on gun club property." Devlin glanced at the others.

"Supposedly there is already a Fae guard stationed outside all of our residences. But if it makes you feel better, send reinforcements with us to watch the parameter while I work. We'll be out of there before your employees report to work."

His mom and dad exchanged glances. "We'll do it. According to my limited information, Summer, you have a houseful including children. Makes sense for you and Devlin to return to the cabin. We'll stay with Josie and Daylan. When he's ready to leave, we'll all rendezvous at the cabin and set things in motion."

Grumbling, Devlin reluctantly agreed.

"Let's get going." Daylan raised his arm. "I should only be a couple of hours and we'll be on our way."

"Wait." Summer held up her hand, glancing at Josie. "I've a better idea. Mom and Josie can bunk in Devlin's apartment at Moon Ridge while dad and Daylan work in the shop. That way Josie has a chance to give her shoulder and body a rest. When Daylan's done at the forge, he and Dad can get some shuteye too, before they all head up here."

"I'm all for that." Josie attempted to stifle a yawn.

Devlin rubbed his hand across his chin. "Better idea. I still don't like it. If anything doesn't feel right, contact us immediately."

"Of course," Vera and Brody chorused.

Summer snapped her fingers. "Devlin's truck is still parked at Moon Ridge. You can drive it up to the cabin when you're ready to leave. Limiting the use of magic."

Devlin tossed his key ring to Daylan. "Don't lose 'em."

"Make sure you disguise your magic and cloak your trail," Summer added.

Rolling his eyes, he nodded. "Of course." *I've...we've been doing that since we were both toddlers. Give me a break.* "Stand close." He waved his arm and the foursome disappeared.

Inside the forge, he flipped on the light. An array of finished weapons glittered from their black velvet-lined display cases inside the showroom.

"Nice set up you've got here." His father surveyed the room. "Much bigger than your one back home."

"Needed a showroom here. Kinda like starting over." He waved his hand in dismissal. "I still have the customers from back home, but here…I've got to earn my reputation again. Devlin's clientele has been a great place to start. Make yourselves comfortable. Josie, don't you want to go to the apartment?"

"Not right now. I've gotten my second wind and my nerves are a little edgy. Devlin's right, it's probably best to stick together."

He shrugged. "The customer area has a fridge with cold drinks, and there are a few bagels on the counter next to the microwave. Help yourselves. I'll be a while."

He pushed through the door to the forging area to survey his unfinished projects and jumped at his father's voice.

Standing in the doorway, his father grinned. "Sorry. Didn't mean to surprise you. Need any help?"

"No, I've got this." He pulled his leather apron off the hook on the wall, crossed to his bench, and donned his welding gloves. Helmet on his head and the settling torch in his hand, he paused for a couple of beats. *Something doesn't feel right.* He flipped up his visor and glanced around. *A bit on edge, I guess.* Before lowering his visor again, he raised his arms over the table and murmured several incantations. A bluish glow with pulsing silver strands emitted from his hands, entering the half-formed steel on the table. Silver strands shimmered as they wound around the blades and melted into the weapons, the glow absorbed into the grips. After placing assorted crystals and gems in the formed indentations around the guards of the swords and hilts of the daggers, he surveyed his work, then snapped his visor down and finished the projects.

A couple of hours later, as he was packing up the weapons they would need, a loud rumble came from outside. Stopped in his tracks, his pulse racing, he jerked up his visor. Josie rushed into the work area followed by his parents, horror etched on their faces.

His earlier premonition had been right, something was wrong. "Josie, under the metal table. Pull the handle just under the front edge, and stay put. Understand?"

"What—Why—" The determined look on his face convinced her to scurry under the table. Eyes wide, she froze for a moment reaching for the handle, staring at the faint orange glow at her fingertips.

"Do it," he barked, leaning over the table.

She yanked down on the handle. Three curtains of chain mail unfolded from around the bench's edges, creating a protective box. On hands and knees, she felt and saw a copper glow heated the floor as she touched her palms to the cold concrete. *Her powers will help protect her.* With Josie safely inside, he moved to another table and turned his attention to his parents.

Pointing to the opposite side of the room, he sent a silent message. *Dad, far corner behind the metal partition. Support my magic. If you get a chance, throw a capture spell.* Knowing his parents were in tune with each other, he jerked his chin toward the door to the bathroom. *Mom, behind the door. Strengthen the magic, and wait.*

*Too late to disperse the daggers.* He reached under the bench in front of him and drew out a silver sword. It shimmered at his touch and wound a protective shield up his forearm. Tightening his grip around the hilt, he knew the sword's golden glow made its way to the tip and arced at the point. With a whoosh, a matching shield appeared out of thin air. A circle of gold wound its way from the outside rim to the center of the shield, where a stone glowed red. "Not this time, bastard. I'm done playing games."

It felt like all the air was being sucked out of the building. All at once the vacuum in the room exploded. Something smashed into the side of a table, shoving it farther against the wall and the chain mail rippled. A quick glance told him the protections were holding.

His attention switched from Josie to the deranged warrior's magic growing behind the building. To his relief, the magic protections held, reinforced by his parents sucking Khellan inside the shop. Khellan's hands were raised in front of him, his eyes glowing an eerie green, but the creature was off balance, and Daylan was ready for him. Lunging at his enemy with his newly created sword infused with magic, he hit his mark, striking the deranged Fae in the gut and jerking the sword up. The warrior stumbled backward, clutching his hand to his chest, but then the Fae conjured a ball of fire and lobbed it toward him. He raised his shield, and the fireball hit full force, knocking Daylan back a couple of feet. It sizzled and smoked before disappearing entirely.

Khellan roared with rage, and lightning bolts zinged from his hand, but he paused and tilted his head as if listening for something.

Sword raised, Daylan took another run at the deranged warrior. This time the Fae turned and was only grazed by the tip of the sword. The warlock drew the sword back, just as Shay and a warrior appeared. Chains and shackles flew overhead, but too late—Khellan was gone, leaving a trail of blood droplets floating in the air and slowly splashing onto the floor, creating a pool of red. The shackles clattered to the floor where Khellan had stood, splattering the blood in all directions.

Leaning back against the bench breathing hard, he wiped his brow. "Well, it looks like I wounded him. Should slow him down." He cursed. "Unfortunately, I hadn't spelled the sword with poison yet. It's a work in progress." He glanced down at the bloodstained sword. "He saw or sensed you coming. You know that. Right?"

Confusion clouded Shay's face. "I'm not sure what you mean. He couldn't have seen or even sensed us. Our magic signature was disguised, as well as our intention and power cloaked."

"How well have you researched your prey? Obviously, his powers have been evolving while you've been chasing him. We believe he can see the future, but his obsession is clouding his visions. Still, he is able to see enough to stay ahead of you."

Shay straightened. "That is not possible. There are no seers in his lineage. He's deranged, cunning, and unpredictable—but able to see the future? Nae." He snorted.

"Then you missed something. It's the only

explanation. How else do you explain his ability to evade you at every turn?"

His parents emerged from their hiding places. Josie grappled with the heavy chain mail until he walked over and jerked the handle again, withdrawing the curtain of metal and allowing her to crawl out from under the table. Reaching down, he grasped her hand and helped her to her feet, holding her tight against him. "You okay?"

"Yes." Voice trembling a bit and forehead creasing, she straightened her shoulders and pushed at him. This time she came across determined and strong. "Yes, I'm fine."

His lips twitched. "I figured as much." He released her and returned his attention to Shay.

"This is how things are going to go down." He explained the plan devised earlier at Earthbound, leaving out the part about using Josie, an innocent, as bait. "Above all, you won't mention this encounter to my sister. Let me handle that situation. We'll simply go forward with our plan. Understood?"

Shay nodded. "Several of my warriors are stationed at the cabin out of sight. Nae reports of anything out of the ordinary there."

"The four of us will continue on as planned." He paused as his gaze swept over the magical arsenal of daggers and swords he'd created. Reaching for a gleaming sword resting on the bench, he sheathed it in a jeweled scabbard, glanced at his dad and tossed to him.

His dad reached up and caught the sword, turning it over in his hand as his fingers traced the intricate scrollwork and the inlay of crystals and gems. "Great craftsmanship, son." His dad gripped the hilt and pulled the weapon free of its scabbard. His eyes widened as a blue glow wound its way up his arm. "That's mighty powerful magic you've infused."

"Had to be. If there's a battle, we will be the victors." He rested his hands on a pair of pearl-handled daggers and swiftly sheathed them in leather, jerking his chin toward his mom. "These are yours."

His mom stepped forward and took possession of the weapons. She whirled them around once in her hands and clipped them to her belt, her hands still gripping the hilts. Red strands of magic wound up her fingers across her hands and disappeared up her arm. "Nicely done, Daylan." Her green eyes glittered as she nodded her approval.

Hands on hips, Josie pinned him with her gaze. "I suppose it's too much to expect a mere mortal like myself to be offered magic weaponry to wield, even though I'm the target of a deranged Fae warrior."

"First of all, you don't know how to wield a magical weapon. Second, you're no mere mortal, since Fae blood runs through your veins. We'll train you up a bit, and you'll be a force to be reckoned with. But time is not on our side." He raised a hand up as she opened her mouth to protest. "However—"

She closed her mouth and glared at him.

Picking up a tri-edged spiraling bladed dagger, he tossed it from hand to hand while peering at her. "I've made this one especially for you. It will recognize your Fae blood and do your bidding without hesitation. In addition, it will return to you with only a thought, should you feel the need to throw it." He slipped the dagger into its leather scabbard and handed it to her. "We'll see to your training before we leave here."

After the family exchanges, Shay glanced at him and nodded in understanding. "Will you be staying here for the moment?"

Daylan yawned wide and sighed. "It might be best to get a little shuteye before we head up the mountain." *Won't be too restful with the twins running wild at the cabin.* "Think he'll be back today?"

"Doubtful. At least not for several hours—until he's healed," Shay said. "Why?"

"We'll stay put, get some rest, while you and your warriors stand guard." He raised an eyebrow. "Would that be all right with you?"

"Certainly." The Fae leader dipped his head solemnly.

His dad approached and put his hand on Daylan's shoulder. "Are you sure you know what you're doing, leaving Summer out of the loop?"

"Yeah. Her fury, not worry, is what I am counting on to sway the outcome. If it comes down to a battle." The vein at his temple pulsed as he scrubbed his hand over his face. "I'll pull Devlin aside when we arrive and explain the situation. If he wants adjustments, I'll let everyone know." He tightened his grip around Josie's waist and strode through the shop. "Let's get some sleep." He motioned to his parents to follow. At the entrance to the forge, he waited for everyone, then closed and locked the door and reinforced the magic protections.

Chapter Twenty-Seven
The Calm before the Storm

As they entered Devlin's apartment, the clock chimed one in the morning. After a shower, Daylan and Josie took the sofa sleeper in the living room and let his parents sleep in the bedroom.

After only a few hours, sunlight poured through the skylights, and the far-off tune of his cell phone played. Rubbing his eyes, he sat up in bed and glanced around, a bit disoriented. The events of last night—or rather, this morning—came flooding back. The offending device vibrated on the kitchen counter. The infernal noise ceased as he swung his feet to the floor and pulled on jeans. He padded over to the counter. The minute he picked up the damn thing it began to ring again. It was Devlin. *Shit.* He touched the screen and put the phone to his ear. "Good morning, Devlin," he said in hushed tones.

"Everything all right?"

"Why wouldn't it be? Got to bed late and slept in. We'll be on our way within the hour." *No way am I going to tell him over the phone what happened.*

"Your sister is wound, sure something has—"

"Bad connection, Devlin. You're breaking up. See ya soon." He quickly disconnected the phone before his soon-to-be brother-in-law had a chance to question him further. He wasn't a good liar. Quietly, rummaging around the kitchen, he located the coffee and coffee maker. Within a few minutes, the aroma of freshly brewed coffee filled the rooms while he showered and dressed and returned to the living room.

Josie sat up and glanced around. "Are we leaving?"

"Not until we do a little work on your wielding of magical weaponry, so you might want to get up and get dressed."

She touched the end table next to the sleeper sofa and wrapped her fingers around the dagger. The hilt pulsed a light lavender at her touch, while the crystals embedded in the leather sheath warmed and glowed golden. Her eyes widened at the reaction.

Leaning over, he picked up a box and laid it on the bed. "Open it."

Eying him with suspicion, she gingerly tugged at the lid. Inside was a pair of black boots with a sleek pouch sewn on the outside of each boot. She looked questioningly at him as she picked up one, rubbing her fingers over the soft leather.

"Your dagger will fit in the pouch disguised by the leg of your jeans. You must carry it with you at all times. It won't do you a lot of good in the seat of the car, or in your bedroom or your apartment."

"I guess shorts are out of the question." She snickered.

"'Fraid so. For now. Unless you want to announce to the world you're armed. Which could be seen as a challenge in certain circles." His lips twitched and the corner of his mouth turned up in a sly grin. "Get dressed, and we'll go out to the forge for a quick practice session while Shay watches our backs."

He scribbled a note and left it on the kitchen table

as Josie dressed.

After forty-five minutes of practice, he leaned over and kissed her cheek. "You're a natural."

She raised an eyebrow, then glanced in his direction. "It's the strangest feeling to have a deadly weapon know what you want and execute it with a thought or action. Didn't do my body a lot of good." She winced and rubbed her shoulder and back.

"Sorry about that. Couldn't be helped. But you'll get used to the magic. We'd better get going, or Devlin and Summer will have our heads."

She sheathed her dagger in her boot and pulled her jean leg down over it, then followed him through the forge and into the showroom. "They'll understand."

"About the training, yes. The fact that I didn't tell them exactly what was going on—not so much." The door *screeched* in protest when he yanked it open.

As they entered the apartment, Josie turned to him. "Do I have time to take a quick shower?"

"Make it fast. I'll load the rest of the weapons and we'll be ready to go. It'll only take a few minutes. We can catch breakfast on the way up Ute Pass to the cabin." He paused to inhale the delicious coffee aroma before padding into the kitchen.

His mom and dad stood in the doorway to the bedroom, fully dressed. "We're ready anytime you are. Coffee would be heavenly."

He poured three mugs of coffee and handed them each a mug. Leaning against the kitchen counter, he blew across the top of his mug and took a drink. "I need to load up a few things from the forge. Then we're ready to go."

Josie greeted his parents and lurched to the

bathroom. After several minutes, she emerged in a cloud of steam, moving better and with a smile on her face. "It's a wonder what warm water will do for your sore and aching body." She eyed the steaming mug in his hand. "Is there enough for me?"

"Of course." He poured her a cup of the hot liquid and handed it to her.

She wrapped her hands around the mug, ran her thumb up and down the ceramic handle, then took a sip. "Mmmm, this is good."

"I'll be right back. Then we'll take Devlin's truck to his cabin."

"I'll join you, son," his father called out.

Inside the forge, he handed his dad the bag of weapons he'd packed last night. "Put those on the floor of the truck in the back." He slid each dagger on the bench into a leather sheath and deposited them into a duffel. Attaching one to his belt, he surveyed the forge. "All set."

The trip up the pass was uneventful. He turned the truck into a cafe in Woodland Park. "The food is great here, but let's make it quick. I'm sure Devlin is wearing a path in the carpet, waiting for us." He took out his cell phone and typed in a text and sent it. "That should hold him for a bit."

With their stomachs full and hot drinks in their hands, his little entourage returned to the truck. Fifteen minutes later, he pulled into the drive to the cabin. A barking Piper greeted them in the front yard, and he fished some beef jerky out of his pocket, then opened the vehicle door. "Piper, we're friends. Where's Summer?" The words were barely out of his mouth and his sister stood at the front door alongside Devlin.

Brody got out of the vehicle and yanked out one of the weapon's bags. Daylan opened the back door for his mom, then reached in and grabbed the duffel containing the daggers.

"Piper. Leave it. Come here." The obedient dog trotted back to her.

"It's about time," Devlin growled.

"We stopped for breakfast to save time and wear and tear on the bride-to-be." Ambling up the path, he tossed the keys to Devlin. "Thanks for the use of your apartment and truck. It was good to get a little rest after I was finished." He dropped the bag inside the front door. His father did the same.

"No problem. Are you saying your evening was uneventful?"

He eyed his sister standing in the door. "Yep. What can we do to help?"

Devlin narrowed his eyes. "Right."

"See, I told you they'd call if there was trouble." Summer waved her hand dismissively. Her eyes, sharp as daggers, pinned her brother. "Right?"

He knew that underlying tone and her dangerous stare. She knew. Not the exact events of last night, but she was aware something had happened but chose to keep up the ruse of normalcy, probably for the benefit of her houseful of guests.

Devlin stared incredulously at her. "Of course." He shook his head.

"Jenny has the food, decorations, and everything inside handled. I could use help in the back yard, stringing the faerie lights. Don't want to use magic to maintain them, for fear of attracting undesirables—if you know what I mean." She winked at Josie, Koda, and Vera. "Come on, I'll show you where the lights are and where I want them. A little magic to install them can't hurt." She walked through the house and pushed open the screen door onto the veranda and pointed to several boxes on the glass-top table.

As soon as the women were out of hearing distance, Daylan caught Devlin's arm. "Hey, Devlin, could I see you for a minute." He jerked his chin toward the study down the hallway, cutting a quick glance toward the door the girls had disappeared through.

"I knew it. 'Bout midnight, Koda, Wyatt, Summer, and I felt a strong disturbance. Then it settled."

He followed Devlin into the study and closed the door. "You're right."

Devlin motioned to the chairs in front of his large desk.

Easing into one of the chairs, he waited for Devlin to settle into the other and brought him up to speed on the events of last evening.

"You should've called." Devlin frowned as the muscle at his jaw worked overtime.

"Didn't really have time. He was upon us with magic immediately after we detected the magic out back. But we were stronger. That's why I don't want to tell Summer. She might hesitate rather than commit to using witchfire if necessary. That moment's hesitation could be fatal."

"You're wrong. I admit killing that vampire with witchfire, and the aftermath, was traumatic for her." He paused, rubbing at the back of his neck. "I don't like keeping her out of the loop, and I may still tell her later. For now, I'll keep your secret. Let's hope it doesn't come to her using that power. We'll be prepared if it does." Devlin pushed up from the chair, strode to the door, and swung it open.

"You bet." Daylan wandered over to where the weapons bags were left. He paused and glanced around. "Hey, where are the kids?"

Wyatt bounded down the stairs into the living room. "Outside, running off excess energy under the watchful eye of Rita. Why? Are Koda and the women still outside decorating?"

"Yep." Brody jerked his chin toward the back yard.

"I've crafted weapons for everyone." He unzipped one bag, searched inside, then moved on to the other. Removing a sword from the bag, he withdrew it with a flourish from its scabbard. What appeared to be sunlight glinted off the blade and bounced around the room, then formed a golden aura around Devlin before fading away.

Appearing a bit confounded, Devlin turned his head from side to side, then leveled his gaze at Daylan. "What the hell?"

"Each weapon is created using the person's known strengths and weaknesses as well as crystals to enhance their abilities. Then I let the magic do its work. I believe this one is yours." He returned the sword to its gem-and-crystal-encrusted scabbard and released the sword. The weapon disappeared with a pop and appeared at Devlin's side.

Wyatt's eyes widened, and he drew in a breath as Daylan withdrew other weapons from the bags, allowing each one to find and bond with its intended individual.

"Best call the gals inside."

Tena Stetler

Chapter Twenty-Eight
Gotta Love It When a Plan Comes Together

Koda unboxed the light strands, handing them to Summer and Vera. The witches levitated the strings of twinkle lights into the tree branches around the yard.

From the ground, Josie pointed toward Summer. "A little to the left, then hang it over the next one." Then she turned to the other side of the yard, where Vera had several strands connected and floating in the air. "Drape them from tree to tree until we have a sparkling outline around the yard."

"Where the heck are we supposed to plug all these lights in?" Koda glanced around the yard careful, not to trip over the folding chairs set up earlier in the day.

Summer giggled. "They're LEDs, so we can make two long strands. Devlin has two electrical hubs at either end of the tree line and several scattered in the yard."

Josie stood next to a huge box sitting next to the veranda's French doors. "What's in here?" She picked up a knife off the glass-top table and held it above the taped end. "Okay if I open it?"

"Sure. It should have all the fiber optic flower arrangements for the tables." Summer put her finger to her lips. "I believe Devlin put the clear sparkly tablecloths and the bags of candy hearts in there, too."

She opened the box and carefully lifted out the

shimmering flower arrangements. "These are beautiful. Battery operated?"

"Kinda." Summer snickered and slid a glance in her direction. "They're wedding arrangements handed down from generation to generation in my family, so the reservoir of magic is complex, deep, and long in them. Since it's not my magic, it would be difficult to trace. I hope." She paused for a beat. "I didn't think I'd ever have a reason to use them, until Devlin." She sighed. "Didn't figure there was a happily ever after in my future."

Josie took the tablecloths and spread them over a couple of the tables, then looked to the sky. "Do you want me to put these out now, or wait until in the morning?"

"Best wait until morning. Can't use magic to keep them safe and in place. Darn it." Summer stared at the beautiful carved wooden gazebo in the center yard, where they would take their vows. The red wooden hearts Koda had designed dangled from pink and purple ribbons on the edge of the structure. Plastic cones attached to the railing of the steps into the octagonal gazebo and around the entrance arch would be full of purple rose bouquets and baby's breath tomorrow.

"You know what? Let's go ahead and leave the tablecloths on the ones you've already spread out. Put a few of the flower arrangements on them, so we can get an idea of what it will look like tomorrow. We'll run through the rehearsal after dinner."

Josie watched Summer for a moment more. "I'll save the candy hearts until tomorrow. You want them sprinkled on the tables?" She turned the bag of hearts over in her hand. "Hey, these bags are defective.

They're all peach colored and say, "Charm Me." That's not right."

"We special ordered them that way." A far away, dreamy look came into Summer's eyes.

"Oh yeah, I remember now. Those are the candy hearts Devlin charmed you with when you were dating." She snickered.

Summer rolled her eyes. "That was bad."

"Off the top of my head, I thought it was genius. Still, the candy hearts are a nice touch." She stood beside Summer and reached out to touch her arm. "Everything is absolutely beautiful. A faerie tale world for your wedding."

"Now let's hope we don't have any monsters ruin the day." Summer snorted.

*If you only knew.* Josie closed her eyes and wished fervently that nothing happened tomorrow. On the flip side, she was ready. She'd stuck inside her boot the sheathed dagger Daylan had crafted.

Piper bounced from person to person, then raced around the yard, kicking up little clods of dirt and grass. Summer frowned. "Piper, stop that right now." The dog skidded to a stop, tilted her head to one side looking at Summer, then trotted over, tail wagging and nose held high sniffing the air. "Down and stay. I can't have you tearing up the sod, then tracking mud and grass into the house." Piper sat down with a huff. She stretched her paws out in front of her, and lay down with her head on her paws, giving Summer a sideways glare of displeasure, ears plastered to her head.

Josie bit her cheek to keep from laughing as the rest of the women joined her on the veranda. They surveyed their work with hands on hips.

"I believe we are done here." Summer brushed her hands together and glanced at the others, who nodded. She called Piper to her, then led the procession into the cabin to check on dinner preparations.

Jenny greeted them at the arched entryway into the kitchen with a smile. "Got everything under control. Prime rib au jus, garlic mashed potatoes, freshly baked wheat rolls, and salad will be served in an hour. Why don't you go relax in the living room until I call you?"

Josie paused at the long oak dining table now covered by a crocheted light blue tablecloth and twelve place settings with wildflower patterned china plates, saucers, and cups. Crystal water and wine glasses shimmered in the candlelight beside each plate. Gleaming silverware lay atop matching light blue linen napkins. The buffet was set up on the wall closest to the table. A large crystal salad bowl with matching plates rested in a bed of ice beside the serving utensils at the far end of the buffet.

"Who knew a bachelor—a retired Navy SEAL, no less—had such fine china and crystal?" Josie mused.

"If I could have everyone's attention for a moment," Daylan called out, motioning the women into the living area. Beside him, a bag lay open with the remaining weapons hovering above it.

Taken aback, Josie glanced around the room at the swords the men either held or had strapped to their sides or back. "What is going on?"

"You didn't think you were the only one?" He sent her a devilish grin.

Recovering from her surprise, she shot back, "I certainly hope not. Safety in numbers—right?" Her gaze shifted to Devlin.

He gave her a thumbs up.

Koda, Summer, and Vera glanced uncertainly from Daylan to her. "Come in and I'll explain." He waited until everyone gathered around. "Last night at my forge, I created weapons for each individual here, as a precaution with the exception of Rita and Brody they'll be safely tucked away watching the kids. Each sword or dagger was crafted using the person's known strengths and weaknesses as well as an infusion of crystals to enhance their abilities. Then I let the magic do its work."

"No shit?" Koda blinked and rubbed her eyes before reaching out to grasp the curved-bladed dagger with a deeply serrated top edge floating in front of her. "This is wicked." She grinned, slicing through the air with the blade, leaving silver trails in its wake.

Two double-edged throwing daggers found their way to Summer, each sheathed in finely tooled leather. She held her arms out from her sides and allowed the weapons to attach themselves to her belt on either side of her waist.

Vera winked at her daughter and caressed the two pearl-handled daggers belted at her waist as they glowed in a multicolor aura. "All set."

Jenny appeared at the doorway of the kitchen. "Dinner is ready. Everyone serve yourself and have a seat." Silverware clattered on the china plates and chairs scraped the floor as everyone filled their plates and settled around the table.

After the family dinner, Koda wandered to the front window that looked out across the meadow in front of the cabin. "Uh-oh—you're going to want to see this."

Daylan, Josie, Koda, Wyatt, Summer, and Devlin rushed to the window. Shay and four warriors stood at the ready, staring at the cabin.

"Oh God, now what?" Josie turned to Daylan as both sets of parents gathered around.

"I'm going to take the kids upstairs," Rita declared. "Come on, kiddos, the last one upstairs has to clean up the room." The twins jumped up from the floor, where they had been playing a board game, and made a quick detour to the front window, where they were whirled around by the adults and propelled toward the stairs. Rita grabbed them both and herded them upstairs.

"One way to find out." He marched to the front door, yanked it open, and stepped outside. "Let me guess. You're here to validate our worst fears. Khellan is still loose." It wasn't a question. It was more of an accusation. The others crowded through the door and out onto the lawn.

"Yes." Shay stood straight, his gaze shifting from Daylan to the others in the group.

Summer rested her hand on her brother's shoulder. The fire in her eyes burned so bright, Josie had to look away. *Good. Exactly as Daylan anticipated.*

"I'm afraid you are correct. If any good has come from our tracking him for a month, it is that we have worn down his stamina and, in turn, his powers. He's not had a chance to rest, and with the injuries Daylan inflicted... We'll stand guard until he shows himself."

"Like hell you will. We've waited long enough. Friends and family have gathered for my wedding tomorrow." Summer shrugged out of Devlin's controlling arm around her waist. Glancing at Daylan and Josie, she gave a sad shake of her head, then switched her attention to her parents, her hands resting on the daggers. "If you thought there was hell to pay after I torched the vampire—If Khellan tries to mess up my wedding, witchfire won't be the only thing I use to reduce him to ash or…"

Daylan interrupted. "Or die trying? Death wouldn't look good on you, Sis. Worse, Devlin would blame me."

Josie stood wide-eyed, shifting her gaze between Summer and Daylan. "I think there is a tiny problem with your priorities."

The corner of his mouth kicked up in a lopsided grin. "We need a plan. You hold the daggers and swords I crafted with strong magic. With our powers pooled, we can defeat him. He won't leave this battle alive." With a grin, he motioned toward the cabin.

Shay held up a hand and shook his head. "I can't let…"

Daylan whirled on Shay. "You've had your chance, and no disrespect—but you didn't get the job done. "We'll take it from here and expect you to support our plan."

"You'll be acting as judge and executioner—that's not done in our realm." Shay took several steps toward him.

Koda, Wyatt, and Devlin's father transformed into wolves and circled the group. Summer, her eyes still blazing, stood next to her brother, flanked on the other side by Devlin, a dagger now in her hand. Devlin eased his hand over hers and gave a quick shake of his head.

Daylan stood his ground. "Maybe that's the problem." He paused waving an arm toward his group. "Look around. This isn't your realm. Again, no offense, but my friend's and family's lives are on the line now. No, this time you'll do things our way. Your duty to safeguard and restore balance in the mortal world or aid humans in need of assistance has been sorely tested and you've failed."

Shay sighed and waved off one of his warriors, who disappeared with a pop.

Eyes narrowed, Daylan stared at Shay. "Where'd he go?"

"To report the situation to the council and gain permission."

"For what?"

"To terminate Khellan if necessary. A mere formality if you go through with your intentions."

"Here's what we have planned. We'll go through our regular routine getting ready for the wedding. Yet we'll all be armed and ready when he makes his appearance. Hopefully that will be tonight, but..." He continued to set out the rest of the plan in great detail.

When Daylan finished, Shay shook his head. "Using an innocent as bait is not our way, and very risky."

"Again, this isn't going to be handled—your way. Josie, are you ready?"

"As I'll ever be." She bent over and touched the twisted dagger at her ankle. "Maybe I should attach it to my waist."

"No. You don't want it visible. We need the element of surprise. You'll be fine."

"Let's start the wedding rehearsal." Summer flipped on the outdoor power, instantly transforming the back yard into a faerie land of multicolor twinkling lights around the perimeter trees, fiber optic flowers glowing on the tabletops, and the burble of the dragon fountain bathed in soft blue lights beside the path to the gazebo. "Places, everyone." The wolves disappeared around the side of the house. After a few minutes, they returned in human form, dressed, and took their places for the rehearsal.

Thundering paws across the veranda drew everyone's attention as Piper barreled out of the cabin and skidded to a halt at the bottom of the gazebo steps.

"Good girl. Now stay." Summer gave her an ear scratch and ambled down the path to the starting point, where her dad was waiting.

He tucked her hand through his crooked arm. "Ready?"

"I am."

The bridesmaids and groomsmen took their places at the edge of the gazebo. Devlin stood at the bottom of the steps, watching Summer and her dad make their way up the path. His dad waited at the top of the stairs inside the structure where he'd be officiating the ceremony tomorrow at twilight. The amber, lilac, and pink lights twinkled around the edge of the gazebo as her father handed Summer off to Devlin.

Josie wiped her sweaty hands on her jeans and breathed a sigh of relief, holding back the urge to applaud when the rehearsal went off without a catch. *Maybe Khellan is too injured to cause a problem.* She followed the rest of the family into the cabin. Daylan caught her hand as they climbed the stairs to their room.

She tossed and turned for a while amid nightmares of impending doom. As the glow of moonlight peeked over the horizon, she silently climbed out of bed, dressed, and crept down the stairs. The French doors *creaked* as she opened them and padded to one of the chairs on the veranda. Easing down, she leaned back and breathed in the fresh mountain air as the moon's brilliance spread across the cerulean sky, with only a few wispy clouds floating in the distance. Sleepy birds twittered quietly in the trees.

Without warning the peaceful night calm shattered at the foreboding premonition washing over her. Breath hitched in her throat and her stomach roiled as she glanced around for the cause. She clawed at her throat—something was closing off her airway, yet nothing was in her line of sight. Frantically searching the area, she frowned as a faint outline of a man wavered in and out a few feet from her. "Khellan."

"Yes, my love. I've come to take you home to prepare for our wedding." In one swift movement, he stood before her, waved his arm, and her airway opened. He extended his hand. "Come with me voluntarily and there'll be no casualties." He paused, a devious grin curled his lips. "Scream, and I'll destroy your friends and family peacefully asleep inside. Their blood will be on your hands." He sneered.

The rustle of leaves and movement across the yard caught her attention. Shay and three warriors materialized without a sound. She quickly averted her eyes back to Khellan.

*It's now or never.* She vaulted out of her chair and over Khellan, landing behind him at the edge of the yard and meeting his angry gaze as he whirled around to grab at her arm. He was a split second too late and she slid neatly out of his reach. "Daylan and I have already consummated our relationship. I'll not be marrying you."

Khellan roared and lunged at her. It was then he noticed Shay at her back, but he was still oblivious to Summer, Devlin, and Wyatt as they streamed out onto the veranda.

She used Shay's diversion to lift her foot and grab the twisted blade dagger out of her boot, aimed and let it fly, hitting Khellan in the center mass of his chest. "Take that, you bastard." *Did that just come out of my mouth?*

He cursed as the dagger flew and let out a blood-curdling scream as it hit its target. She stood rooted to the spot. A green glow surrounded the wound and spread as he clutched at his chest. Someone else screamed, followed by a stream of obscenities filling the air. *Shit, was that me?* Though her throat was raw, the screaming continued.

Daylan appeared at a dead run out of the forest that edged the property and skewered the deranged Fae through with a sword he'd forged and spelled with poison. He jerked upward before withdrawing the sword. He dove for Josie, grabbed her, and rolled out of the way as his sister took Josie's place.

The werewolves circled and kept guard at the perimeter of the back yard where it met the thicket of trees and bushes. In awe of the feeling surging through her, Josie felt the added magic support from Summer's parents to Shay and his warriors in an effort to disable Khellan's power and attempt to disappear. To her relief, their endeavors appeared to be working. Yet how did she know? Magic was so far out of her wheelhouse she didn't understand what was happening to her. Suddenly, a searing heat flashed above her. She blinked and tried to focus on where it was coming from.

Everything was happening in slow motion around her.

Summer leaned on her back foot, witchfire bow in her hand. She placed the flaming arrow on the string of the bow, pulled it back, and let it fly. The first one hit Khellan in the sternum next to the dagger. He howled in pain switching his grasp from the dagger to the shaft of the arrow. She pulled her arm back and a second fiery arrow appeared. This one struck him right between the eyes. The stench was horrendous as his body sizzled and fell to the ground in a pile of ash. Summer raised her arms, and the witchfire disappeared. Brushing her hands together, she let a satisfied but sad smile curve her lips. At the pile of ash, she bent down and retrieved Josie's dagger, wiping the blade through the earth before she rose to Devlin's embrace.

He kissed her lips, then wiped the tears and streaks of dirt from her face. "My li'l witch warrior. It's over."

Summer sighed and leaned into him for a few moments. Clasping his hand, she propelled them to where Daylan stood with his woman. The werewolves faded into the trees. The others formed a loose circle around them.

"You all right?" Daylan picked Josie up off the ground and balanced her on her feet. Supporting her with one hand, he wiped his sword on his jeans and sheathed it.

She nodded, unable to form any words. Her gaze riveted on the pile of ash. Taking a life, any life, had to have serious consequences. Before she committed to the plan and made her decision to try to lure Khellan here, she'd talked with Summer at great length about the possible outcomes. How it felt when she'd taken the vamp's life even though it was the vamp or her brother.

She'd hoped capture would be possible and it wouldn't come down to this. But it had, and she was numb. She'd been instrumental in taking a life.

Summer eased a comforting hand on Josie's shoulder and said quietly, "We did what had to be done. You live in a world of magical creatures now. Life will never be the same, but what's to say it won't be better. Well—except my little brother." She grinned. "I was born first. He'll always be a challenge. But it's one you've chosen—knowingly, I might add." Summer elbowed her lightly in the ribs. "Huh, kid." Summer handed the twisted dagger back to her.

Her eyes flew open wide at the realization that someone else knew how she felt. Still shell shocked, she shook her head in an effort to make sense of what had just transpired and what Summer was saying. She blinked several times before the world snapped into place. "I guess you did warn me," she croaked, her own voice unrecognizable. *Was that me screaming during the whole episode?* She lifted her foot and sheathed the dagger.

"Hey, wait a minute." Daylan wrapped an arm around each woman. "I think we make a pretty good team. Don't want to do this every day. But today we saved the world from a deranged and dangerous creature. In my book, that's a win. Not to mention we have a wedding to celebrate without worry. Another win." He glanced at her uncertainly. "You still with us?"

"I think so. It's a lot to take in," she said haltingly. "What happens now? We acted as judge, jury, and executioner. That can't be good."

Chapter Twenty-Nine

The Aftermath, a Wedding & Visit to the Fae Realm

Shay, flanked by two warriors, strode over to where Summer, Devlin, Daylan, and Josie stood. A warrior paused and took out a crystal cube from a leather pouch at his side. As he swept the cube through the air over the pile of ash, the smoldering remains were sucked into the cube, turning it a sparkling silver edged in shimmering black. "He wasn't always evil," the warrior murmured. "Once—a long time ago—he was decent." The warrior tucked the cube back into his pouch. "We will return Khellan to the Fae Realm."

Josie and Summer exchanged glances and sucked in breaths simultaneously. Summer found her voice first and squeaked, "Wedding's tomorrow at twilight, and you're all invited."

Shay, a bit taken aback, raised an eyebrow. A full-on smile turned up the corners of his mouth. "We accept. Though we are here with news. There will be no accountability or consequences for your actions." The Fae leader's gaze shifted between the women. "Khellan's behavior left him to the mercy or not of those he threatened. His fate, though unorthodox by our standards, is sanctioned by the Fae council." Shay and his warriors bowed. "The Fae realm owes you a debt of gratitude."

Wordlessly Josie and Summer glanced at each other, then to the Fae. "Thank you," they chorused reverently.

"I am positive we are all anxious to put this sordid affair behind us. The hour grows late, and with your permission, we'll take our leave and return in time to join in the celebration. A good way to spend the summer solstice." Shay paused for a beat. "Unless you wish us to stand guard until the festivities are over."

Devlin stepped forward and glanced at Summer, who nodded to some unspoken communication between the two. "Not necessary. We'll see you tomorrow." He slung his arm around his bride-to-be's shoulder and motioned the rest of the group toward the cabin. "Celebration dessert anyone?"

Summer put on the coffee and Josie sliced the two chocolate pies Jenny had left on the counter when she went home for the night. She put the pie on plates and carried them outside where everyone had gathered. The battle and outcome was the topic as the group settled into the seats, coming to terms with what had happened. It wasn't long until the conversation shifted to the wedding and the few preparations left for the next day.

Josie yawned wide and snuggled her head onto Daylan's shoulder. Whether or not she could sleep tonight was yet to be determined.

Summer smiled sleepily, leaning over to put her head on Devlin's upper arm. "I'm with you. Time for bed."

Devlin reached up, his fingers caressing her strawberry blonde curls. "I can't wait until tomorrow. It's been a long time coming."

"Good night, everyone. See you all in the

morning." Daylan pushed up from the porch swing and offered his hand to her. Hand in hand, they made their way through the house and up the stairs to their bedroom. Once inside, he swept her up in his arms like a medieval knight, closed the door with his foot, and carried her to the bed. A dozen lavender roses arranged in a crystal vase sat on the nightstand. It was one of the most romantic expressions she'd ever experienced. She slipped her arms around his neck and trailed kisses to the hollow of his throat. Gently, he nudged her cheek with his chin. She turned her face up, and his lips captured hers in a searing kiss. Her lips parted and his tongue thrust inside, teasing, tasting, exploring the soft recesses of her mouth until her tongue joined with his in a sinuous dance. The kiss sent her stomach into a wild swirl as spirals of heat flowed through her like molten lava. Tired as she was, she wanted more. She wanted him. Now.

He lowered her legs until her feet momentarily touched the floor. She wrapped her legs around his waist and arched against him, feeling his heat and arousal at her core.

"So this is the way it's going to go." He lowered her to the bed and murmured, "Too many clothes." With a wave of his hand, they were both naked. He slid between her legs and up her body until his mouth closed over the rosy peaks of her breasts. She moaned and writhed beneath him, her fingertips caressing the flexing muscles of his back.

His hands explored the soft lines of her waist, her hips, and eased between her thighs, where his fingers teased and caressed the soft folds where she was hot and wet. He slid one finger inside, then another, reaching her sweet spot. Arching her body against his hand, she buried her face in his chest to muffle a scream as she crashed over the edge of ecstasy.

"Like that, did you?" he whispered, his breath hot against her ear. "Wait until you see what's next." His tongue sent shivers of desire racing through her as it teased her nipples and circled her belly button. His warm breath on her intimate parts nearly drove her crazy. When his tongue slowly caressed the soft folds at her center, she was lost in a wave of fiery sensations.

"Oh, Daylan," she moaned as he continued his ministrations. Her hands tangled in his hair as waves of pleasure throbbed through her once again.

He snickered. "One more time with feeling?" Her legs spread wider as he slid up her body, his mouth covering hers hungrily. Her curves molded to the contours of his hard lean body. His hands slid up to fondle her breasts, then grasped her shoulders. He pressed his erection to her entrance, and she welcomed him inside her. The heat of his body coursed down the entire length of hers. He roused flames of passion inside her, and his own grew stronger as the rhythm that bound their bodies became more urgent. He thrust deeper, and together they soared to an awesome, shuddering climax like nothing she'd experienced before. Breathing hard, he rolled off and lay beside her. Her heart still pounded in her chest as she cuddled into him, her head resting on his shoulder. Their legs tangled, they fell into the deep sleep of sated lovers.

**\*\*\*\***

She awoke snuggled in Daylan's arms as the sun's bright yellow rays filtered through the lace curtains at the window. Rubbing her eyes, she reviewed the events of the last evening as memory came rushing back. Her pulse quickened. Then Daylan's bright emerald eyes met hers. "Morning, my little warrior."

Her eyes widened. Unsure of how she felt about that, she licked her lips and gave him a shy smile. "Morning, my magic man."

"Hope that's in reference to our escapades last night—or rather, in the wee hours of this morning." A seductive smile curved his full luscious lips, and he winked at her.

She licked her lips, remembering in vivid detail his lips on hers and their wild lovemaking the night before. His reference chased any thoughts of the battle from her mind. Today was Summer's wedding day, and it would be a glorious day.

She slid out of bed and stretched her arms high over her head. Letting her arms fall to her side, she padded into the bathroom, turned on the shower, adjusted the water temperature, and stepped inside. A soft click of the door made her smile.

Daylan pushed aside the shower curtain. "Mind if I join you?"

"Feel free." She felt his smoldering gaze on her and turned to face him. "You can't possibly be…"

"I wouldn't bet on that." He chuckled and tugged her against him. "You are the sexiest creature I've ever known." His hands lightly caressed her breasts and wandered down her body.

Against her better judgment, she let her body curve against him, reveling in his arousal. "We're going to be late. They are going to wonder where we are."

"I doubt that." A seductive laugh rumbled up from his throat.

****

Standing in front of the gazebo, she watched Summer walk down the path to join Devlin where they would be joined together. Her gaze wandered out over the family and friends seated in the back yard awaiting the ceremony to begin. Harp strings played the "Wedding March" with such emotion she swallowed hard to keep from tearing up. Never one given to tears often, she blamed the urge on the roller coaster of events over the past month. As a reminder, twelve Fae warriors stood in the back of the crowd. She couldn't help but wonder if someday this family would be part of hers one day.

Try as she might, she couldn't keep her heart protected from the ravages of Daylan. The realization that she was head over heels in love and not just lust with him was a shock, as were the numerous recent revelations her mother had kept from her. That woman had to have known, yet she left discovery to chance. An extremely dangerous decision, in her book. She, Josie, was able to wield magic, she was a magical being…well…part anyway.

How could her own mother betray—Loren's voice penetrated her thoughts as he began the ceremony; the harp music had stopped. Darla fidgeted beside her, holding a basket with a few purple rose petals in the bottom, while her twin brother stood beside Devlin with a small heart-shaped lavender pillow in his hands, on which white ribbons secured two golden bands glimmering in the twinkle lights twined on the gazebo as the sun sank below the mountains. A glorious display of orange, red, and yellow slowly faded to purple and maroon spread across the dusky sky as the vows were pledged and Summer said, "I do," followed by Devlin. The radiant smile on Summer's lips and reaching up in her eyes gave Josie goosebumps. This was a union that was meant to be; she could feel it. The sensation in and of itself was new, but oh, so magical.

"I now pronounce you husband and wife. Devlin, you may kiss the bride." Loren's words resounded in the air.

Devlin pulled his new bride into his arms, kissing her with reckless abandon. After several people cleared their throats, the couple reluctantly broke apart. Summer's cheeks flushed. Devlin—well—he looked like a man who had conquered the world. Josie grinned and turned to follow Summer and Devlin back down the aisle with the best man, Devlin's brother, Cabe, who'd barely made it in time for the wedding due to work constraints.

During the reception, a calm washed over Josie. An unusual feeling, for sure, but she'd been a magnet for the bizarre in recent weeks. At least it was positive rather than foreboding. She'd had enough of that to last a lifetime. She sighed, observing the idyllic scene in front of her. Daylan and Summer were chatting with their parents. The previous tension between Summer and her family had given way to a friendly camaraderie. Daylan's goal of reuniting his family had been achieved. She smiled. *He'd done good.* Glancing around, she wondered if Ghost Daylan would make an appearance.

In Daylan's arms, she danced the night away at the reception, and in the wee hours of the morning, she snuggled against him. "We'd better head home." She scrunched up her face. *Where was home? Summer's apartment above Earthbound? Her carriage house? It wasn't ready. Devlin's apartment?* They'd stayed so many places recently in the name of safety, she wasn't sure.

"It's really late. Maybe best to spend another night here, then head back to the Springs tomorrow morning."

"We need to leave really early. I teach the first class tomorrow morning and the rest of the week. Mandy is taking the afternoon and the few evening classes. Summer is taking a few days off to spend with Devlin here at the cabin. They'll be going to Hawaii on their honeymoon after the holidays in January."

"Oh, why wait so long?" Daylan's eyebrows squished together.

"Summer claimed Colorado summers are too beautiful to spend them away from the mountains."

"True enough."

Before making their way to the bedroom, they said their goodbyes to everyone. By morning she and Daylan would be long gone before most were awake.

After only a few hours of sleep, they tiptoed downstairs and out to her SUV. A quick stop at a little café in Woodland Park and they were ready to take on the day.

"How about I'll drop you off at Earthbound and go on to work at the forge. I'll check on Moon Ridge for Devlin. Call me when you're ready to leave, and I'll pick you up."

"We can figure out living arrangements then."

"Good plan."

Out of habit, he drove around Earthbound before easing the SUV into a parking space behind the yoga studio. She dodged the rain puddles in the gravel lot as he walked her to the entrance.

She unlocked the door and disarmed the alarm with a shiver. "It's darn cold in here. Summer must have turned the furnace off—again."

"The rainstorm early this morning cooled things down." He studied the fireplace stoked with logs, flicked his hand toward the hearth and a roaring fire erupted. Brushing his hands together, he grinned. "That will do for now. By the time it burns down, the sun will probably have this place warmed up." Placing his hands on her shoulders, he stared into her eyes. "You've been so brave to have weathered the events of the past week without going screaming into the abyss." Eyebrow raised, he shook his head. "Most mortals would have."

Hands on hips she snorted. "I'm not a mortal, or so I've discovered. My throat will attest that I've done my share of screaming. But I always knew you had my back. Mostly."

"It takes a village or a family to raise a magical being—right?" He chuckled and drew her close, his lips pressed against hers light as a summer breeze and her arms wrapped around his waist. "I've got to go. See you soon."

The touch of his lips was a delicious sensation that started spirals of butterflies in her belly as she held tight to his waist and deepened the kiss.

"Unless you want your students to find us writhing on the floor in ecstasy, you might want to loosen your grip," he murmured against her lips.

Reluctantly she released her arms. "Until tonight."

"I'll hold you to it." He kissed her once more and disappeared out the door.

She locked the door behind him, glanced at her little desk, and climbed the stairs to Summer's apartment, where she showered before she dressed in her pink yoga pants and a bright tie-dyed shirt. Bounding down the stairs, she felt a mental tug from the desk. *This is different.* She waved her hand dismissively. *Not now. I need to get centered for class. Yeah, that's going to work.* The room was much warmer now, and she hurried across the floor to spread out her mat. One half hour later she rose, unlocked the door, and peeked outside. Students were climbing out of their vehicles, shouting greetings to each other. She smiled.

Leading her mixed class of advanced beginners and intermediates settled her and brought her back to actual center. It made her realize she'd not been centered, really centered, in a long while, only going through the motions. As the class rolled up their mats, she padded to the front door and stepped outside. inhaling deeply the fresh, rain-washed air that was warming quickly. After waving goodbye to her students, she closed the heavy door and leaned her back against the cool wood. The fire had burned itself out, and the sunlight streaming through the front windows heated the room.

She crossed to the secretary and ran her hand over the scarred wooden top. It warmed to her touch. Yanking her hand away, she stared at the desk, then back at her tingling hand, and wiggled her fingers. *What the heck?* Something was drawing her to the desk. She eased into the antique wooden chair Summer had given her, which nearly matched the intricate flower-and-leaf carvings on the edges and legs of the secretary.

Her grandmother's worn leather book materialized

on the desktop. The catch released and the cover flipped open. Several pages flipped of their own volition until stopping at a page where flowing longhand words glowed violet on the yellowed parchment. With a trembling hand, she reached, touched the page, and the room spun. Multicolored ribbons streamed in a vortex that sucked her in. Her stomach roiled, and she covered her mouth, hoping to keep her stomach contents in place. As suddenly as it started, the motion stopped. She blew out a breath and glanced around. One thing was for certain—she wasn't at Earthbound any longer.

She stood at a garden gate, the trellis overhead covered in beautiful blooming flowers. The sweet fragrance was familiar, but she couldn't place it. Rose bushes with the biggest red, yellow and pink blooms she'd ever seen were at the far end of the garden, at either end of a wooden settee. The bench had the same floral carving across the back and down the legs as her grandmother's desk, only the color on the carved flower petals and leaves wasn't worn but vibrant. A light touch on her shoulder had her whirling around, hands fisted in front of her.

A willowy creature with huge blue eyes and silver hair cascading around her shoulders to the middle of her back touched her fists. The caress was warm and calming. "No need to fear me. I mean you no harm."

Josie's heart thundered in her chest as she tried to quell her fight-or-flight response. "Who are you? Where the hell am I?"

"Welcome to the Fae Realm. I'm Dalia, your Fae guardian. Your grandmother requested I keep an eye on you, should your talents be awakened during a time of desperate need." Dalia put her hand on the gate and pushed it open. "Come, let's sit on the bench and chat for a while."

"What… What? She knew all the time and didn't tell me?" She followed Dalia through the gate and into the garden. Waiting for her Fae guardian to take a seat, she settled on the bench beside her.

Dalia held up her hand. "Let me finish. Olivia, your grandmother, had no choice. After your mother married a mortal, it was her wish that none of her children be made aware of their lineage. Though it was difficult for your grandmother, she acquiesced to her daughter's wishes, though she saw the magic in you was strong, and she tried to convey an inkling of understanding in you by way of faerie tales and bedtime stories."

She thought back to all the wonderful stories Grammy had woven for her as a child.

"Olivia believed your mother saw magic in you and tried to squelch your free spirit." She smiled and shook her head. "Olivia knew you'd be the one to defy your parents. So as her time of passing drew near, she asked me to watch over you and intervene if necessary."

"That's why she bequeathed me the secretary."

Dalia nodded. "The book and the desk together in the hands of a Fae became a portal to our world. It was her way of giving you a safe haven should you need it. Thanks to your stubborn nature and determination, you did pretty well on your own until…"

"Until Kurt—uh, I mean Khellan."

"Sadly, yes. We had no idea he saw Tautha in you and a way to get even with the warlock and his family. Your talents awakened when he kidnapped you. I had to help you temper them until you were safe. Yet with Shay and his warriors searching for Khellan, I was forbidden to get involved, even with Olivia's decree. Shay guaranteed your safety to the council early on."

"So if Daylan and his ghost hadn't arrived at Earthbound, none of this would have happened?"

"Not exactly. Khellan had already discovered your Fae blood but failed to make the connection until Daylan and Ghost Daylan showed up. Fate has a way of making things that are supposed to occur—happen. Magical creatures, even ones that are unaware of their talents, will seek out other magical creatures. Which explains you being drawn to Daylan, despite his sister's dire warnings." Dalia tapped her finger to her pursed lips and narrowed her eyes. "Come to think of it, probably that's why you and Summer became so close even before Daylan was in the picture. Fate was at work even then."

"Why now? Why not contact me when I inherited the desk? I assume you made the portal open today."

"Yes and no. Word has spread of Khellan's demise partially at your hands. I became worried. Blood on one's hands is a terrible burden to bear. I took my concerns to the council and got their permission to contact you, to check on your well-being. I didn't disclose that I wanted to explain some of your family's history. That's going to have to be our little secret. Neither Olivia nor her daughter would approve, but I can live with that. You needed to know."

Far off, a door slammed, a phone rang, and someone called out Josie's name.

"Our time here is at an end. Your mortal world is beckoning. At this time, sharing our conversation wouldn't be prudent." Dalia paused for a beat. "Well, maybe with Daylan, but no one else. If you ever need me, you know how to find me. The portal is now open to you."

The garden swirled with the same multicolored ribbons, taking her along with them. Without warning she found herself sitting in the chair at her desk, with Mandy patting her arm.

"Josie, Josie, are you all right?" This time Mandy gave her shoulder a little shake.

"Yes, I'm fine—just lost in my thoughts."

Mandy blew out a breath. "Oh, that's a relief. Your phone was ringing when I arrived. When you didn't answer it, I became concerned."

"No problem. Thinking about Summer's beautiful wedding." She glanced up at her co-worker.

"It was wonderful. I only wish Clay and I'd been able to make the rehearsal dinner. But I'd already committed to meet Clay's parents at dinner that night."

Josie swiveled in the chair. "Things are getting serious between you and Clay?"

Mandy's cheeks pinked. "I think so. His parents seemed to like me. After I voiced concern over their opinion, Clay said it didn't matter anyway." She fanned her face. "And he said he loved me."

"Wow! Congratulations."

"Oh, don't jinx it." She wiggled the fingers of her left hand. "He's not put a ring on it yet." Mandy dissolved into a nervous fit of giggles.

"I've a feeling it will be soon." To her surprise, Josie knew her feeling was right. Her phone rang, and she checked the screen to see Daylan's name pop up. "Hi, handsome."

Mandy winked and walked away.

In a concerned voice, Daylan said, "Thank goodness you answered. I was about to send out a scouting party. Oh, wait a minute. That's me."

"Sorry I missed your call. I was tied up with things at the studio. I'll tell you all about it when you get here."

"Good enough. I've a couple more things to wrap up, and then I'll be on my way."

"See you soon." She touched the screen to end the call and helped Mandy set out the extra yoga mats for the students who didn't have their own.

Chapter Thirty
Finally a Resolution to the Ghost Problem and a Carriage House Surprise

Relieved to have reached her, he disconnected the call. This morning he'd made good progress on special orders received from regular customers. He cleared off the bench he'd been working on and cleaned up his tools and put them away. Connections he made with the Scottish games throughout the East Coast had been a boon to his business. He needed to look up those organizations out west now and get in contact. Sitting down at the computer, he pulled up his newsletter list. It had been several months since he'd sent out information. It was time to let his customers know he'd moved and how to contact him. He pulled up an old newsletter and revamped it with all his new information. Satisfied, he proofed it and sent it on its way. Since he owned the building in Martha's Vineyard, he'd have it remodeled and lease it out.

Grabbing his jacket off the back of his seat, he shrugged into it, set the alarm, and locked the door to the forge. The sun shone bright with only a few fluffy clouds floating in the blue sky. A stiff breeze tugged at his jacket as he jogged to the SUV. When he pulled into Earthbound's parking lot, Josie was sitting on the steps. She jumped up and sprinted to the vehicle, barely giving him time to exit the SUV.

She wrapped her arms around his neck and gave him a smacking kiss. "You are never going to believe what happened after my class today." Breathlessly, she proceeded to tell him everything.

Sliding his arms around her waist, he pulled her to him. "Wow, what a morning. Well, you got a lot of your questions answered." He hesitated for a few seconds. "Where does that leave you with your parents or siblings? Going to tell them?"

She chewed on her bottom lip for a beat. "No. Or at least not until I've had time to process it all. Remember Dalia said it wasn't a good idea to tell anyone except maybe you." Pausing she glanced at him uncertainly. "For now. What do you suppose she meant?"

"I don't know. Maybe there's something yet to happen?" He shrugged one shoulder and leaned back against the vehicle.

Raising her arms up, she let them drop to her sides. "I certainly hope not. I've had all the paranormal activities I can stand for a while."

"On that note, do you want to take the desk back to your carriage house? We can load it in the SUV. Might be safer there now rather than in the yoga studio."

"Sounds good. Mandy's class will be over in a few minutes. Then we can move it. I don't want to interrupt her class."

"No problem. So about living arrangements…" He rubbed his chin with thumb and index finger.

"I was thinking about that while I was waiting for you. It would be more restful for both of us if we moved out to the carriage house."

"That's exactly what I was thinking. Did you see anything of Ghost Daylan?"

"Nope. But I didn't go in your room. Decided to avoid any possible distractions until after class. Then I sat down at the desk and you know the rest. Do you suppose Khellan's demise released the curse and he's been able to join his wife?" She glanced hopefully at the studio.

"After all the trouble he caused, I'd think he'd at least say goodbye." He frowned, following her gaze. "Let's walk around to the back door and check out my room." Reaching for her hand, he twined their fingers and strolled to the back of the studio. He eased the back door open silently. They crept down the hall and into his room. It was just as he'd left it. Nothing out of place. "Daylan. You here?" the warlock whispered. No answer.

"I don't feel his presence either." She turned in a slow circle in the middle of the room.

"Look at you using your new abilities like a pro," he teased.

A red flush crept up her neck and spread across her cheeks. "I have a long way to go, I fear." She chuckled.

Voices drifted down the hall. Sounds of rolling up mats and stacking them against the wall accompanied goodbyes. "Class must be over." She opened the door a crack and a sudden gust slammed it shut. Sucking in a breath, she whirled around to see her Daylan grinning at Ghost Daylan and a beautiful woman with flowing red hair standing beside him. "Wow, it did break the curse."

"Apparently." The ghost chuckled and tilted his head toward the woman. "This is my Tautha. We owe you a debt of gratitude. How can we ever repay you?"

"By returning to the afterlife and staying put." He waved his hand in a shooing motion.

"Very well. Just wanted to say goodbye and thanks."

Daylan reached for the ghost, but his hand went right through him. "Seriously. I'm glad it all worked out. Our family is healing, and all is well."

"I'm so glad." The ghosts waved their hands in parting and faded away.

Josie put her hand to her heart and sighed. "A faerie tale ending."

"Yep. Let's get the desk and chair loaded and be on our way. Is there anything you need from the apartment?"

"I'll run upstairs, grab my duffel and toiletries. That should be it." She bounded out the door, nearly running smack dab into Mandy.

"Whoa! I thought I heard something." Her co-worker took two steps backward.

"Hey, is Clay here?" Daylan glanced over Mandy's head.

She turned and pointed out front. "He's waiting out in the car. Why?"

"Think I could get him to help me move Josie's desk and chair into the SUV? She's going to put it in the carriage house."

"Sure." She frowned. "Josie, you're not leaving?"

"Oh, no. The desk is a family heirloom that I was storing here until I had the carriage house ready to move into."

"Whew. With all the chaos around here, I was concerned." Mandy mimicked wiping her brow. "I like working here."

"Me too."

He jogged down the hall and out the front door to

where Clay sat. "Can I get you to help me move Josie's little desk to her SUV?"

"Sure." Clay pushed open the car door and unfolded himself out of the car. "Gotta get Mandy a roomier vehicle. "This one is on its last legs anyway. I'd like her to have a four-wheel drive by this winter."

"Always a good idea." He led the way into Earthbound. Josie was waiting for him with a roll of tape.

"Thought we should tape the drawers shut before you take it out to the vehicle."

"Good idea." He taped the drawers shut while she ran outside and lowered the back seats. They carried the desk out to the SUV and slid the antique into the vehicle. Mandy brought out the chair and handed it to him. "Thanks for your help." He slipped the chair inside and shut the back hatch.

"See you tomorrow." Mandy waved as they pulled out of the parking lot.

****

Josie's eyes flew open wide when she pushed the door open to the carriage house. The walls had all been painted a light cream she'd picked out. The worn carpeting had been replaced by a new frosty gray with muted pastel swirls running through it. New hardwood flooring polished to a gleam greeted her when she entered the kitchen. She turned to face him. "Did you do all this?"

"Yep. I was the cause of the chaos in your world, so I figured it was the least I could do to set things right."

"I love it. How'd you know what I wanted?" She wandered around the kitchen touching the new countertops and appliances.

"Paid attention when we were here scoping out the place during the walk-through."

She padded down the short hallway and put her hand on the newly painted bathroom door. "When did you have time?"

"Oh, Devlin knew a guy." He put his hand over hers and pushed on the door. The new fixtures and large sunken tub gleamed under the revamped lighting system. White tile with veins of light pink and turquoise covered the bathroom floor. The tile continued on the walls of the meandering maze leading to her large shower with three heads, a glass shelf recessed into the wall and a little bench formed on the opposite end from the shower heads.

Staring, she opened and closed her mouth, but no sound came out. Finally, she squeaked, "How did you—the bathroom wasn't this big—was it?"

He tented this fingers and rocked back on his heels. "Not exactly. A bit of magic expanded the area. Truth be told, Mandy showed us a bathroom you'd admired in a home improvement magazine."

"Oh, wow, no wonder it looks familiar." She drew in a breath. "She didn't say a word."

"We told her it was a surprise. Summer shared our secrets with Mandy and a bit of the situation. Just in case she was around when all hell broke loose. Didn't want her freaking out. She took it all in stride and swore never to divulge what she'd been told."

"I guess it's better that everything is out in the open."

"Not everything, but most. Where do you want to put your desk?"

She ambled back into the living area, where several stacks of boxes were waiting to be unpacked and her paintings were leaning against the wall. "Beside the front window, so I can look out at the flowers I'll plant in the garden as soon as I get a moment." Turning in a circle, she surveyed the room, then pursed her lips. "A fantasy mural on that wall will bring the room to life. Don't you think?" Pointing toward the far end of the room, she tilted her head and peered up at him.

Shoving his hands into his jean pockets, he shrugged. "Decorating is not in my wheelhouse. So you're on your own." He walked to the door, stepped outside, and glanced around. Finding no one in the vicinity, he waved his hand toward the vehicle. The rear door to the SUV opened. With a flick of his wrist, the desk and chair appeared in the exact spot Josie suggested.

"What happened to 'no magic for personal gain' rule?"

Sighing heavily, he leaned one shoulder against the wall. "Not personal gain. It's to avoid dropping in my tracks. In case you hadn't noticed, it's been a rough couple of weeks. I'd say the universe will grant us a little magic without retribution. Speaking of a bit of rest and relaxation..."

"I didn't know we were," she teased.

"I don't know about you, but it's been on my mind." He hesitated for a beat. "A lot. I talked with Devlin and Summer earlier. When they return to work, we're going to disappear for a few days. Rocky Mountain National Park has been calling to me for quite a while. We need to answer that call." With a devilish grin, he picked up a box marked "bedroom" and turned on his heel.

"Wait. You're ready to drop in your tracks, but you pick up a box and carry it to the bedroom? I can unpack tomorrow."

"Already headed that way." Shifting the box in his arms, he turned and winked at her.

Eyebrow raised in question, she followed him to the bedroom and let out an ear-piercing squeal. Her old full-sized bed was gone. In its place stood a brand new king-sized, light oak sleigh bed with under-bed drawers and cabinets. A plush comforter in a pink, blue and purple fantasy design spread across the bed. Matching curtains shimmered at the windows. A color-coordinated moon-and-stars throw rug rested on the hardwood floor beside the bed.

Setting the box down at the bottom of the bed, he spread his arms wide. "Décor courtesy of my sister."

"Wow—just wow!" She sat on the bed and bounced. "I love it. But how am I ever going to repay all of you?" With a sigh, she reached over and picked up a small pink envelope sealed with purple wax and the Earthbound logo placed on top the pillows. Turning it over, she slid her fingernail under the seal and took out a small pink piece of paper with scalloped edges. In flowing purple ink it read, "Josie, happy carriage housewarming. Wanted to let you know, if Daylan ever figures out you are the best thing that ever happened to him and acts appropriately, you have my and Devlin's blessing. Love, Summer." She held the note to her heart for a moment, then tucked it back inside the envelope and slipped it into her backpack.

"From Summer. I recognize her seal." He sat down beside her. "Going to tell me what it said?"

"The comforter and curtains are a carriage housewarming gift from her and Devlin. The rest is girl stuff." Smoothing her hand over the quilt, she tilted her head to glance over at him. "Now, what were you saying about a few days of R and R?"

"Reserved a premiere spot at one of the campgrounds in Rocky Mountain National Park."

"How in the world did you do that? Those sites are reserved six months in advance and are full minutes after they are made available. Do you have a tent?"

"Apparently, someone canceled. I don't have a tent, but the big fifth wheel parked at Moon Ridge is mine."

"Really? Did you go camping on Martha's Vineyard?"

"Not quite. I bought the truck and trailer when I discovered how much my blade-making talents were in demand at the Scottish get-togethers and games across the country. They have a large gathering during September in Estes Park. It'll be a good place to drum up some business. I don't want to wait until then to take a few days off, so we leave the week of July fourth.

"Sounds like fun. There is a fantastic fireworks display over Lake Estes if there's not a fire ban." Covering her mouth, she tried to hide a jaw-popping yawn. "Feels like the weight of the world has been lifted and my body is drained. I could sleep for days." She fell back onto the bed.

"Not surprising. You half-mortals aren't built to withstand the type of stress you've been through the past few weeks. However, I'm not sure Mandy would appreciate that." He snickered.

She bristled. "I did fairly well. Helped dispatch the

bad guy. Didn't I?" She sat up and took a swing at him.

He dodged the blow, catching her hand in his and kissing it. "Yep. You sure did." Relief flowed through him. She was processing the events of the last few days without it becoming a big deal or damaging her psyche.

A Cheshire cat grin spread across his face. "Race you to the shower."

"What does the winner get?" She giggled, pulling her top over her head. By the time she reached for the button on her jeans, he was naked and sprinting toward the shower. "Hey, no fair using magic." Wiggling out of her pants and underwear, she unclasped her bra, pulled off her socks, and groaned. "I had more clothes on than you."

"Not my problem," he called from the entrance to the brand-new shower.

"Okay, so what was up for grabs?" She pushed by him and waltzed into the curving path to the main shower area.

"You." He swept her into his arms and kissed her.

\*\*\*\*

Josie's doubts that life would ever return to normal disappeared, leaving her free to enjoy the classes she taught. The administrative end of the business was a bit more daunting, but she managed without calling Summer once.

The week flew by without incident. Never had she felt so free. A couple of times when she was alone, she tried to make her hands spark, which resulted in burning a hole in the office carpet. Daylan fixed it and no one else was the wiser. The next time, she practiced over the dry empty sink.

Monday morning they met Summer and Devlin at

the forge for juice, coffee, and bagels. She and Daylan had packed the fifth wheel the night before. He hooked up the truck, and they were ready to hit the road when Summer and Devlin arrived.

"So how'd it go?" Summer hugged her and Daylan. Piper trotted up to him, sniffed, then went about her doggy business.

Daylan grinned. "Finally I've been accepted."

"For now." Summer laughed and turned her attention back to Josie.

"Not bad, once I got the hang of your accounting system and software. We may need to add classes to accommodate the new students. Seems the word spread at the college down the street, and we've had a lot of new sign-ups." She handed Summer a glass of juice and pointed to the plate of bagels.

"Great news, good job." Summer patted her on the back. "Thanks for covering." She picked out a blueberry bagel and took a bite, then handed Devlin a cinnamon apple.

"So how about you? Enjoy your days off as a married woman?"

"Of course. Wasn't ready to come back." Summer sent Devlin an affectionate look.

He slung an arm around her shoulder and kissed her cheek. "Glad to finally make it official. The wedding was fun, with all the extended family, but we were ready for alone time."

"You can say that again." Summer glanced at her brother. "It was good to be a family again. Thanks for that."

"No problem. It's a weight lifted off me." He bumped shoulders with Summer.

"I didn't hear from any of my staff." Devlin glanced at his brother-in-law. "Any problems at the gun club?" He took the mug of coffee Josie handed him.

"Not really. Ran short of cash the second day. Apparently, Kevin deposited all the cash in the bank, failing to keep some on hand for the drawers. I went to the bank, got a couple hundred, and he paid it back the next day. And kept operating cash after that." Daylan snorted. "I guess you handle all the cash and deposits?" He blew across the top of his mug of steaming coffee and reached for a bagel.

"I have up until now. Had some staff problems and never got around to sharing the info after the problems were solved." Devlin took a bite of his bagel and wiped the crumbs from his shirt.

"While I was at the bank, I opened up operating accounts for the apartment building. Josie and I signed the signature cards, but you and Summer need to go by and sign them too. Checks are ordered and internet access set up." He handed a slip of paper to Devlin with all the info.

Josie added, "I set up the account information on the computer at Earthbound, so you're all set, Summer. Lizzy will be acting manager while Daylan and I are gone. Thought you two would have enough to catch up on without the added apartment management stuff." She took a swig of orange juice and popped the last bite of her asiago cheese bagel in her mouth.

Daylan got up from the table. We're going to hit the road now. If you need us, you know where to find us, though cell service is spotty in Rocky Mountain National."

"You guys go on and get out of here. We got it

handled." Devlin clapped Daylan on the shoulder. "Thanks for all your help. See you when you get back."

Chapter Thirty-One
Sometimes a Romantic Getaway Puts Things in Perspective

Avoiding I-25, he took the back roads to Estes Park, Colorado. With rush hour traffic and road construction, the highway was nothing short of a parking lot most days. Besides he wasn't in a hurry, but he preferred to set his own pace. They arrived in Estes Park in early afternoon. He wheeled into the shopping center that contained a pizza place one of the Moon Ridge customers had recommended. Negotiating a parking lot with a one-ton, long-bed truck and a thirty-six-foot fifth-wheel trailer was not for the faint of heart. Finally, he parked truck and trailer at the far end of the parking lot and pointed to the pizza place.

"Is this lunch?" Josie yanked up the door handle and jumped out. "How'd you know about this place?" She rounded the front of the truck and waited.

He joined her and they walked hand in hand to the pizzeria. "Ray, one of the clients at Moon Ridge, wandered into my shop. He commissioned a couple of knives and a claymore sword. Paid in advance."

"Gotta love that."

"Yeah, and when I told him it'll be a few weeks, he didn't have a problem with the time frame. I told him we were taking a few days off to go camping at Rocky Mountain National Park. Ray indicated he was a

Tena Stetler

frequent visitor to the park and highly recommended this pizza place. So I thought we'd try it."

"Good choice. That way we can build a fire when we get to the campground and go straight to the s'mores." She licked her lips, then glanced around the establishment. "I'm going to run to the ladies room and wash my hands."

"Me too." At her raised eyebrow, he snickered. "Men's room. I'll grab a booth first." After washing his hands, he returned to the booth, slid into one side, and fingered the small box in his pocket. No doubt he was ready to settle down. *But is it too soon to… Will she feel rushed? Maybe the best course of action is to let things unfold naturally. Yep, that's the ticket. I'm over-thinking the whole thing.* Pushing the doubts away, he perused the menu.

She came bouncing up to the booth and plopped down beside him. "Do you think we could get the pizza to go? I can't wait to get to the park. We'll still have time to hike around Bear Lake before sundown."

"Sure, and we have cold drinks in the cooler."

"Did you bring graham crackers, chocolate bars, and marshmallows?"

Chuckling, he reached out and stroked her cheek. "Never leave home without them."

She wriggled impatiently in her seat.

The waitress sauntered over to the table. "What can I get for you folks?"

"A large pizza with lots of meat, sauce, and extra cheese." Josie turned to Daylan. "Is that all right?"

"Yep, works for me." He glanced at the waitress. "We'll take it to go."

"Sure thing. Do you need drinks, paper plates,

304

napkins, forks?"

"No drinks. But napkins, plates, and forks would be helpful."

"Great. I'll have it out in a jiffy or two." She grinned at them and hurried away.

True to her word, several minutes later she appeared with a big pizza box and a paper sack with plates, forks, and napkins inside, and handed it all to him.

Anxious to be on their way, he handed the box to Josie, left a tip on the table, and paid for the pizza.

Inside the truck, she opened the lid to the box and inhaled deeply as steam rose off the pie. "Wow, does this ever smell good."

He dumped out the paper bag on the console. She stuck a fork under the first piece and lifted. The plastic fork broke as she lifted out the piece. Cheese stringing everywhere, the slice landed upside down on the paper plate with a plop, the handle of the fork stuck through it.

She laughed, licking the sauce and cheese off her fingers. "This one is my piece." She took a bite and huffed out a breath. "It's hot!" She waved her hand in front of her mouth for a couple of beats. When able to chew, she closed her eyes. "Mmmm, this pizza is wonderful."

He roared with laughter. "Nothing like dinner and a show." Reaching for the pizza box, he skipped the fork and picked up a piece, wrapped several strings of cheese around the slice before sliding it neatly onto his plate. "And that's how it's done." Still laughing, he closed the box and put it in the back seat. He took a bite. "Mm-hmm, this is great." Reaching behind Josie, he grabbed a couple of cold drinks out of the cooler. "Do you want me to open this for you? I'd rather not have cola-colored stains all over my truck."

She shot him the evil eye, but politely said, "Yes, please." Dabbing her mouth with a napkin, she eyed him speculatively.

Resting his plate on the console, he pushed open the truck door and twisted the cap off the bottle outside the vehicle. With a hiss and pop, but no overflow, he handed the bottle to Josie.

She grinned. "Show off."

He opened the other bottle, set it in the cup holder, and took another bite of pizza. "We're off."

Thirty minutes later he turned onto Loop C in Moraine Campground. He backed into the site with a panoramic view of the Rocky Mountains and a herd of elk in the meadow below. A moose wandered by several yards from the site, paused to watch with mild interest, then meandered on his way toward the meadow.

Leaning out of the window, she glanced up. A few wispy white clouds floated across the bright blue sky. "We've time to make it to Bear Lake." She stepped out of the truck and breathed in the cool mountain air. "On second thought, let's get set up and spend the evening around the campfire. We can hike Bear Lake, then follow the trail up to Emerald Lake and Nymph Lake tomorrow. If we get an early start. The parking lot fills up fast, so we need to beat the crowd."

"I like the way you think." He unhooked the truck and parked it beside the fifth wheel trailer, barely missing a huge boulder sitting off to the side.

Josie reached into the truck bed, pulled out several

logs and pieces of kindling, and carried them over to the fire ring. "This should get us started."

He flipped up the door to the storage area on the trailer and pulled out two high-backed orange camp chairs and set them around the fire pit. Next, he snapped his fingers toward the fire ring. The kindling and logs formed a teepee, then burst into flames.

She shook her head. "Somehow that seems like cheating."

Snickering, he lifted a brow. "That's the closest I can come to witchfire. Unlike my sister."

Her eyes widened, and she blew out a breath. "Your sister's power is impressive and a little scary."

"Tell me about it. Now, no more talk about recent events. Let's relax and enjoy a peaceful camping trip."

"I'll get the s'mores fixings." She bounded up the trailer's steps and paused in the doorway, holding the screen door open. "Where are they?"

"In the plastic bag I set on the counter...or maybe on the bed. I didn't want it sliding all over or spilling on the floor. We need graham crackers, not crumbs."

"Okay. I'll find it. I'm going to grab a jacket from the closet. Want yours?"

"Sure, it'll get nippy up here when the sun goes down."

"You bet." She let the screen door close.

He arranged the chairs and placed a folding table between them. Pulling out the wrought iron fire scepter, he leaned it up against his chair. It was just a huge pair of tongs that gripped large pieces of wood. There was nothing like a roaring fire to chase the demons away. He loved to stir the fire, add logs, and keep it a maximum flame.

Everything set, he eased into his chair and watched the flames lick the sides of the logs, racing up the kindling, leaving nothing but red-hot embers. Somewhere off in the distance an owl hooted, while crickets chirped until he scraped his chair as he changed position against the smoke that curled in his direction. *Never fails. Wherever I sit the smoke follows.* He picked up the scepter, repositioned the logs, allowing more air to circulate, and the smoke dissipated.

"Hey, Daylan, since when do you wear skirts?"

"They're kilts," he corrected without turning around. "I used the trailer as living quarters while I joined the Scottish games. They're some of my best customers. Gotta look the part. By the way, what are you doing nosing in my clothes?"

"Searching for a jacket." She pushed the door open and held out a blue-and-red plaid kilt. "So…tell me, do you wear anything under this?"

"Never tell, but maybe I'll demonstrate tonight," he said seductively.

Snickering, she flounced back into the fifth wheel and quickly returned with his jacket slung over her arm. "That's quite a fire you got going there." She descended the steps and joined him at the campfire. "What would you think about getting a puppy?"

He turned and stared wide-eyed at her. "Where did that come from?"

"Well…as a child, I wasn't allowed a pup because they were time-consuming and made a big mess. Mother insisted I needed to pay attention to my career path." She spread her arms wide. "We see how that turned out. Cavorting with witches, faeries, and werewolves. What has become of me? My parents would never approve." She laughed. "Besides, I love Piper. Summer usually leaves her at the studio when she runs errands. Piper is a wonderful companion. A pup would love it out here camping with us." She shifted to face him. "There'll be more of these activities?"

He nodded. "Of course."

"Great. I love camping." Pausing for a moment, she tapped a finger to her lips. "The carriage house has a yard, whereas my apartment didn't. It wouldn't have been fair to a pup to be cooped up like that. Now is a perfect time, and I have the perfect place."

"Piper hates me," he grumbled.

"Only until she got to know you. A pup of our own would love you—us—and provide protection and companionship. Maybe we could check in with a rescue organization."

He scrubbed his hand over his face and scrunched up his forehead. *She is planning a future together, so that has to be a good omen.* "Sure, we could do that, once we get settled into a routine. It wouldn't be fair to bring a new pup into our lives otherwise."

"True enough. I'll talk with Summer about training and rescues." She slid her fingernail under the tab of the graham cracker box, popped open the flap, and dumped out a pack. Tearing open the wrapper on a chocolate bar, she stacked the crackers and chocolate squares on paper plates.

He skewered several marshmallows and held them over the flames until they were golden brown. "Done to perfection?"

"Wow, that's great. Mine always seem to catch on fire." She held out a plate as he shoved a marshmallow off the skewer onto the cracker topped with chocolate. She squished another cracker on top and took a bite. Gooey, stringy, toasted marshmallow clung to her upper lip and corner of her mouth as she tried daintily cleaning the sticky mess with the tip of her tongue.

He sat transfixed, watching her. *A woman should know better than to do that with her tongue in front of a man.* Shifting, he tried to ease the growing interest in his crotch, covering his lap with his own plate and s'more. Finally, she resorted to spilling water out of her bottle onto a napkin to clean her face and fingers. *Thank God.*

Oblivious to his discomfort, she took another bite of the s'more. "I'd forgotten how messy these things can be. But oooohhh, so worth it." She glanced over at him again, licking her top lip. "What?"

"Don't you have any idea—never mind." He took a big bite of his s'more, careful to keep his plate in place.

As they were finishing the last of the s'mores, the bushes several feet behind them rustled. Josie twisted in her chair, her gaze following the sound. Glowing eyes appeared among the leaves. Her hand flew to her mouth. "Oh no," she squeaked, jumping out of her chair. A huge buck elk stepped out of the brush and bounded down the trail. The air whooshed out of her. "For a moment—I thought..."

"We were going to be attacked by demons?" He laughed.

"Given our recent experiences, I don't think my reaction was out of line," she said indignantly standing hand on hips. After a couple of minutes, she glanced at the fire. "Want me to add another log?"

"No, we probably should go to bed. According to

you, we need to be up before the crack of dawn to get a parking place at Bear Lake."

"You got that right." She gathered up the chairs and leaned them against the trailer as he took the five-gallon bucket of water set near the fire and doused the flames. He stirred the steaming muck and poured more water on it.

"So are you going to model the skir—kilt for me?" She grinned down at him as she ascended the stairs.

"You bet."

****

Stars twinkled across the dark sky as he pulled into the nearly full parking lot at Bear Lake, with just a thin glow of orange spread across the eastern horizon. He parked, and Josie hopped out of the truck.

"Wow, this is perfect timing. We can warm up on the trail around Bear Lake, then start up the trail to Emerald Lake. Then if we have time maybe Mirror Lake?"

"Sounds like a full day."

"Yep. Not a cloud in the sky." A gentle breeze through the trees brought a fresh pine scent as they walked. A family of ducks paddled their way along the shoreline a few feet from the trail, the adults quacking and trying to keep their ducklings in line. A wide smile turned up the corners of her mouth, and she couldn't help but giggle. *This is the life.*

"What's so funny?" He quirked an eyebrow.

"Everything and nothing. The ducks scolding their young ones, trying to keep them out of trouble. Not unlike parents do their children. Some listen. Others, like that one making a break for it in the opposite direction from their little flock, complicate life."

"True. I guess we both were like that little duckling." He watched as one of the adult ducks set out after the wayward one and brought it back into the flock. He reached around her waist and guided her toward the trail marked Emerald Lake.

Following him up the rocky trail strewn with pinecones, she paused for a beat, leaned toward him, and brushed her lips over his. "You've put your flock back together. Something to be proud of."

He sighed. "Fact remains, had I listened in the first place, the family discord could have been avoided."

"And you never would have met me—or Summer wouldn't have met Devlin. Those two are soul mates for sure. Sometimes, fate is in control and you can't do anything about it." She reached for his hand and twined her fingers with his as they climbed up the gravel path.

Raising her hand up to his lips, he lightly kissed each knuckle, then gazed into her eyes. "Which begs the question, what about you and your family? Seems you have a lot to talk about. I don't mean to stick my nose where it doesn't belong…"

She shook her head. "Sadly, magic, Fae, and things of that nature will never be in my family's vocabulary. Which is why Grams willed the secretary to me. She saw inside me, knew I would be different." She snickered. "If she only knew how right she was." Her eyes flew wide open and she sucked in a breath as the lake came into view between fragrant pine boughs. "Wow, this is beautiful."

"It is. But not as beautiful as you." He knelt down on one knee and gazed up at her, then took the small pink box out of his pocket, holding it in the palm of his hand. "Josie, I'm not trying to rush you. I mean… Oh hell, Josie, I'm not good at this." He paused to wipe a bead of sweat off his brow. *Some romantic I am.* "I want to spend the rest of my life with you by my side. Will you marry me?"

**\*\*\*\***

Her eyes met and held his gorgeous sparkling green eyes. Her heart thundered in her chest and her mouth went dry. This man in front of her was everything, and he was asking, really asking, her to be his wife. *Am I dreaming? Is this really happening?* She pinched herself. "Ouch." *Yep, really happening.* Her cheeks warmed.

His face scrunched up in puzzlement, he blinked. "What?"

"Oh, Daylan, I'd love to be your wife and spend the rest of my life with you. I didn't think you were ever going to..." *There I go again, engaging mouth before brain.* She giggled, remembering her Gram's words of reproach. "Some things are better left unsaid, little girl." A warm breeze caressed her face and was gone. She looked around—the air was still, not a tree, leaf, or branch moved. She touched her cheek. Her Gram's voice whispered through her mind: "Have faith, my wild one. All will be well. I'm proud of the woman you've grown to be. But you must not hold it against the family if they fail to see the magic. You, my dear, are the special one."

"Josie, Josie. Are you all right?"

Daylan's concerned voice became more insistent as her Gram's voice faded away. "I'm fine. But yet again I'm...seeing, no, hearing... I can't believe... My Gram just touched me and..." Her voice trailed off.

"And what?" He gave her shoulders a little shake.

"She's proud of me." She rubbed her cheek again, describing to him what her Gram had said. "What do you think it means...she means?"

He snorted. "That's easy. You're the one who inherited your Gram's Fae talents, through blood and belief. You have to confront—no, tell your mother, parents, siblings about the desk, your experience in the Fae world, everything. If they choose not to believe, then that's on them. You have to try."

"Aren't you the wise one."

"No, I grew up with the benefit of knowing magic exists." He glanced at the sky. "We'd better start back. Looks like a shower is headed our way. Mirror Lake will have to wait until tomorrow."

Chapter Thirty-Two
Epilogue—Nearly Six Months Later

A huge evergreen wreath adorned the solid wooden carved door. *This is different. I don't remember Mother ever decorating the front door.* Josie fingered the pine bough decoration while standing on the steps of her parents' mansion in Evergreen, Colorado. A few huge storybook snowflakes landed on her dark eyelashes and melted in her hair, while others fluttered to the ground around her. Her hand poised to knock, she blew out a breath. "I can't do this." She turned to Daylan, who stood supportively beside her.

"Well, they can't come to the wedding if they don't know about it."

A sharp bark came from the truck parked in the circular driveway.

"We can send them invitations. Magick is seconding that action." Josie pivoted on the porch and prepared to bolt.

He caught her by the shoulders and whirled her around to face the door. "No, the pup has no idea what is going on here. Only that we left her in the truck in the crate and she's not happy. Therefore, the sooner you get this over with the sooner we can let her out." He nudged her with his hip.

She sucked in a breath and raised her hand again—just as the door opened. Squealing in surprise, she

315

blinked at the entrance, where Deborah, her parents'
housekeeper, stood.

Deborah frowned. "I thought I heard voices. Are
your parents expecting you?" She lowered her voice.
"Pam and Rod are here too. With their families."

Regaining her composure, she returned the
housekeeper's stare. "Nope not expecting me."

"Well, okay then." Deborah opened the door wider,
inviting them in. Her questioning glance followed
Daylan.

"Deborah, this is my fiancé, Daylan Rylie." A
smirk spread across her face, but she couldn't help it.
"That's why we're here."

Deborah's eyebrow winged up for a second, then
she schooled her features into a reserved expression,
one Josie had seen most of her life. Deborah had snuck
her food when she was sent to her room without supper
for speaking her mind or various other violations of the
Mackenzie family code. Secretly, she always thought
Deborah enjoyed the fireworks caused by her defiance,
right up until her parents ordered her not to darken their
door ever again and cut off her access to trust funds.
The housekeeper had witnessed that final argument
with her parents, in silent disapproval.

She had seen compassion and understanding in the
housekeeper's eyes as she gathered what possessions
her parents allowed her to take and vowed to never
cross their threshold again, slamming the door in her
wake. Yet here she was, already across that threshold,
and at the holidays to boot. *Am I crazy?*

As if Daylan had read her mind, he slid his arm
around her waist and leaned over to whisper, "You've
got this."

Her legs turned to jelly as the twinkling lights of the huge Christmas tree in the foyer reflected off her mother's face as she strode toward the entrance.

"Deborah, who is it?" Her mother's eyes widened, and her mouth fell open. She stood speechless.

Never in her memory had she seen her mother left speechless by anyone. "Hi, Mother." She wondered at the surprisingly calm voice coming out of her mouth. "I'll only take a few minutes of your time. "Daylan, my fiancé, thought we should personally invite you to our wedding on Valentine's Day. I told him you wouldn't be interested—but here we are." Finally, the words stopped flowing out of her mouth. *I really have to do something about this nervous habit.*

Daylan smiled wide and offered his hand. "Good to meet you."

Her mother, as if still in shock, finally closed her mouth, extended her hand, and took his. "This is a pleasant surprise." Her gaze searched the entrance, then switched down the hall. "Sean, I think you better come here." Then, as an afterthought, she said, "Josie is here with her fiancé."

*Wow. I didn't expect that.* Josie straightened her shoulders and stepped forward. Slowly she released the breath she'd been holding and stared at her mother. "How have you been?"

Her father's footsteps echoed on the polished tile floor, preceding his larger-than-life form that strode from the family room into the hall. Rod, her brother, and her sister, Pam, followed close behind the man.

"Well. And yourself?" her mother asked in a friendly tone.

*This isn't how I expected things to go.* She dared a

glance at Deborah, whose lips twitched as if holding back a smile or maybe even a laugh. She replayed in her mind the scene of the last time she'd spoken with her parents, and shuddered. Yet remarkably the vibes she was picking up were amicable. She raised an eyebrow as her father skidded to a stop, her brother and sister nearly running into each other.

"Josie." Her father's eyes shifted from her to Daylan and back. "This is an unexpected surprise. Come on into the family room." He motioned for them to follow him.

*Who are these people, and what have they done with my parents?* Her brother and sister hung back, whispering to her mother, which allowed her and Daylan to follow directly behind her father.

"Have a seat." Her father motioned to the couch on the other side of the coffee table filled with Christmas cookies and hot chocolate. He took the chair opposite them and glanced at Deborah as she entered the room. "Two more mugs of hot chocolate." He paused, peering at them. "Unless you'd like something else?"

"No, hot chocolate is fine," she replied. Daylan echoed her response.

Her sister leaned over to the group of children seated in the center of the floor and whispered something. The four children, of varying ages, stood and peered at Josie.

"Josie, I'd like you to meet Jeff and Hannah—they are our two munchkins." She glanced at her husband sitting near the fireplace. "My husband, Jerry."

Jerry nodded in their direction. He was clearly uncomfortable with the present situation and wanted to stay out of any line of fire.

Pam placed her hand on the other two children, the older ones of the group. "These are Rod's two kids, Merry and Charles." She handed each child a cookie. "Now run up to the playroom. Merry and Charles, see that Jeff and Hannah don't get into trouble." Pam took a seat next to her husband.

She thought she saw her sister send a scathing look to her brother as he took a seat next to a pleasant-looking woman, but the exchange was so fleeting she could have been mistaken.

Her mother slipped into an empty chair and waited expectantly. After exchanging glances with his wife, her father stood and paced in front of the huge moss-rock fireplace, pausing to run his fingertips across the mantel. This was his habit since she could remember when he had something unpleasant or uncomfortable to discuss. These discussions were usually held in the study.

She shifted in her chair. Her father liked to control things. Set the tone, he'd always said, but this time— she'd take the reins. "I came here at my fiancé, Daylan's"—she paused for a moment to glance at him—"urging tonight to invite all of you to our wedding on February fourteenth at two in the afternoon. The nuptials will take place at a friend's cabin in Divide, Colorado."

Her father cleared his throat as if about to speak. She held up her hand. "Let me finish. In recent weeks, my life has been turned upside down because neither you nor Mother saw fit to inform your children of our heritage, along with the fact that the bedtime stories Gram told us were true and not the ramblings of an old woman."

Her mother's lips formed a perfect O before she put her hand over her mouth and stared at her husband.

On a roll now, she decided to spill all the beans in front of the whole family before they had her escorted out of the house. "Yep, that old secretary Grams left to me, the one you so badly wanted, is a portal to the Fae Realm." She looked accusingly at her mother. "You knew, didn't you?"

Her mother nodded. Tears glistened in her eyes for a moment, before she blinked them away.

"And the family book, the leather-bound one in the secret compartment in the desk—why didn't you list your children's names? Only my first name, in Gram's handwriting, is in that book, and it should have included our family history."

Her father's expression was thunderous as he opened his mouth to speak. This time it was his wife who silenced him with a stern look.

*Wow, have things changed. I can't wait to see what happens next.* Daylan wrapped his arm around her shoulder and squeezed.

"Sean, it's time we pay the piper," her mother said, shifting her gaze between her children. "First of all, none of you showed signs of Fae abilities. Rarely do half-breeds raised in a mortal environment ever inherit—*demonstrate* Fae talents." She paused and locked eyes with Josie. "We figured you'd inherited my wild-child behavior, but never in a million years did I suspect you'd be able to…wield the magic."

"You were wrong. Way wrong…so wrong it could have been fatal." At the horror on her mother's face, she softened her voice. "But that's a story for another time. I've said my piece, extended our wedding invitation, and now we'll take our leave. Sorry to have spoiled your evening."

As soon as the words were out of her mouth, she regretted them. Her parents had been nothing but civil, even inviting, and part of her was still reeling. "Sorry, I didn't mean that." She shoved up from the couch. Daylan following her cue and got to his feet. They'd gotten only a few steps toward the door when her father called out to them.

"Hey, even the condemned get a chance to be heard," her father barked in his courtroom voice. "I respectfully request to be given that opportunity."

She was speechless for a moment or two. Expecting to be escorted from the house, she paused. "Granted."

Her father's voice softened as he slid his arm around his wife, who was now standing at his side. "We've regretted our decision and words said in anger on that day a few years ago. Parents should never do to their children what we did just because…because they don't like or understand the life path they've taken. Your mother knew you were different, from the day you were born. We were scared of what you might become without our strict guidance. A free spirit, a wild child or adult, was unacceptable in our circles."

Her mother interrupted. "Besides, I'd disavowed all connection to your gram's world long before you were born. As you can imagine, the Fae Council was unhappy, to say the least, when I married a mortal, and a lawyer to boot. To add insult to injury, I chose to live in his world. The Fae said, Don't come back. Which was fine with me. But your gram was well respected and allowed visits as long as our heritage wasn't revealed." Her mother shook her head. "She knew. I am so sorry for the pain my decision has caused."

"Wait…What??" She stared incredulously at her mother. *Boy, had things changed. Mother never interrupted Dad, let alone apologized.*

"We tried to contact you, but you never returned our calls," her mother said softly.

"It was blind ego that made us—me—decide it was meant to be," her father interjected. "So we quit trying to contact you…until…"

Her mother and father exchanged looks. Her mother continued, "We had a couple of visitors a while back. Shay and Dalia were not pleased with our decisions and were only too happy to describe our failings in great detail." Her mom took a breath.

Her dad took that opportunity to continue the story. "They appeared in our home out of thin air, I might add, with several ultimatums. You have no idea how disconcerting it can be when people appear out of nowhere right in front of you." He wiped a bead of sweat off his brow and shook his head.

She bit her lip in an effort to keep from grinning, having a good idea how the conversation went. "Yeah, Shay and Dalia can be opinionated, maybe even a bit intimidating."

"You've met them?" her mother asked.

"Oh, yeah." Not wanting to divulge anything further, she turned to the door. "We have a puppy waiting in the car. I've delivered our message and will send invites with the pertinent information on the location of the wedding and reception. It's up to all of you whether or not you'll attend. Please RSVP to Summer Sawyer, or she'll have your heads and ours too."

"Summer Sawyer?"

"She owns the yoga studio I teach at. We've become good friends. She's graciously consented to have our wedding and reception at her and her husband's cabin."

"Summer is my sister. She kinda introduced us." Daylan beamed.

"Son—what do you think of all this magic talk?" Her father narrowed his eyes at Daylan.

"I'm not sure what you mean." He paused for a moment. Then the light dawned. "Oh, I've lived with it all my life. I come from a long line of powerful witches."

Her father's adam's apple bounced up and down as he swallowed hard. "I see."

Wishing she had a camera, she bit back a grin. Never had her father looked so much like a fish out of water. But she had to give him credit. He recovered quickly. In fact, the whole family appeared to take Daylan's announcement in stride. She was ready to make an attempt at smoothing things over when—

Pam stood up. "Count me and my family in. We'll be there. Do you need our address to send the invites?"

"Nope. I've kept track of you and Rod over the years." Josie smiled. "Didn't want to cause any problems by making contact."

Slowly surveying his family, her dad tented his fingers and rocked back on his heels. "It's time for this family to put our differences aside and act like a family," her father declared. "Your wedding will be the first step." Her mother nodded in agreement.

Rod's wife elbowed him in the side. "We'll be

there too." She stared defiantly at her husband. He gave a curt nod.

Josie once again bit the side of her cheek to keep from laughing. "I'll let Summer know."

Deborah entered the room with two mugs of steaming hot chocolate. She glanced from person to person, then handed the mugs to Josie and Daylan.

"Won't you stay at least long enough to drink your hot chocolate? You know Deborah's frosted sugar cookies are the best."

She couldn't deny her mother's hopeful expression. Reaching down, she snatched a cookie from the plate, took a bite, and closed her eyes. *Mmm, just like I remember. Heavenly.* "We can't stay long, or we'll have puddles." She handed Daylan a cookie.

He took a bite and meandered to stand beside Sean in front of the cozy fire. "These are fantastic."

"I'll gather a dozen for you to take with you." Deborah smiled and bustled off to the kitchen.

Her sister laughed and jerked her chin toward the back of the disappearing housekeeper. "Some things never change. She always did like you best."

Josie set her mug down and popped the last bite of cookie in her mouth. "We have to get going. But thank you for everything."

Deborah brought in a holiday container filled with cookies and handed it to Daylan. "This way at least you'll get a few before she devours them all."

"Thanks so much." She put her hand on Deborah's arm. "You're invited to the wedding too, you know."

"I appreciate that, I'll be there."

"Maybe we'll see you at Christmas?" her mother asked hopefully.

"Maybe." She smiled. "Summer and Devlin already invited us to the cabin for Christmas, though."

"But we'll work it out," Daylan put in with diplomacy. "I think you'd like my sister and her husband." He winked at her parents.

"We'd love to meet them."

"I'll arrange it." A few snowflakes fluttered inside as Daylan opened the heavy wooden door for Josie. They chorused, "Goodnight."

Walking hand in hand toward the snow-covered vehicle, snow crushed under their feet as they sauntered up the sidewalk. Through the openings in her crate, a little black nose was plastered against the glass and a paw swiped at the steamed-up window.

"Bet she's been watching for us the whole time."

"Naw, she has sleepy face." Opening the SUV door, Daylan released the catch on Magick's crate. She came bounding out, wiggling all over. He hooked her leash on the harness, put her on the ground, and turned to Josie. "Didn't go at all as you imagined."

"No, it sure didn't. But I'm glad. After all these years, it's good to be accepted for who I am and have become."

"With all the family drama behind us. Now we can focus on our wedding and our future together."

"I wouldn't have it any other way." She snuggled against him, lifting her face up to peer lovingly into his.

He bent down and brushed his lips over hers. "Me either."

## A word about the author...

Tena Stetler is a best-selling author of award-winning paranormal romances. She has an overactive imagination, which led to writing her first vampire romance as a tween, to the chagrin of her mother and delight of her friends. After many years as a paralegal, then an IT manager, she decided to live out her dream of pursuing a publishing career.

With the Rocky Mountains outside her window, she sits at her computer surrounded by a wide array of witches, shapeshifters, demons, faeries, and gryphons, with a Navy SEAL or two mixed in telling their tales. Her books tell stories of magical kick-ass women and mystical alpha males who dare to love them. Travel, adventure, and a bit of mystery flourish in her books along with a few companion animals to round out the tales.

Colorado is home, shared with her husband of many moons, a brilliant Chow Chow, a spoiled parrot, and a forty-five-year-old box turtle. When she's not writing, her time is spent kayaking, camping, hiking, biking, or just relaxing in the great Colorado outdoors. Oftentimes you can find her curled up in front of a crackling fire with a good book, a mug of hot chocolate, and a big bowl of popcorn.

Visit Tena at:

http://www.tenastetler.com